Prairie
Gothic

Also by the author

Mad Dog & Englishman
The Grey Pilgrim

To receive a free catalog of other Poisoned Pen Press titles, please contact us in one of the following ways:

Phone: 1-800-421-3976
Facsimile: 1-480-949-1707
Email: info@poisonedpenpress.com
Website: www.poisonedpenpress.com

Poisoned Pen Press
6962 E. First Ave. Ste 103
Scottsdale, AZ 85251

Prairie Gothic

A Mad Dog & Englishman Mystery

J. M. Hayes

Poisoned Pen Press

First Edition 2003

10 9 8 7 6 5 4 3 2 1

Library of Congress Catalog Card Number: 2002114467

ISBN: 1-590580-50-8   Hardcover

Poisoned Pen Press
6962 E. First Ave. Ste. 103
Scottsdale, AZ 85251
www.poisonedpenpress.com
info@poisonedpenpress.com

Printed in the United States of America

For Barbara, of course,

and for Jodi, Kita, and Charlie,
three sisters to an only child.

Which leaves Kansas just about the same
as anyplace else that hasn't as yet
had the benefit of the civilizing
influence of the Mafia operating on
the local level. Where ordinary man's
sins, repentances, and hopes are
of no more consequence than some
long gone Indian vision quest.
        —Earl Thompson
            A Garden of Sand

Deep in the heart of a country trying desperately
to remember itself.
        —John Stewart
            "Ghost of the Superchief"

Mad Dog parked his Saab behind the Texaco by the row of evergreens that defended the gas station from the north wind. Their ranks were bent and wounded from the strain. In winter, winds from the north assault everything in Kansas with the ferocity barbarians from that direction traditionally employed to savage civilization: Huns, Goths, Mongols, Athabascans—even Cornhuskers. At 5:30 on an icy-gray January morning in Buffalo Springs, Kansas, the open Texaco was as close to an outpost of civilization as you could find for a good fifty miles in any direction.

Considering his cargo, he probably shouldn't have stopped at all, but, with the hatchback open to accommodate the old man's height, Mad Dog was about twice as cold as he'd expected, and he'd expected to be damn near freezing.

Mad Dog skittered across the icy parking lot, past the vacant gas pumps, and let himself into a bright and cheerful interior, a shrine to American commercialism and the antithesis to most of the rest of economically depressed Buffalo Springs. The place was filled with virtually every form of candy and snack food—a cornucopia of items guaranteed to heighten your risk of cancer, stroke, heart attack, or simple obesity. There was also a huge display of tobacco products by the front counter. Mad Dog found himself wondering why they didn't just add a rack for cocaine and heroin and be done with it.

And speaking of addictive substances…He made his way to the row of coffee machines, now offering a limited range of exotic flavors like Mocha and French Vanilla and even Sinnamon spelled with an S, confirming the suspicions of many a local fundamentalist.

"Morning, Mad Dog." The woman behind the counter raised her head from a Nancy Pickard mystery and gave him a friendly wave. It diverted Mad Dog's attention just long enough to put him face to face with the deputy sheriff before even noticing him. Under the circumstances, Mad Dog would have jumped and gasped, only he was too cold for his body to react. He jerked just enough for the hood to his parka to slide off the back of his shaved head. His hair was too curly for the braids he wanted so he'd been shaving it instead for years.

How had he missed the sheriff's cruiser that must be parked out front? Maybe he really was on the verge of hypothermia.

"Geez, Mad Dog. You crazy, driving around with the hatch on your Saab open on a morning like this?" The thermometer outside the front door read twenty-six degrees, though it hung in a comfy spot insulated from the wind chill factor.

Mad Dog's advantage in these situations was that most folks did think he was crazy. He had, over years of carving out his niche as village oddball, established a tradition of acts so strange and monumental that almost nothing he did anymore caused real surprise.

"Morning, Deputy," Mad Dog managed. His mouth was cold enough to fumble most of the consonants. "I'm in desperate need of some coffee."

Deputy Wynn stepped aside and leaned casually against a rack of potato chips. He and the rack tipped too far to make a recovery and both ended up on the floor, colorful bags of chips scattering the length of the aisle.

Wynn had a reputation too. Folks in Benteen County had given him a nickname, "Wynn Some, Lose Some," on account of the young man's tendency to do the latter.

Mad Dog and the woman from behind the counter helped Wynn set the rack back in place and rearrange the bags of chips so the ones he'd crushed weren't too obvious.

"What you transporting so early and on such a rotten day?" Even the chips hadn't diverted the deputy's troublesome curiosity.

"Just some more of those signs," Mad Dog fibbed. He'd added to his reputation since the Supreme Court stepped in to settle the presidential election in George W. Bush's favor in December. Conservative, solidly Republican Benteen County had been more than a little shocked that Harvey Edward Mad Dog wanted to impeach five members of the court as a result, or, failing that, persuade folks it was time to man the barricades and reclaim American democracy. Mad Dog thought the Court's ruling had suspended it. He had petitions he wanted them to sign. These weren't proving nearly as popular as the ones he'd circulated demanding Mr. Clinton's resignation for lying about Ms. Lewinski.

"Lord have mercy, Mad Dog. Does the sheriff know you're still doing that?"

"Englishman knows. The rule of law may have been rescinded in America, but my brother's still in favor of free speech. Aren't you, Wynn?"

"No wonder they call you Mad Dog," the deputy observed. "You get your teeth into something, you just won't let go."

Actually, they called him Mad Dog because that was his legal name. He'd been born Harvey Edward Maddox, but disgust with his long-gone father and fascination with his Cheyenne heritage (until she died, his mother, Sadie Maddox, always explained she was half Cheyenne, half wildcat) had caused him to formally adopt his nickname. He'd earned it as the star of the last Buffalo Springs High School football team to win more games than it lost.

Mad Dog's nickname had proved inadvertently responsible for the sheriff's, as well. Sheriff English was Mad Dog's half brother. They shared the same Cheyenne lineage on their mother's side, though the sheriff, who sort of looked the part, didn't take it very seriously. The sheriff's father had come along years after Papa Maddox left the county. When Harvey Edward earned his sobriquet bowling over defenders, setting a record for yardage gained that still stood decades later, his little brother found himself stuck with a nickname of his own. "You got a Mad Dog," Sadie had said, "you got to have an Englishman." Mad Dog adored his nickname as much as the sheriff hated his. Only family got away with using it anymore. Most folks called him Sheriff, but if you mentioned Englishman, everyone in Benteen County knew who you meant.

"I got a petition to recall those five justices out in the car. You want to sign it?" That was about the surest way he could think of to keep Wynn away from the Saab. "Or, I've still got that one that says Kansas' schools should teach evolution."

Mad Dog paid for his coffee at the counter, and, because he was too nervous to eat at the moment, passed on the chocolate-covered donuts he'd been anticipating. In spite of his threats to Wynn's political soul, and the cruel cold, the deputy trailed him out the door.

"You see anything suspicious as you drove through town this morning?" Wynn inquired, taking on a tone of grave importance.

"Just the vacant buildings and the boarded-up windows that argue Buffalo Springs is already a ghost town. Why?"

"The phantom snowballer struck again last night. Put one square in the middle of the windshield of Supervisor Bontrager's car as he drove in on Main Street, coming back from a Blue Dragon's basketball game over to Hutchinson. Pretty near put him head first into the building across from Klausen's Funeral Parlor."

"Supervisor was probably speeding, like usual."

Wynn nodded and, to Mad Dog's surprise, continued to follow him toward the Saab.

"Then shouldn't you be patrolling?" The last person Mad Dog wanted to explain the old man to was Deputy Wynn.

"Yeah, maybe. But then I figure anybody's out this time of morning, before Bertha's Cafe or Dillon's Grocery opens up, they're eventually gonna end up here to get warm. I got me a list of customers who've been in. Maybe I'll see one or two more. The phantom snowballer likes to strike real early or real late. Likes to hit folks on the way to work. He even got my dad last week."

Wynn's dad was most of the reason Wynn Some, Lose Some had managed to keep his badge over the years. Wynn Senior was Chairman of the Benteen County Board of Supervisors and had a lot to say about the annual budget for the sheriff's office.

Mad Dog paused against the side of the Texaco. The wind was sneaking through gaps in his clothing he hadn't known existed. It threatened to crystallize his ears. He paused and snugged the parka up around his face. There was no way Mad Dog was going any closer to the Saab with Wynn along. In fact, the deputy already seemed far too interested in what was protruding from the Saab's interior and resting on its back bumper.

Mad Dog turned and started back toward the entry to the Texaco. "You know, I think maybe I need to go back in. Get me the key to the restroom and take a whiz."

"What's that you got in there?" Wynn asked, bending down and peering into the wind as if a few inches would give him a better angle on the Saab.

"Hey, maybe that's the snowballer pulling into the pumps out front," Mad Dog offered, getting a little desperate. The pickup belonged to a seventy-something farmer on his way to the usual breakfast gathering at Bertha's. The man had rheumatism so bad he could hardly drive, let alone hurl snowballs.

"What's wrapped up in that blanket?" Wynn was staring at what Mad Dog knew were a pair of bare feet atop his bumper.

Mad Dog briefly considered crowning the deputy with something hard and heavy and making a break for it. He couldn't. He was a pacifist. Besides, nothing suitably club-like was handy.

Wynn took a couple of steps beyond the corner of the building. The wind rocked him and he skidded on a patch of ice. He started to turn back toward Mad Dog with a puzzled look on his face. His hat flew off and the deputy dropped like a stone, the back of his head plastered with the remains of a snowball that had come from somewhere in the vicinity of the row of cars awaiting repairs at the other end of the Texaco.

Wynn did a Charlie Chaplin imitation regaining his feet. Mad Dog would have found it funnier if Wynn hadn't drawn his service revolver and inadvertently pointed it Mad Dog's way.

"Who did that? Where is he?" Wynn demanded.

"Over in those cars." Mad Dog pointed with a coffee cup already too cool to steam.

"I'll get him this time," Wynn howled, slip-sliding across the lot and into the maze of cars. Mad Dog took advantage of the moment to reclaim his Saab. As he aimed it onto the blacktop and headed south, he glanced in the rearview mirror. Wynn Some, Lose Some was on his hands and knees, impersonating a hockey puck on its way to a goal on the far side of Main Street.

The man with the dark complexion, the high cheekbones, and just enough votes in the last election to retain the office of sheriff parked his pickup in the lot beside the former Hotel Benteen. In its day, the three-story brick structure had boasted the finest accommodations on the Great Plains—at least between Hutchinson and Dodge City. Its day was more than seventy years gone, though, corresponding with the brief boom that created Buffalo Springs, then ended in the Great

Depression and a pretty fair Dust Bowl. After a series of incarnations that included offices, a cheap rooming house, and cheaper yet storage, it had recently blossomed again as a bastion of the latest growth industry, the retirement home—a warehouse for the elderly.

The parking lot was hardly crowded. Not many visitors this early on yet another gloomy January day. The morning commuter jam crowded nearby streets with a car every few minutes. The sheriff slipped his truck between a patch of ice and a muddy snowdrift, pushed open his door, snuggled down in his jacket, and fought the wind and the uncertain footing to the entrance.

The man who met him in the reception area was short and pudgy. He wore an expensive suit that couldn't be purchased in Buffalo Springs. The reception area was bright and cheerful, a remarkable contradiction to the deteriorating downtown just outside. A cage full of brilliantly colored birds sang delicate melodies at the far end of the room. A pair of ancient white heads nodded unconsciously to the rhythm, but turned their attention to the entry the moment the sheriff swung it open.

"Thank you for coming, Sheriff. We're all terribly concerned." The man in the suit had a soft voice and a similar handshake.

The sheriff wasn't wearing a uniform, just Levis over long johns, boots, work shirt, and a wool-lined leather jacket turned up against the wind. Pinned somewhere under there was a badge, but folks in Benteen County didn't need to see it. Everyone knew him.

The sheriff doffed his hat. His momma had taught him gentlemen didn't wear hats indoors. The Kansas wind made it difficult to wear one outdoors as well, but tradition demanded otherwise. He wished he could remember the chubby guy's name. He was a Sorenson, the sheriff thought, but on his mother's side. Better just get down to business.

"Where's the baby?"

"Baby? I'm sorry. No babies here, Sheriff. This is a retirement community. It's poor old Mr. Irons we're concerned about. He's terribly ill, you know. Terminal, really. And now he's gone and disappeared. If he's outside, he won't last long in this weather."

"I'm confused," the sheriff said. "I just got a message from Mrs. Kraus over at the office. She said she had a call from here about someone finding a baby."

"Oh dear, no. That can't be. There must be a mistake." The soft man turned to the woman behind the front desk. "Lucille, do you have any idea what this baby thing is about?"

Lucille Martin was a big woman, as old as some of the clients she was serving. She was well known for the authoritarian efficiency she had perfected in her previous career as an elementary school teacher. The sheriff recalled her enthusiasm at applying rulers to knuckles. She was hardly the sort of caregiver he would want seeing to the welfare of his elderly parents, but fortune had already carried them beyond her reach. His mother had died years ago and he had no idea who or where his father was. A foreign soldier doing temporary duty at a nearby weather station, rumor had it. Most folks thought his mother, Cheyenne Sadie, hadn't even known the man's name, that she'd just chosen his nationality when it came time to put something down on English's birth certificate.

"Good morning, Sheriff," Lucille Martin said. Though he was the authority figure these days, her disapproving glare still inspired guilt feelings. He felt like he'd neglected a homework assignment.

"Baby? That would be Dorothy again. She's been fretting about that doll of Alice Burton's this morning." Mrs. Martin leaned in the sheriff's direction and confided in a tone that probably carried only as far as the second floor. "Alice has the Alzheimer's, you know. Doesn't know anyone anymore. Used to cry sometimes and disturb the other residents, until we got that doll for her to cuddle. It calms her."

"Mrs. Kraus didn't say anything about anyone being missing."

"No," Mrs. Martin explained. "I hadn't gotten around to calling in that one yet. Old Tommie Irons can hardly get to and from the bathroom anymore. They turned him over to the Hospice people months ago. He hasn't the strength to go far. I thought we'd turn him up in a few minutes. Mr. Deffenbach here gets panicky over the littlest things. I didn't want to trouble you, Sheriff, unless Tommie's really missing."

The sheriff noticed that Mr. Deffenbach—he remembered now, Stan Deffenbach of the Cottonwood Corner Deffenbachs—wasn't prepared to challenge Lucille Martin's assumption of his authority. Some people were born leaders. English wished he'd inherited a few of those genes, instead of the ones that were making it so hard for him to keep his waist from hanging over his belt buckle.

"Oh, good. Someone's finally come about the baby." The tiny woman, maybe all of five feet tall and ninety pounds, ducked through a pair of swinging doors across from the entrance. She was wearing a bulky gray sweatshirt, matching sweatpants, and a pair of iridescent red tennis shoes. Her white hair was chopped short in a bob that was becoming fashionable again.

"Now Dorothy," Mrs. Martin admonished, shaking a finger almost as big around as the birdlike woman's wrist, "I've told you to forget about that baby. It's just a doll. You shouldn't have called the sheriff's office, but as long as he's here maybe he'll help us look for Tommie."

"No need for that." The little woman was undeterred by Lucille Martin's efforts to deflect her. She slid under the bigger woman's arm and into the sheriff's face. "Tommie's dead, but so's that baby and somebody needs to do something about it."

"Dead?" Martin, Deffenbach, and the sheriff made the query into a three-part harmony.

"Tommie died about supper time last night."

"If Tommie Irons is dead, Dorothy, then why can't we find his body?" It was really less a question than Lucille Martin's effort to demonstrate the fault in her student's logic.

"That would be because nobody around here checks on us much, unless we demand it of them. And because that man came and took him away this morning."

The sheriff felt like he needed to regain control of the discussion. "That man? Do you mean somebody from Klausen's Funeral Parlor?"

"No, don't be silly." The little woman wiped the suggestion out of the air with a dismissive gesture.

"Doc Jones, then?"

"Not him either. It was that big guy who got to be friends with Tommie this last fall. I'd tell you his name only I'm having a senior moment and it won't come to me. But that doesn't matter. Tommie died natural. That baby probably didn't."

The sheriff glanced at Martin and Deffenbach. "Either of you know who she's talking about?" Neither responded. "Don't you think you should?"

"Guests are supposed to sign in at the front desk," Mrs. Martin said.

"Will you forget about that," the little old lady interrupted. "I'll remember his name in a minute and I'll tell you. But you need to come see to that baby."

"I'll check on the baby soon, Ms...." The sheriff didn't know the old woman's name. That was unusual, but it wasn't because he was suffering one of his own occasional senior moments, though he was decades less entitled to them. It was because he'd never seen her before.

"Dog," she said.

"Your name is Dog?" The sheriff was nonplussed.

"No, no. I'm just Dorothy. Dog, that's the man's name. Mr. something Dog."

"Mad Dog?" the listening trio chorused, the sheriff dismayed, the others clearly more accusative.

"Yes, that's right. Mr. Harvey Mad Dog. That's who came for Tommie Irons' body."

The last buffalo in Benteen County watched mournfully as Mad Dog's Saab went by his pasture without stopping. He was the only surviving member of the dozen feeder calves Mad Dog had decided would be the start of his effort to repopulate the Great Plains with the great herds. It was another of his occasional attempts to be a born-again Cheyenne that hadn't quite worked the way he'd planned. The veterinary bills had been phenomenal and the skills of modern medical science insufficient to maintain a herd of more than this one solitary bull.

He was a magnificent creature, inspiring what Mad Dog hoped were racial feelings of kinship within himself. The animal stood at the corner of the fence line, his breath smoking with such ferocity it seemed possible he might be responsible for the clouds that hid the rising sun. He was proud, noble, immortal—well, maybe not immortal. A shadow detached itself from the evergreens on the other side of the fence row and Mad Dog hit the brakes, tumbled out of the Saab, put two frozen fingers to his mouth, and blew. The silver-gray wolf paused in its tracks and looked from the buffalo to Mad Dog. The buffalo pawed at the frozen earth. It had seen the predator as well. The wolf seemed to shrug powerful shoulders, as if deciding to leave the bison for another day. It turned and loped easily to the fence, leapt it without pausing before charging Mad Dog and lunging at his face.

The pink tongue with the single black spot slathered him with wet kisses. The force of her affection sent Mad Dog tumbling back into his seat. His timing with the buffalo herd probably hadn't been the greatest, since he'd gotten involved in wolf-hybrid rescue about then, too. Mad Dog's pack had cost him part of his herd, and the ill will of several local sheep men, before he found most of the animals new homes and built proper pens for the rest.

Mad Dog hugged her and she submitted, for just a moment, then scrambled across his chest and into the passenger's seat.

"How'd you get loose again, Hailey?"

Her answer was a wide yawn, then a polite sniff at the bundle behind the seats. She didn't seem to mind sharing the Saab with Tommie Irons' corpse. She settled into her accustomed spot, overflowing the passenger seat's cushion, her nose comfortably fogging the window she preferred in the down position.

Hailey was the only one he'd gotten as a puppy. The Wichita attorney who'd imported her from Alaska had the money to afford an exotic pet, but not the patience to deal with one. After she dug through his new leather sofa, searching for the source of a faint squeak in one of its springs, he sent her to the vet to have her euthanized. Mad Dog had just mailed out a batch of fliers advertising his services as a foster home for wolf-hybrid rescue to central Kansas veterinarians and this one hadn't reached the circular file yet. The vet was soft hearted enough not to destroy an obviously healthy puppy. In spite of the attorney's unqualified instructions, the vet had called and Mad Dog brought the puppy home the same day.

Hence her name. She came from an all but hopeless situation. She was like one of those last-second, desperation passes he fondly recalled from his days playing for the Buffalo Springs Bisons. Time running out, fourth and long, nothing to do but throw up a Hail Mary and pray. Mad Dog had caught a couple and salvaged unlikely victories during his football career. He figured this pup was one more. Feminized, Hail Mary had become Hailey Marie, the smartest animal he'd ever known, and his problem child. Given her propensity for finding a way out of any combination of restraints he applied, he thought he should have feminized a version of Houdini instead.

Tommie Irons had been one of Mad Dog's neighbors. He lived down where the great flat stretch of farmland southwest of Buffalo Springs began to show a little topography on its way to the once mighty Kansaw River. He was older than Mad Dog. The two men had known each other only well enough to exchange the occasional "howdy" or a wave as their vehicles passed going to and from town. Irons would have seemed just another Kansas farmer, except, like Mad Dog, he turned out to be an Indian—part Choctaw on his mother's side.

It didn't mean much to Mad Dog at first. A Choctaw wasn't anything like a Cheyenne. Choctaw were East Coast Indians, driven out by early white settlers and relocated to Indian Territory. They weren't Plains Indians like Mad Dog and his kin.

Irons and Mad Dog might never have progressed beyond neighbors and casual acquaintances but for Doc Jones. There weren't that many doctors in Buffalo Springs anymore. Not that many people either. The town, and the area which it served as county seat, had been losing population steadily for a good fifty years. Doc Jones was Benteen County Coroner as well as one of its best-liked general practitioners. Mad Dog and Doc knew each other through the sheriff. It wasn't like Mad Dog trusted Western medicine that much, but there were times when even a natural-born shaman couldn't perform a self cure. Doc had proved up to Mad Dog's occasional small emergencies. So far. He also happened to be the man who diagnosed Tommie Irons' cancer. He told Mad Dog when Irons' health forced him into a full-care residential facility, and caused the old farmer to ponder philosophical questions he'd previously avoided.

"He's heard about your vision quests and stuff," Doc explained to Mad Dog on a bright day in October so filled with promise that it still seemed possible this could be the season Kansas State went to its first Orange Bowl. "Probably isn't anybody in Benteen County who doesn't know how you shave your head, cover yourself with body paint, and set yourself out in the middle of Veteran's Memorial Park every summer. Well, Tommie Irons has some curiosity about what you're up to, and whether you've come to any conclusions about the way the universe works. He doesn't know much about being a Choctaw, but he's thinking he'd like to find out. He's dying, Mad Dog, and he'd like to talk to someone who can tell him how an Indian's supposed to do that, where he might be headed, if it's any place other than just some hole in the ground out at Southlawn Cemetery. Doesn't matter whether you know what you're talking about as long as you'll take some time and listen too. I can't help him anymore. And you can't do him any harm."

By then, Mad Dog was less certain of his own philosophy than he'd once been. One of his first efforts to practice his "people's" shamanistic beliefs had been linked to a couple of deaths. He felt at least partially responsible. His talks with real Cheyennes had been disappointing. Most didn't know as much about their belief system as he did. The exceptions wouldn't take him seriously. As far as they were concerned, he was just another white man playing new-age games, pretending to be Indian. Still, Mad Dog started visiting Tommie Irons and sharing his beliefs. He did some research on the Choctaw and taught the dying man what he could about the religion and customs of his mother's people.

Mad Dog helped Tommie Irons die confident of his soul's destination. The Civilized Tribes, of which the Choctaw were one, were the source of the concept for the "Happy Hunting Grounds." The old man couldn't remember any better days, he confessed, than walking a slough with a shotgun or snuggled into a duck blind watching his breath and the sky. That's exactly where he wanted to spend eternity. It was his mortal remains that concerned him. The Choctaw interred their dead in burial mounds, but not until the corpse had been picked clean of flesh by Bone Picker or Buzzardman. If that was how it should be, then that was how Irons wanted it. It was close enough to Mad Dog's Cheyenne world view, and the way he wanted to be treated when he died, that he'd agreed to help the old man's final wish come true.

Irons had farmed a section less than five miles from the old Maddox place, now Mad Dog's. The land there sloped gently down toward where Calf Creek joined the Kansaw. One minor drainage curled through an edge of the section with a tiny stream that stayed wet in all but the driest years. Another, dryer slough zigzagged from the northwest corner down to meet the creek. Those were the hunting grounds Tommie Irons dreamed of stalking again. And he had built a pond near their confluence, grading up a small dam just below where the slough turned damp and natural springs seeped sweet, clear water. It was the only mound Irons had ever made, and a perfect destination from his perspective.

Getting there took Mad Dog time. The roads that were clear of the last snow tended to get used. The Saab was remarkably nimble on snow and ice, but it wasn't a four-wheel drive. It had limitations. And the county's infrastructure had seriously deteriorated. Old bridges seldom got repaired or replaced when they wore out or washed away in spring floods.

Mad Dog parked the Saab just short of where the trees along the slough became thick enough to allow snow to drift across the road. No one had driven through there since the last storm and that seemed a good indication that Mad Dog could finish his business uninterrupted.

Tommie Irons was stiff as a board. Rigor was already at an advanced stage by the time Mad Dog picked up the body. A long drive on an icy morning hadn't done anything to soften him. Because he was unbendable, Mad Dog had been forced to dangle Irons' feet over the rear bumper. They were probably frozen solid by now. Mad Dog could sympathize. Most of him felt similarly chilled.

With Hailey delightedly investigating the slough for something to chase, Mad Dog dragged, towed, and slid Tommie down to the grove of cottonwoods above the pond. The concept of Bone Picker/Buzzardman seemed to indicate that birds should handle the task of defleshing Irons' bones.

Mad Dog wrapped him in the mesh hammock he'd purchased with that in mind, chose a high branch unlikely to be spotted by humans, and started climbing. It wasn't easily done while wearing two layers of clothing and a quilted down jacket of a thickness to make him resemble the Pillsbury Dough Boy. Good handholds were scarce for thickly gloved fingers, but the cottonwoods cooperated. One leaned inward at an angle suitable for scaling, then another offered massive limbs at conveniently ladder-like intervals. Irons' final perch was difficult to view from below and out of the reach of coyotes, bobcats, and other carrion eaters without wings. Come spring, when the birds had presumably finished their work, Mad Dog would return, move the bones a few yards south, and plant them in the side of the dam. Tommie Irons, Choctaw Moundbuilder, would finally rest in peace.

By the time the job was done, Mad Dog was exhausted. You're too old for this, he thought. It wasn't something he liked to admit. In his mid-fifties, Mad Dog could still pass for a decade younger. He jogged, he exercised regularly, and he ate right—except for an addiction to chocolate. There were plenty of men two decades younger who couldn't have done what he was doing for Tommie Irons. Still, that didn't help Mad Dog find the reserves he needed to climb down and return to the road. He sat, for a moment, in the crotch of a tree, behind a massive trunk that blocked a little of the wind that had already turned Tommie Irons into a frozen pendulum, counting its way from now to forever.

What would anthropologists call this, Mad Dog wondered? Was there such a thing as an extended tree burial?

If he hadn't been so cold and exhausted, Mad Dog would have appreciated this view of Tommie's Happy Hunting Grounds. Even in the frozen grip of the harshest winter in a decade, the stream and sloughs were an enchanted place, crisscrossed with game trails, prints, and spore. It was the kind of location Mad Dog would have enjoyed hunting in his youth. No more, though. Killing for sport had lost its appeal. When he hunted these days it was with a camera or binoculars.

A harsher gust nudged him, a reminder he'd better get down before his aging muscles began to stiffen in the cold. It was nearly too late already, but he made it.

Tommie was barely perceptible in the jumble of branches above. When there were leaves, he'd be absolutely invisible.

Mad Dog put his fingers to his lips again. It was time to reclaim Hailey and head for home. He stopped short of whistling. Something, besides the frozen wind, prickled the back of his neck. He was being watched. He moved his eyes and pivoted his head.

It was only Hailey, come up behind him with her usual stealth, an ability that made her seem able to beam herself instantly from place to place. She smiled at him, but only with her eyes since her mouth was filled by a big oval rock.

"Drop it, babe. Let's get out of here. Go back to the house for some coffee and a rawhide chew toy." He didn't try to take things out of her mouth anymore. There were ways in which wolf hybrids were different than domesticated dogs, even ones like Hailey who adored you. She stepped up beside him, though, and put the rock gently on the snow at his feet. It was a peculiar rock with regular indentations. Mad Dog bent and picked it up and found himself wanting to quote Hamlet's line about poor Yorick. It wasn't a rock. It was a human skull.

"**N**ot likely we'll have visitors on a morning like this," Deffenbach said a little defensively. The young woman they'd found to replace Mrs. Martin at the front desk of the Sunshine Towers seemed overwhelmed by the possibility she might have to answer a phone or look up a room number. Minimum wage, minimum skills, the sheriff thought.

There was a long hall just off the lobby, offices on one side, a cafeteria on the other. None of it lived up to the reception area's bright promise.

"Our multipurpose room," Deffenbach explained as they passed.

"We call it the mess hall," Dorothy said. "Mess is the perfect description for what they serve in there."

"It is a little bland," Mrs. Martin admitted, "but wholesome." There wasn't much of a breakfast crowd and most of those were just nursing cups of coffee.

"How could Mad Dog, or anyone, walk in here in the wee hours of the morning and leave with a dead body?"

"Inside help." Mrs. Martin shot an accusing glare at the little woman with the red tennies. "We secure the doors every night at nine, then unlock at seven the next morning. They can all be opened from inside so people can't be trapped in case of some emergency, say a fire, but an open door sounds an alarm at the front desk. If he came through a door, we should have known. The windows are supposed to be secured too, but I've found a few that have been jimmied from time to time. This isn't a prison you know."

"Coulda fooled me," Dorothy grumbled.

"Were you the one who helped Mad Dog come and go?" The sheriff bent to focus his question on the little senior.

"One of them, but let's talk about that after we see to the baby."

One of the offices was a nurse's station. A frazzled woman was counting out prescription medicines into labeled cups. "Mrs. Burton's in her room, far as I know," she said, in answer to Mrs. Martin's query. "Haven't seen her on this level and I haven't managed to do rounds upstairs because I've been persuading one of our ladies she doesn't need a morning-after pill on account of last night's indiscretion."

"Card games get pretty boring after awhile," Dorothy muttered again.

There was an elevator midway along the hall. It took a long time to arrive, during which the bird woman entertained them with further examples of the Sunshine Towers' many shortcomings. From what he could see, the sheriff agreed with her.

A Mutt-and-Jeff pair of elegantly dressed matrons were on the elevator when it finally arrived. They took one look at the group that was going up, then stepped aside to make room rather than get off.

"Not much excitement around here," Dorothy said. "We get hungry for it, grab onto most anything."

Lucille Martin rolled her eyes as the elevator began to ascend. "Perhaps we should explain just who our Dorothy is, Sheriff."

"Surely he recognizes her?" the Mutt woman wondered.

"Why, those ruby slippers give her away," her Jeff counterpart replied.

"Yes, visiting from Oz." Mrs. Martin tapped her skull gently in an indication that Dorothy's might be softer than normal.

"No autographs," the little woman said. The elevator let them out into a hall with open doors every few feet. Nearly all were occupied with ancient women sitting in chairs that varied from folding to wheeled.

"Kinda reminds you of that street in Amsterdam, doesn't it," the visitor from Oz observed. "Whores on display. Only these are ladies of the morning, and they aren't selling a substitute for love, they're eager buyers. They'll settle for anything that resembles affection."

The fifth door to the right of the elevator was closed and empty. Mrs. Martin did the honors without a knock. She swung it open on a cramped room into which a few pieces of ornate furniture had been stuffed.

"We encourage the families to let residents use their own furniture," Mr. Deffenbach explained. "It helps them feel at home."

The room felt anything but home-like. Temporary storage, maybe, which, English decided, many families, as well as the management, probably considered it to be.

Alice Burton was sitting in a rocker nearly hidden behind a dresser so out of proportion for the small room that it blocked half of the only window. She didn't look like an Alzheimer's patient. She was clean and well groomed, her hair only lightly peppered with gray. She was wearing corduroys and boots below a hand-knitted sweater with a gold pin. She held a baby swaddled in a thick blanket.

"Let me do this, it'll be easier." Dorothy ducked past Mrs. Martin.

"The Sheriff's here, Alice. He's come to take this baby back to her rightful mother. You understand why that's got to be."

Alice Burton did seem to understand. She looked at the bundled form sadly for a moment, then delivered it to Dorothy without complaint.

"You see," Lucille Martin began, then faltered as the tiny woman began peeling back the blanket. No one would make a doll in quite such a pasty shade of gray.

"Sweet Jesus!" Deffenbach exclaimed.

"Sure don't smell sweet, and there's no indication he'll rise from the dead. I'd guess this ain't him." Dorothy passed the dead infant to the sheriff's open arms.

It was a small skull. Until he reached down and picked it up, Mad Dog let himself hope he was wrong and this wasn't human. When he touched it all doubts vanished. He had one of those moments he couldn't explain. It made him believe in himself again. He was, in fact, a natural born Cheyenne shaman.

What he felt was kinship. He was related to this tiny orb of weathered bone. They were both Cheyenne. He didn't know how he knew, but he was sure.

He held the skull up and looked at it as if he might recognize its features. It didn't work. It remained only vacant bone, but bone that had once been one of his people.

So much for Tommie Irons' uninterrupted journey to the happy hunting grounds. Englishman was going to have to know about this, and once he came to this place, finding Tommie was a virtual certainty. Unless…Mad Dog considered the apparent age of the skull again. Maybe, if this were some prehistoric Cheyenne, he could just replant it.

"Where did you find this, Hailey?"

The wolf didn't make any Lassie-like efforts to lead him where he wanted to go. She just wagged her tail and danced around as if she expected him to toss the skull and involve her in a game of catch. Her games of catch, however, involved darting to within inches of his grasp and then tearing away, holding whatever prize she was currently using to tempt him into trying to catch her. Trying was the key word.

Mad Dog opened one of the big Velcro pouches in his jacket. The skull was small enough to fit inside. Discovering where Hailey had found it shouldn't be hard. He was Cheyenne, after all. Well, one-quarter Cheyenne, or, if Englishman's wife's genealogical researches were correct, more like one-sixteenth, that quarter being broken into equal parts Cheyenne, Sans Arc, Buffalo Soldier, and Mexican cowboy. Not that his heritage was necessary. Backtracking her through the snow in the sloughs should be simple. There would be no other wolf tracks.

Benteen County, Kansas lay smack in the middle of the Bible belt. Fundamentalist Christians were common. Those with liberal interpretations of the holy book—Episcopalians, say—tended to be viewed with suspicion. Non-Christians, like born-again-Cheyenne Mad Dog, were considered aberrations. They were suffered because this was a free nation, tolerant of other views, so long as they were insignificant enough to be crushed the moment they threatened. You couldn't drive out of Buffalo Springs' city limits without encountering a pro-life billboard. Many citizens might send contributions in support of Planned Parenthood, but they didn't mention it over a cup of coffee at Bertha's Cafe, especially not when steak knives were part of the place settings.

The sheriff accepted the sad little bundle with a doubly heavy heart. He mourned this small innocent, whose life had ended almost before it began, and he mourned for the community as well. Buffalo Springs wouldn't rest until someone paid for this. God help the mother, he thought, unless there proved to be a simple explanation for how her child came to be here instead of up the street at Klausen's Funeral Parlor.

"Two dead bodies?" the sheriff inquired of Mr. Deffenbach and Mrs. Martin. "One that should be here and isn't, and one that shouldn't be and is? Your security is worse than you imagined."

"I'll get you the name and address of the man on the front desk last night," Mrs. Martin offered, shifting blame. Deffenbach just directed his horrified stare at the infant and trailed along as they headed back toward the elevator.

"I'll need Doc Jones over here right away. Then I'll want that name, and a chat with anybody else who knows anything about this."

The women of the morning quietly watched them pass. Dorothy of the ruby tennies trailed along, silent now, looking faintly ashamed of the way she'd behaved.

Mrs. Martin hurried ahead to punch for the elevator. Surprisingly, it opened almost immediately.

"Freeze!" a voice shouted from inside. Everyone did pretty much the opposite. A .357 magnum poked cautiously into the hall. "Which of you is the phantom snowballer? Fess up."

"Wynn?" The sheriff's voice hovered somewhere between outrage and astonishment. "Put that gun away!"

Before the deputy could obey, the door hissed shut. Wynn frantically pulled his hand back inside. His hand made it, but the .357 stayed behind.

◇◇◇

Hailey hadn't chosen her path with Mad Dog's convenience in mind. Still, he hadn't been up in the cottonwoods long enough for her to have ranged far. He went around the thick stands of undergrowth that she'd cut through. Her path was easy to pick up again on the other side. She'd come from downstream of the dam that held Tommie Irons' pond.

Sometime over the years, the pond had filled to overflowing. Gradually, it must have built its own spillway. The soaked earth suffered years of freezing and baking. The spillway eroded its way toward the pond. Recently, a fresh chunk of earth had tumbled into the stream. That's where the footprints led and, when Mad Dog clambered up onto the side of the dam to examine the icy avalanche from above, he saw more bones protruding, both from the wall of earth that remained and in the debris that had fallen.

Tommie Irons' dam really was a burial mound. Mad Dog suddenly remembered that Tommie had been specific about where he wanted his own bones placed—at the other end of the dam, about as far as you could get from where these were.

Mad Dog dropped to his belly and leaned over the edge. Hailey sat by his side, proudly sharing her find. The bones had taken on the texture of the earth that held them. Mixed with bits of ice and snow, they were hard to make out. One thing was immediately clear, though. Most were far too large to go with the skull Hailey had brought him.

There was something else down there among the earth and bones. It was a splash of color that didn't belong in a January Kansas landscape. Mad Dog reached and brushed at it. It came loose and he snagged it with his gloved hand before it could fall into the breach.

It was plastic, a battered ID card. Mad Dog could barely make it out without his reading glasses. There was a picture and part of the name that faded away toward the end. HORNB was all that remained.

The picture was of a young man with dark hair and smiling lips. It could be an old shot of County Supervisor Ezekiel Hornbaker, only this face had a broad, flat nose that appeared to have encountered a determined fist. Mad Dog was sure Supervisor Hornbaker's nose had never looked like this.

Doc Jones arrived in his aging Buick station wagon that doubled as ambulance or hearse, depending on circumstances. It was beige, speckled with mud, not unlike the streaks of tired snow that remained between the elms on the lawn in front of the Sunshine Towers Retirement Home.

The sheriff met his old friend on the sidewalk. The wind reminded him just how cold it was. Doc slumped into his heavy overcoat, his droopy, hound-dog face looking even sadder than usual.

"Morning, Sheriff." Doc extended his hand. "As coroner, I get to come over here all too often, but never after an infant before. What's up?"

The sheriff escorted him to the entry and through its first set of doors. In the space between inner and outer doors, the cold was only a threat, not an adversary.

"I don't know much yet, Doc. What I do is pretty bizarre."

"I assume you're keeping me from getting somewhere warm for a reason." Doc gestured to where a small crowd filled the lobby and stared at them with an intensity normally reserved by residents here for a few soap operas or the odd global tragedy.

"Everybody in the county is going to know about this before dark. I'd just as soon not share more than I have to."

Doc nodded and snuggled a little deeper into his coat.

"Tommie Irons died last night," the sheriff told him.

"Not a surprise. The cancer was all through him. So you've got two bodies for me?"

The sheriff sighed. "Tommie's not here. Apparently Mad Dog's been coming to see him. They've been sharing their indigenousness, or something. I guess Tommie decided he wanted a traditional Choctaw burial and persuaded Mad Dog to help. Some of the residents called Mad Dog and smuggled him in this morning. Damned if I know where my brother or the body have got to."

Doc's droopy mouth straightened into a half smile. "Sorry, Sheriff, that's partly my fault. I persuaded Mad Dog to come talk to Tommie about Native American religious notions. The old man wasn't going easy and I thought...No, hell, I should have thought. Your brother always carries things to their illogical extremes. But what's that got to do with a dead baby?"

"After Mad Dog left with Tommie, some of the seniors went for an early morning stroll. Alice Burton was one of them. You know about her?"

"She's not one of my patients, but yeah. I know. She's been diagnosed with Alzheimer's, but she's not as far gone as her family seems to want to think. This got something to do with that doll they gave her?"

"I guess she took the doll along. Nobody noticed anything until after they got back. Somewhere, she seems to have traded plastic for the real thing."

"And I assume they didn't traipse through any nurseries. You're thinking this child was abandoned?"

"Shortly after birth from the look of things. Part of the umbilical cord is still attached. I'm hoping this kid belongs to someone who was just passing through town."

"I can appreciate that sentiment," Doc said.

"We may end up with a lynch-mob reaction to this. Can you suggest any likely candidates for the baby's mother?"

"Half the teenage girls in this county. We don't teach our kids sex education. We don't offer much recreation. The nearest Planned Parenthood office is halfway across the state. Having a 'premature' kid six months or less after the wedding is pretty much the norm around here."

"I meant specifically."

Doc turned his face away from the crowd in the lobby. "You know I don't do abortions, Sheriff. Not because I don't believe they're occasionally a better option, but because if I did, even an occasional secret one, word would get out and I couldn't live here anymore. Literally. You and I could list a dozen people in this county who would seriously consider shooting me if they believed I was killing unborn babies. So, I'd have to say no in answer to your question. No one's come to me for a solution to an unwanted pregnancy, and even if they had, I'd never admit it. I took an oath. If anyone told me something like that, I couldn't reveal it."

"Sorry, Doc. The possibilities of this thing scare me as much as they do you. I was thinking of myself more as coming to someone's rescue rather than leading a rush to punish."

"I know." A shiver ran up Doc's spine that the sheriff didn't think came from the cold. "Let's take a look. I'm coroner here and I'll share with you anything I learn from performing my duty. What you do then is between you and the law, or you and your conscience."

The sheriff couldn't recall ever seeing Doc so obviously upset. Neither of them knew a thing about this baby yet, and already both of them were as skittish as a pair of taxpayers facing IRS audits.

He opened the inner doors and shooed people aside. They pushed through to the hall that led to the cafeteria and offices and headed for the one where Deputy Wynn stood guard, one hand hiding his empty holster. The sheriff had locked his deputy's .357 in the glove box of his truck and wasn't sure he would return it.

"Mornin', Doc," Wynn said.

"If there's a disaster, I can always count on you being there, can't I, Deputy?"

Doc really was in a mood. If there was one man in the county who was never unkind to those who meant no harm, it was Doc Jones. Wynn didn't seem to notice the insult. He just opened the door to the nurse's office, then followed them inside.

"Ah, damn!" Doc muttered softly. He peeled away the blanket that swaddled the infant with a touch so gentle it seemed he must believe the potential for suffering survived beyond death.

The room felt too small for three adults and a dead baby, though not for want of square footage. All of Kansas was too small for the blend of horror and tragic innocence the tiny corpse represented.

"At least we can rule out the Golds and the Eisenbergs," Wynn said.

The sheriff was surprised. Not that either family had been high on his list, but he thought it was going to be tough to narrow down suspects.

"Why's that?" Doc asked, his tone equally tinged with doubt.

"You didn't notice?" Wynn was clearly shocked, and, from the flush that suddenly spread over his face, maybe a little embarrassed.

"Notice what?"

"His pee pee. Look at his pee pee," Wynn said. "Boy sure ain't Jewish."

Bertha's Cafe was jammed. All the booths along the windows were occupied and the excess had spilled over to flood the seats at the counter. People milled around, waiting in the remaining floor space, making a mockery of the capacity sign the fire marshal had tacked up by the front door. Bertha delivered monstrous platters of bacon and eggs and home fries, and brimming mugs of coffee strong enough to wake Sleeping Beauty. Buffalo Springs wasn't ready to trade large doses of cholesterol and caffeine for bran muffins and juice just yet.

County Supervisors Bontrager and Hornbaker were nursing their coffee and discussing the outrage of Mad Dog making off with Tommie Irons' corpse. Irons was Ezekiel Hornbaker's brother-in-law. The supervisors were occupying a booth Bertha could make better use of. That's why she asked them about the baby.

"What baby?" they replied.

Bontrager was a big man in the dairy cattle industry. He raised registered Holsteins on a couple of sections a few miles north of town. He'd been handsome when he was younger. Now, in his early seventies, he just looked weathered and maybe a little beaten down by the losses he'd been taking on his tech stocks.

Zeke Hornbaker was taller and maybe five years younger than Bontrager, but he looked younger still. He didn't farm. The family had inherited money, and Zeke, to hear him tell it, was a successful investor in the commodities market. His boots and western-style suit were custom made and helped him look fit and young, as did regular applications of hair coloring.

"That dead baby they found over at the Sunshine Home this morning. Folks have been talking about it since I opened. I figured two government officials, such as yourselves, would know everything. Or should."

Parties at several adjacent tables turned to listen to Hornbaker's response. "You sure about this, Bertha?"

"It's true," a farmer in a pair of clean, starched bib-overalls at the counter replied. "I dropped the wife off there to visit her mother a bit ago. They say it was a newborn that somebody just disposed of. Threw away. Englishman and Wynn were over there investigating. You didn't know about it?" The tone of that last part seemed faintly accusatory and was met by a general grumbling from Bertha's clientele.

"Maybe you should check in at the courthouse?" Bertha suggested. There was enough nodding to indicate a chorus of Amens might have been heard had this been a gathering of those seeking sustenance for the soul instead of the flesh.

"Maybe we should," Bontrager agreed, uncertainly.

"No maybe about it," Hornbaker replied, wadding up his napkin and climbing to his feet. "If a baby has been murdered in Buffalo Springs, I personally will not rest until the guilty party is caught and punished." His statement had the ring of a campaign promise. Hornbaker and Bontrager grabbed their coats off the rack and headed for the door, trailing a few loyal political followers and leaving some badly needed table space.

"Gertie and Abe Yoder, party of five," Bertha called. She grabbed a stack of dirty dishes with one arm while she swiped a gray cloth across the formica, leaving it smelling of antiseptic and covered by a film the Yoder children could draw in while their parents studied a menu that changed about as often as Kansas gave its electoral votes to a Democrat.

Doc Jones had taken the baby to Klausen's Funeral Parlor, where one of the back rooms made do for official Benteen County Coroner's business. Wynn Some, still unenlightened about circumcision, had been sent to retrieve the cruiser, keeping his eyes open for the doll that Alice Burton had presumably traded for the real thing on the way. His eager efforts to make a report about his pursuit of the phantom snowballer also remained on hold. His shift was over and he was off duty. The sheriff needed help, but it was clear things would go smoother without Wynn.

The sheriff was in the room of the little woman with the red tennies. It resembled Alice Burton's cramped quarters, only without the massive furniture. The room felt seriously institutional. A metal-framed bed stood flanked by a couple of chairs, a dresser, and a nightstand. They looked like rejects from a going-out-of-business-sale at an economy motel chain.

Nothing personalized the room, not even the stack of news-papers and paperbacks on top of the dresser.

"Just call me Dorothy."

She sat primly on the edge of her bed and watched as the sheriff paced over to the window. It offered a stunning view of vacant lots and abandoned businesses over which the Buffalo Springs grain elevator loomed from a few blocks away.

He reached up and rubbed the back of his neck, trying to loosen muscles that felt tight enough to snap. "We don't really know each other, ma'am. I was taught to maintain a certain level of formality in situations like this."

"Murder investigations?"

"Well, we don't know that yet, and I hope not, but an investigation anyway."

"They call you Englishman, don't they?"

The unexpected use of his despised nickname turned him from the window and brought her his full attention. "Some do. Mostly not to my face."

"You'd rather be called something else?"

"Yes ma'am. Sheriff or English, or the combination."

"I started out as Ruth, but I didn't like it much. I prefer Dorothy."

He got it. "OK, Dorothy."

"How can I help you, Sheriff."

"Well, we've got a pair of unusual circumstances this morning. One body that should be here is missing. One that shouldn't be, turned up here. What can you tell me about how that happened?"

She glanced out the window, as if the answer might be found in the weathered words printed atop the elevator where it threatened to scrape fresh snow from the low clouds rushing just above.

All it said was BUFFALO SPRINGS CO-OP, though you had to have good eyes to pick out the fading letters.

"Tommie died," she said.

"I'm sorry."

"Oh, don't be. He was past being ready for it. In fact, he was getting a little cranky that it couldn't just be over and done with."

"Was anyone with him?"

"About half a dozen of us. I'm not gonna tell you who the others were. It's up to them, whether they want to talk about it or not. I'll take responsibility for myself, but I won't give up any names."

It was like she was playing the tough gal role in a movie—hard but honest, and with a code of honor she planned to live by. He suppressed another smile. "I understand. When did it happen?"

"Six-fifteen or so. We were watching the news on his TV. One minute Tommie was eyeing that cute little weather gal, the next he was gone."

"What did you do then?"

"We called your brother, like Tommie asked us. Then we prepared his body."

The sheriff raised his eyebrows.

"Oh, nothing peculiar. We just washed him and rolled him up in a blanket. Then we waited. Your brother came for him about four. Unless there's some kind of emergency, even the night staff is always asleep by then. We let him in the back door."

"I thought there was supposed to be security on all the doors. Some kind of alarm."

"Oh, yeah, but we've wired around some of that stuff. This is a pretty boring place. Every now and then we need to get out without our keepers riding herd on us. We've got several escape routes, in case they find one and it takes us awhile to get around to unfixing it again."

"And Mad Dog, what did he do?"

"Nothing. He just thanked everyone for helping Tommie get his final wish. Then he took the body and left."

"He didn't bring anything? Nobody came with him? Could the baby have gotten in then somehow?"

"No, no. Alice brought the baby back later."

"You left the building after Mad Dog took Tommie Irons away?"

She paused and looked back at the grain elevator. Fitful snowflakes blew past her second-story window and played tag among the branches of skeletal elms.

"Some of us don't sleep too good. It was practically morning, almost time to get up. Didn't seem worth going back to bed and there was nothing to do around here. We decided to go for a walk."

"Where?"

"Just out. No place in particular. We prowled around downtown some, where nobody much goes anymore, especially not at that hour. Some of them like to remember the way it used to be when those businesses weren't boarded up. There used to be good shopping, nice restaurants, and movies at the Strand. Buffalo Springs was alive then, and they were younger and healthier and able to enjoy it. No, we just wandered. Tried to stay out of the wind and off the packed snow and patches of ice. Old bones break easier than young ones, and heal slower."

"And that's where Alice Burton found the baby?"

"Well, I think so. Must have been, 'cause I know good and well it was that cheap plastic thing she had with her when we went out. Blond hair that was painted on. I remember noticing the way it reflected the light in the hall. Now, I don't know where she found it, but that baby had dark hair when we came back. I tried to get a look, but she wouldn't let me. I thought it might still be alive. That's when I called that Kraus woman at your office. After Alice settled down a little, I managed to get closer. That's how I knew the baby was dead when you got here."

"Did you see anything, hear anything unusual while you were out?"

"Maybe. Over near Klausen's. I thought there were some kids there when we went by."

"Kids? Who, and doing what?"

"Well, actually I didn't see them. Just thought I heard them. And I'm not sure why I say kids. High voices, kind of excited like. Could of been girls, though I never saw 'em, never made out any words. I can't even say for sure they were there, though I saw some toilet paper on the bushes of a house in the neighborhood. That's a trick kids have been playing for a long time. It was windy and we were getting cold by then, hurrying back to warm up before they start gathering us for that stuff they call breakfast. And then, one of us girls was in an awful rush."

"Why's that?" the sheriff wondered.

"Her beau usually wakes up with an erection. She didn't want to waste it."

The Buffalo Springs educational system was housed in a pair of brick buildings of similarly nondescript early twentieth-century design—red squares with big windows—connected by a breezeway with offices and classrooms added in the fifties. For reasons that had always escaped the sheriff, that connection was made without concession to matching what it attached. It was yellow brick and hideously mid-century modern with tiny windows and occasional rows of glass bricks to admit light. Viewing the place had been known to induce nausea—just like when a test (essay, multiple choice, or of character) loomed behind its doors. The sheriff still couldn't approach it without the queasy feeling that he was about to be hit with a pop quiz for which he'd neglected to prepare.

Like most public buildings in Benteen County, you entered through two sets of doors. The design feature was meant to act as a heat or cold trap, keeping out whichever you didn't want. They held back wind and dust, too, at least hypothetically. At school, both doors tended to stay open and defeat the design when assaulted by crowds of kids hurrying to or from the line of yellow buses that gathered them from the far corners of the school district.

The sheriff joined one such crowd, along with a frigid cold front that swept through the main doors and down the corridor within. The kids peeled off toward the lockers that lined the halls. The sheriff made for the offices.

"Good morning, Sheriff English." The student secretary was blond and cute. "You here about the horrible Heathers or has the vice principal called you into her office again?" She grinned to make it clear she was teasing, but the humor didn't extend to her eyes. She was a year older than his daughters, "the horrible Heathers," and ran with the rich kids, a very different crowd.

"Hey, Englishman!" The sheriff's wife stuck her head around the corner of a door labeled JUDY ENGLISH, VICE PRINCIPAL. "I've got to get to a meeting. We're about to decide to turn the kids around and stick them back on the buses and send them home. The weatherman says scattered snow showers, but it's getting nasty out there. Come on in. I can spare a couple of minutes."

She greeted him with a warm, but appropriate, kiss as he entered her office and closed the door behind them. The space within gave new meaning to the word cramped. The sheriff felt NBA-sized in here.

As the door clicked shut she came out of the embrace, took him by the arms, and pushed him back to look at his face. Not that far back. Arm's length would have required her to slam one of them against a wall or her desk.

"What's this about a baby?"

"You know?"

"The whole school knows, and is actively involved in speculations. Is it true? What can you tell me?"

"Yeah, it's true, and not much. It was a newborn. Doc's got it now. He'll let me know whatever else he can find out about it. Him, actually, it's a boy. Looked Caucasian to me, which shouldn't be surprising in Benteen County. Do you know about Tommie Irons?"

Judy backed away and sat on the edge of her desk. The sheriff took the only full-sized chair on his side of the room, then tried to figure out where to put his feet.

"Tommie died last night. I guess Mad Dog had been filling him with stories about afterlife in the happy hunting grounds. He stole Tommie's body from the Towers to dispose of it 'properly' sometime before dawn. Some of the residents helped smuggle Mad Dog in and Tommie out. Then they went for a walk..." He shook his head. "When they came back, one of them had a real baby instead of the doll she usually carries to calm her."

"Alice Burton." Judy echoed his disbelief with a shake of the head, though hers was more dramatic because of her shoulder-length auburn curls. "And you don't have any idea whose it is?"

"Not yet. Nor where it came from. Wynn was going to take a quick look before he clocked out, and Mrs. Kraus is calling around to find me a deputy to give me some backup. You know how short-handed we are."

Judy knew. It was a topic he brought home for complaint about as regularly as she did the county's teacher shortage and the lack of competent substitutes. "So what do you want from me, the names of our sexually active girls? Did you come here for rumors, Englishman? Are you that desperate?"

Her voice got a little loud near the end. The sheriff could just picture the blond girl with her ear to the door. He held up his hands.

"Yeah, I suppose. But me getting there in a hurry might be important. If somebody disposed of an unwanted baby, there are people in this community who'll want to punish her. Maybe she deserves punishment, but not without all the messy checks and balances our legal system has to offer. And then, Doc said some things that set me thinking. Had me worrying about our daughters."

Judy's jaw dropped. "You think one of the Heathers…"
She started to laugh, but something clouded her face. She
shook her head emphatically. "No way. Not possible. They've
both been on the pill for years."

"The pill? Our little girls are on the pill?"

"They're not that little anymore, or haven't you looked
lately. They're both sixteen. How old do you think I was the
first time we…"

Picturing the blond at the door again, the sheriff waved
her off. "You've made your point. But how long has this been
going on? When were you going to tell me?"

"More than three years. Since Heather number two came
to live with us. There's a lot of sexual abuse in her background.
Sometimes that gets inherited. I decided not to take any
chances. Especially after I found some rubbers in her drawer.
The girls are the same age. I couldn't get pills for one and
not the other. And, I was going to tell you when you asked,
or when it came up, which it just did."

"Are they sexually active? No. Never mind. I'm not sure I
want to know. "

"I'd accuse you of a really irresponsible attitude, only I
haven't wanted to know either. I don't think our Heather has
gone that far yet. Two, though, I'd guess has had several partners
already."

"Could she?" the sheriff began. "I mean, is there any way…"

Judy bit her lip and ran her fingers through her thick hair,
considering it a lot longer than he liked. "I don't see how.
Something like that would be almost impossible to hide and
I think they would have told us. But you hear about parents
being caught by surprise sometimes. Englishman, the girls
didn't come to school this morning. Two locked herself in
the upstairs bathroom. She was still in there, being sick to
her stomach, when I came in. One wasn't feeling that chipper
either, so she stayed home to keep an eye on her sister. I
mean, I can't imagine it, but all of a sudden, I can."

And that was the trouble with imagination. If Judy could, so could the sheriff.

It was only a few blocks from the Buffalo Springs schools to the two-story frame house in which the sheriff, Judy, and a pair of Heathers lived. Judy and the Heathers usually walked to school, though not when the day's high was threatening thirty and wind gusts made it feel like that should be thirty below. The sheriff dallied along the way more than he normally would. When you haven't properly done the birds and bees bit, how do you walk through the door and ask your daughters if one of them has just secretly had a baby and then disposed of it? The closer he got, the slower his pickup moved.

The sheriff was good at laying guilt on himself. It wasn't like he and Judy had provided a June and Ward Cleaver atmosphere for the girls to grow up in. They fought all the time. Not knock-each-other-around fights, but arguments, most of which weren't about anything and weren't serious. But they'd learned how to hurt each other too. Enough that their marriage was on its second try. They'd divorced after their first eight years. Not a great example for One of Two, the only Heather they'd had at the time. Even after the divorce, though, their romantic life hadn't stopped. He and Judy were prominent figures in Buffalo Springs, big fish in the smallest of ponds. Benteen County was the antithesis of modern-urban America in which a sexual revolution and a multitude of personal freedoms made for all sorts of acceptable alternative relationships. It all happened in Benteen County, of course. It was just still "dirty" here—unacceptable—something to keep in the closet and out of the public eye. It wasn't proper for a teacher or the county sheriff to be involved in extramarital affairs, or at least not to get caught at them, so the two had soon fallen back into bed. Their daughter, Heather, was an excuse for spending a lot of time together.

The community could pretend it wasn't unusual for divorced parents of a child to discuss her future until all hours, even if they were pretty certain a lot more was going on behind the family's drawn blinds.

Then along came the other Heather, Two of Two. She was only a few months older, and so physically similar that the pair looked enough alike for strangers to think them twins. And they were actually related—distant cousins by a series of improbable twists the sheriff preferred not to think about. He preferred not to think about them because they were painful, Two of Two having come from about as dysfunctional a family as he could imagine—a family that had met its tragic end right here in Buffalo Springs. The second Heather had suddenly needed a foster family, and remarkably, turned into the linchpin on which he and Judy hung their second pledge to love, honor, and cherish, until death did them part.

Having two Heathers in the house was a complexity that probably should have been solved by name changes. Though neither Heather had been especially fond of her name before that option presented itself, neither proved willing to abandon what she was used to. And soon, both were arguing it wasn't necessary. It was no problem to them to call each other Heather. They always knew to whom they were speaking. The solution finally developed from the first Heather's addiction to Star Trek. The moment the character Seven of Nine appeared on the Voyager series, she knew how they would do it. She would be One of Two—after all, she was the first in the house and the natural child and deserved that minuscule privilege. Two of Two didn't have a problem with it. She was grateful for a place to go and people who wanted her. She retained her own last name, Lane, so that at school, there weren't two Heather Englishes, but around the house for the last three years, two girls answered together, or avoided answering, when addressed as just Heather, but responded with Borg-like enthusiasm to their Trekkie designations.

The sheriff parked his Chevy in the street in front of the house and tried to think of an excuse to put off his mission and go do something else. There were plenty of other things that needed doing, but, although he was sure the infant's mother wouldn't be found here, he needed to expand belief to certainty. They were going to be hurt by what they would perceive as his lack of trust, and they were going to be angry when he asked them to betray what they knew or suspected about their friends. He didn't want to do this, as sheriff or as father, but both positions required it of him.

The wind tried to tear the storm door off the house while he fumbled with the latch and let himself in. It stung his face with occasional snowflakes as well, though he couldn't tell whether the clouds were fulfilling their threat or the wind was just rearranging what was already lying about.

Boris, the family's aging German Shepherd, provided a suitably enthusiastic greeting as the sheriff entered, but the house was ominously silent.

"Heathers?" he shouted, but he already knew there was no one home.

The note was on the dining room table.

Don't worry. We're fine.

Small emergency. Back soon.

Love! One & Two

"Five-hundred to 501," Mrs. Kraus said into her walkie-talkie from her desk in the Benteen County Sheriff's Office. She spoke with dulcet tones, something similar to a metal file taking a burr off a plowshare.

A particular file was most likely to come to mind if you wished to describe Mrs. Kraus—the rat-tailed bastard file, named for its long, narrow shape, and its medium coarseness. Both were apt descriptions. Not that she was tall. She wasn't, she just seemed tall because she was so slender—roughly the same dimensions from top to bottom. And no one would accuse her of being either too coarse, or insufficiently so, at least not for an employee of the sheriff's department for nearly forty years.

The phone started ringing again and Mrs. Kraus reached over and took it out of its cradle and told it to hold on a minute before setting it down to repeat her numerical mantra into the radio. The office was five hundred. The sheriff was 501. Deputies ranked on down to 510, based on the assumption, untrue during her tenure, that the department was fully staffed.

"I read you five hundred."

"I hate to intrude," she informed the radio. "I know you're a busy man, but your office—that being me—could use a briefing about what's going on out there. We're swamped with calls wanting to know about that dead baby, and a missing body, and I don't know what to tell folks."

She had taken the original call about the baby and he'd told her about Mad Dog and Tommie Irons, so she knew he wasn't exaggerating much when he replied, "You know almost as much as I do."

She looked across the counter at the small crowd gathered in the office. "Well, sir, there's a county supervisor down here who'd like to be filled in. He's suggesting maybe you should drop everything and come over and make him happy. Pretty much otherwise ignore public safety and well being for his convenience."

Supervisor Bontrager had the good sense to look embarrassed, but not enough to hold his tongue. "Supervisor Hornbaker is handling a small emergency, but he and I have constituents who want to know about this baby. Mr. Hornbaker heard rumors it was a late term abortion. He's going to look into that. It's the kind of horrendous criminal act we aren't about to tolerate here."

"I heard," the sheriff said. "I haven't got time to care what anybody wants just now. The supervisors get in your way, Mrs. Kraus, use your Glock. You find me any spare deputies?"

"Hank Wilson is coming from over by Cottonwood Corners. It's gonna take him some time to navigate his way to the plowed roads, he says, but he's coming. No luck otherwise. If you're looking for Wynn, I don't know where he is. The manager of the secondhand store at Main and Monroe called earlier about him trying to confiscate all their dolls. When they wouldn't turn them over, he left. I've tried calling him on the radio and his cellular. No luck. He most likely forgot to turn them on."

The radio caught the tail end of an expletive. "If you hear from him, send him home. Hank or I'll deal with the missing doll. Now, is that all? I've got problems I need to deal with."

"I'm not just trying to pass the time, Sheriff. Amongst the fifty or so calls I've answered in the last hour, there's two you might want to know about. Some of Tommie Irons' kin are over at the Sunshine Towers. They say Tommie isn't the only thing missing from his room. They say there was an heirloom, something valuable, and they want to know what's become of it. Seemed a lot more upset about it than about Tommie."

"I'll head back over."

"You might want to make a stop on your way. Doc called, says he's got your autopsy results. Said he wouldn't give them over the phone and you should come by and talk to him when you got time."

"I'll do that. Tell our supervisors to go on about their business. I don't want any volunteers getting in the way. Five-oh-one out."

Mrs. Kraus smiled pleasantly at the crowd on the other side of the counter, set down her radio, reached into her desk drawer and extracted her Glock. She put it on top of her desk.

"You all heard what the sheriff said. Get on out of here and keep out of the way. I've been authorized to use this."

Bontrager sputtered, pounded his fist on the counter a couple of times, then spun on his heel and stomped out, followed by an angry retinue.

"Mrs. Kraus," a tiny voice whispered.

She remembered the phone. "What can I do for you?" she inquired.

"Mrs. Kraus," the phone told her. "This is Mad Dog. I got a problem. Englishman isn't there?"

"You got a problem all right, and no, he's not."

"I tried his cellular but it reads out of service. Can you get in touch with him?"

"Course I can, if it's important."

"I think this qualifies. I found a body."

"Mad Dog, the whole damn town knows about the body you found, and just where you found it."

"No ma'am. I mean another. Maybe more."

"**E**nglishman, I told you before. I won't give you a list of our school's sluts." Judy had exactly that list in front of her and was checking them off against today's attendance. No way she would admit that to Englishman, though.

"The car's not at the house," he said. "You drove to work this morning, right?"

"You having trouble with the Chevy? You can have the station wagon if you want. I can walk, or get a ride home if the weather gets worse. You need me to come pick you up?"

"So you drove?"

"Didn't I just say that?"

Only three of the girls had been missing from school this morning. She thought she would start with phone calls. A little cautious inquiry to eliminate suspects and she could tell Englishman to leave them alone. If she happened on something troubling, maybe she would point him, discreetly, in the right direction.

"No, you didn't tell me. And you still haven't. Is the station wagon at the school?"

"Yes, of course. I was late. I was lazy. It was cold and windy, and I wanted to be able to run home if the girls needed me. But you can have it if you want it."

"You're sure it's there? You're sure nobody's borrowed it?"

Judy shoved aside her list. This was turning into one of those conversations that felt like they were speaking alien languages at each other. They had so many of those she sometimes wondered if this second try at marriage had been a mistake. And she still wanted to live somewhere other than Englishman's beloved Plains.

"Who would borrow it?"

"Can you see it from your window?"

"Sure. You know where my parking space is."

"No, I mean can you see it from your window right now?"

"Englishman, what are you doing to me? Is this some kind of test-your-wife's-patience exercise from the morning paper?" There was no morning paper in Benteen County, but they subscribed to a rural edition of *The Wichita Eagle*.

"Humor me, Judy. Just look."

Judy leaned back in her chair and rubbed at the condensation that frosted her window. A fine hail of snow crystals peppered it from the other side. The Taurus huddled in a forlorn row of vehicles behind the school. It seemed to peer at her with an accusing look, wondering why it had to give up its warm space in the garage to save her three blocks of exercise she probably needed anyway.

"OK," Judy told the phone.

"OK, what?"

"It's there, Englishman. It's in the lot, right where I left it. Are you satisfied? Is there anything else you want? Should I double check the location of our school buses for you?" The school buses were returning students home in advance of what the weather bureau had decided might be a major storm after all. "Why do you want to know where our car is?"

"Tell you later."

"Englishman!" she howled, startling a couple of nearby administrators. The sheriff didn't hear her though. He'd hung up.

◇◇◇

Aside from the new addition to the Texaco, Klausen's Mortuary was far and away the most prosperous piece of real estate in Buffalo Springs. It stood, perfectly manicured, freshly painted, and flawlessly maintained at the corner of Washington and Main. It blended into the neighborhood, among those businesses that were still occupied and not verging on bankruptcy, like a peacock among sparrows.

The sheriff parked his Chevy in the lot at the side of the building. Even though the lot was almost empty, he avoided the main entry. It was all soft carpets and dark woods, soothing paintings that hinted at a gentle eternity, vases of fresh flowers, or now, in the dead of winter, the finest silk blossoms. If you lived in Benteen County, you could hardly avoid going through those doors for many rites of passage. Too many. Your last would probably be here as well. He followed a neatly shoveled walk around to the rear and let himself in the back door.

It opened on an antiseptic white hallway. The building embraced you back here in a way that was less friendly but more honest. Englishman's boots echoed reassuringly, an indication that he hadn't left his body behind when he passed into this lifeless place of light and silence. The third door on the left was rented by the county at a minimal rate. The sheriff knocked and Doc Jones told him to come in.

Doc was alone. His desk was uncharacteristically cleared of papers. It appeared that he'd just been sitting there in the dim light that filtered through the small high window behind him, eyes lost in the thousand-mile stare of someone contemplating the mysteries of life and death. This place must lend itself to such considerations. The sheriff resolved to spend as little time here as possible.

"Been waiting for you," Doc said, shoving himself up from his chair. "Come on, let's go have a look at our uninvited guest."

"That necessary?" The sheriff had been in the mortician's room that doubled as autopsy lab too many times. "Can't you just tell me what you found?"

Doc kept moving. He made his way down the hall to the first door on the opposite side. The sheriff felt like Doc was punishing him. Not because he was to blame, most likely, but just because he was available to take the abuse. A dead baby was hard on everyone.

Doc's office held some personality. He'd hung a couple of paintings, stuck some photographs on his desk, added shelves of heavily thumbed texts that gave the room a lived-in feel. The lab was the opposite. It felt died-in, but that wasn't the case. People didn't die here. They came to be embalmed, repaired, and groomed for open-casket funerals, boxed and tagged for transport to a crematory, or to lie on that cold steel table and wait for the coroner's unwelcome intrusions. No, not people, the sheriff amended. Their shells. Whatever made them people was gone by the time they came to Klausen's workrooms.

Against the south wall was a door that looked a lot like the one to the meat locker down at the Dillon's. Not without reason. Doc opened it and disappeared into the refrigerated interior for a moment. He came back carrying a little zippered bag. The sheriff had stuffed buddies into similar versions when he was in Vietnam. He'd come close to needing one himself.

Doc laid it on the stainless-steel table and worked the zipper. The baby looked like it had been fitted with zippers of its own. It had been sliced open, examined and then closed back up. The scars were neat enough, but they lacked the sort of precise small stitches reserved for flesh that might heal. The sheriff wanted to look somewhere else, but he couldn't. He found himself staring at the child's face, seeking resemblance to his family and hoping not to find it.

Where were the Heathers? Where could they have gone without the car? Or had they gone in someone else's car? He wanted to be outside this room, searching for them in the land of the living, not back here worrying in the land of the dead.

"Stillborn, full-term boy. That's what my report will say."

"Stillborn, can that be true?" That might take some of the heat off from the outraged locals, but it sure didn't take away the heat Doc suddenly radiated.

"You think I'd file a false report?" Doc was steaming.

"No. That's not what I…"

"You ever know me to lie? You ever know me to falsify anything? As Coroner, I won't do that even to make it easier for those who're left behind."

"Doc, calm down. What's with you and this case? You've had a burr up your ass from the moment you found out about it. You know I think you're the least likely public official in Benteen County to play other than by the rules. But you're making me think there's something about this that you aren't telling me."

Doc got himself back under control. "I'm sorry." His voice was calm again, but he was still stiff and anything but relaxed. "There's just something about a baby that didn't have to end up this way that angers me."

"Are you implying this was a wrongful death?"

Doc turned back to the task of removing the little corpse from the body bag. "I don't know. This child might have lived if it had been delivered in a hospital, if the mother had seen fit to consult with a physician through the course of her pregnancy. But that's not what happened. It never drew a breath. That's what I'll say in my report. The lungs never inflated. All kinds of maybes, but the result's the same. This baby's dead."

Neither Doc nor the sheriff referred to the baby as "he" or "him." Maybe using "it" kept this impersonal, distancing them from the pain.

"And you couldn't have just told me that?" The sheriff was a little pissed now too. It wasn't like finding dead babies was a cause of good cheer for him either. He still had to find a mother, determine how and why this little body had ended up where an old woman with Alzheimer's could find it.

"You remember what Wynn had to say about the baby being Jewish?" Doc asked. It seemed a strange segue, and this time it was the sheriff who exploded.

"When I have time, I will explain about circumcision to my deputy. Meanwhile, I've confiscated his weapon and sent him home. I know, as a law enforcement officer, he's an embarrassment. If I didn't need this job so badly, or wasn't always winning re-election by such narrow margins, I'd probably fire his ass and tell his father what to do with my department's budget. I might even try to run Wynn Senior out of office, only he's the most popular political figure in this county and about the only one on the board who knows what he's doing. Folks around here are fond of Deputy Wynn. They find him an amusement, as long as he isn't screwing up their cases or ignoring their legal rights. And, damn it, he means well."

"Guess I'm not the only one who's a little touchy this morning," Doc said. For the first time there was a hint of warmth, evidence of their close friendship in his voice. "That's not what I meant either. Come over here. Take a look."

Doc reached down and gently brushed thick black hair off the child's forehead. There was a mark there. The sheriff bent closer.

"You see it," Doc asked, and the sheriff did.

In the center of his forehead, just below the hairline, someone had drawn a tiny swastika.

The weather was deteriorating. By the time Mad Dog and Hailey got back to the Saab, all his extremities were numb. His face was raw from the stinging snow that had begun falling, driven by the wind so that it blew almost parallel to the ground. He couldn't get a cellular signal and had to step back out of the Saab to try his phone in the open. Hailey refused to follow. If a tundra wolf preferred to snuggle near the heater vent on the seat of an aging Saab Turbo instead of sniffing about for bunnies—or more skeletons—it was definitely turning unpleasant out.

Mad Dog finally got the phone to work. The connection was weak, but he discovered his brother's cell phone was turned off. When he punched in the number for the sheriff's office next, it actually rang. Of course Mrs. Kraus didn't really answer, she just told him to hold while she dealt with something. It sounded like a madhouse there, only his signal was so poor that he couldn't make out much. Could all that be because of Tommie Irons?

Just as he was about to abandon hope, Mrs. Kraus came back on the line. For a moment, her voice was crystal clear. "What can I do for you?" she asked.

Englishman wasn't there and it was clear folks were pissed that he'd helped Tommie Irons on his journey to the Happy Hunting Grounds. Englishman needed to know what Hailey had discovered, though, so Mad Dog swallowed his pride and began trying to explain to Mrs. Kraus.

"I found a body," he told her.

"Mad Dog, the whole damn town knows about the body you found, and just where you found it."

"No ma'am. I mean another. Maybe more."

He stomped his feet to try to get some feeling, and then there was way too much feeling on the left side of his face and when he turned to look for the phone it wasn't there anymore, just some wires and shattered plastic hanging over his bare, bloody hand. Moments before that hand had held a cell phone and been enclosed in a thick mitten.

Mad Dog hadn't thought the Saab could get through the drifted snow just downhill of the slough, but it did, and faster than he would have dreamed. The plastic had nicked his hand, but it was his ear doing most of the bleeding. He couldn't hear out of it quite right, not that he was complaining. Right now it was about putting distance between himself and the white pickup truck that had followed him down the road by the slough. If, when he found time to check, he resembled

Vincent Van Gogh in the ear department, he would still count himself lucky. The shooter with the white truck had put a bullet through his phone. The Nokia was dead. He wasn't. If the Saab proved better at negotiating snowdrifts than the shooter's truck, he would keep it that way.

"I don't think I can do it," Two of Two said.

"Spread your legs a little. Put your left foot up there and push."

"Don't forget to breathe," One of Two suggested.

"OK," Wynn said, shifting his butt around nervously and wringing his hands. The deputy leaned forward and looked out the windshield, checking the street ahead. It was empty, just as it almost always was. "Your foot on the floor?"

"My left one?" Two wondered. "Yeah. Pedal's all the way down."

"All right, now. Take ahold of the shifter here and shove it to the left and forward so's you're in first gear." Two did as instructed. "Now, gently, push your right foot down on the accelerator as you lift your other foot off the clutch."

"Like this?" The sheriff's cruiser spun its back wheels, then the tires chirped and grabbed and the car jumped forward like a dragster coming off the line.

"It would be good if you stayed on the street," One observed from the back seat. Wynn wasn't saying anything because he was too busy cringing as they climbed the curb. The front bumper avoided an oak by inches. Heather Lane got them back in the street as the engine approached red line on the tach. She took her foot off the accelerator half a moment before she put her other foot back on the clutch. Everyone jerked forward until she shifted gears and popped the clutch again. This was executed even less smoothly than her initial effort, but there were so many cubic inches of ancient Detroit iron under the hood that it was almost impossible to stall, even when you managed to miss a couple of gears and go directly into fourth.

"How was that?" Two wondered, proud of the success she'd managed on her very first try.

"I think she's getting the hang of it, don't you, Deputy?" One said.

Wynn couldn't find his voice to answer. They accelerated out of town, headed south along Adams Street, racing the wind and beginning to win.

"You are such a sweetheart, agreeing to teach us how to drive a manual transmission," Two told him, taking her eyes off the road just long enough to bring the tires on Wynn's side to the edge of an especially deep ditch.

"Ulp!" Wynn responded graciously. He couldn't get enough breath for a terrified scream.

Judy English studied the names on her list and remembered their faces, figures, and characters. The sophomore had to be too skinny. No way she could have hidden a pregnancy in that scrawny body of hers, and yet...Judy remembered noticing a bit of a tummy on her last week. She'd thought it might be evidence of malnutrition. The other two, the seniors, seemed more likely. One of them was Marilyn Monroe voluptuous. Lots of room in those ample curves to hide an extra bulge. The other was a strikingly beautiful girl with a weight problem. She had trouble saying no to food—or sex. Self-esteem issues, Judy decided.

She probably ought to tell Englishman, Judy thought, but she was still pissed at him for that bizarre call about the car. She reached out and picked up a picture from her desk. Englishman stood in the front yard, a Heather at either shoulder and an explosion of morning glories erupting behind them. He could make her so angry...or so horny.

He still looked good at forty-seven. His face was more weathered; the crinkles around his amazingly blue eyes were

deeper than she remembered all those years ago when she
was a teen and he was a wounded war hero. She'd looked across
the gym at a Bison's basketball game and decided he was the
one. His hairline was a little higher, just a hint of gray dusted
his temples, but he still had that calm, noble look that had
turned her on. The Cheyenne heritage Englishman and Mad
Dog's mother had claimed, and Judy's genealogical research
appeared to confirm, was evident in his high cheekbones, his
Roman nose, and his dark complexion. She, and plenty of
other girls, had thought he looked exotic and dreamy. Hot!

Judy smiled. They'd been right. He was hot. He certainly
lit her romantic fires. There'd never been any shortage of
passion in their relationship, either when they loved or when
they fought. He'd told her, once, that was what first intrigued
him about her. She was feisty. If she didn't agree with him,
and she usually didn't, she let him know. And fighting with
him was fun because it was so much more fun making up
afterwards. Though, for a while there, it hadn't looked like
there would be an afterwards. They'd gotten divorced. Even
then, they'd gone right on fighting...and loving.

But damn Englishman. What was that call about the car
really about? It wasn't like him to try to annoy her. Not on
purpose. These days, when she got mad, he seldom showed
his own temper. He usually just backed off and let her have
the last say. He was trying hard to make it work this time.
She loved him even more for that.

Why would he care where the Taurus was if he didn't want
to use it? She glanced back down at her list of potential sex
kittens and suddenly knew.

She was breathing hard when she picked up the phone.
She fumbled, punching in their home number. Had to do it
twice to get it right. The answering machine clicked in after
the first ring.

"Hi!" One of Two greeted her. It wasn't their usual message.
Englishman was on that one. "We're ill. We're trying to nap.
Please call later, or leave a message and we'll return your call

when we can." Judy thought she could hear Two talking to some-one in the background. And just the hint of a masculine reply before the recording stopped and the machine beeped at her.

"Girls. It's me. Pick up the phone please." No one did, not even when Judy repeated her plea a couple of times in an increasingly higher register.

Before the machine beeped to tell her she'd run out of time, Judy was slinging on her coat and digging in her purse for her keys, already out of the office and on her way to the parking lot.

◇◇◇

"Where have you been?"

Stan Deffenbach was hopping around the lobby of the Sunshine Towers like a child in desperate need of a potty break. Lucille Martin took Deffenbach by the shoulder and gently pushed him aside. She looked older than she had earlier.

"We do have a problem, Sheriff," Mrs. Martin said. "Tommie Irons' family came shortly after you left. Becky Hornbaker's son, Simon, and one of his young brutes."

Becky Hornbaker was Tommie Irons' sister and Supervisor Hornbaker's wife. Simon was their only child, and his twin sons, Judah and Levi, were a pair of hulking bullies.

"Apparently there's some family heirloom missing and they're upset about it. Simon went so far as to accuse poor Mr. Deffenbach and the Sunshine Towers staff of stealing it. Simon and Levi are still up there looking. They've terrified most of the residents. Perhaps you can make them leave and stop disassembling furniture and searching people's rooms."

"What are they searching for? What's missing?"

"They won't say."

"They won't tell you what's missing, but they want you to give it back?" The sheriff found such lack of logic hard to imagine, except of Hornbakers. It was also hard to picture Lucille

Martin not getting a satisfactory answer or being disobeyed by anyone, even if she was currently without a ruler.

"Precisely. It's something small, I think, from some of the places they've looked for it. And from the energy they're bringing to the search, it must be valuable. I told them they would have to leave, but they ignored me."

Was ignoring Lucille Martin permitted?

"Please stop them," Stan Deffenbach whined. "They're ruining my business."

"W̲hy did I let you talk me into this?" Wynn complained.

"'Cause we blackmailed you," One of Two said.

"'Cause when you caught Gloria Ramirez on the street after midnight and accused her of being the phantom snowballer, you searched her," Two added from behind the wheel. "Too thoroughly. I mean, who's going to hide snowballs inside her bra?"

"Now listen," Wynn swiveled in his seat to fix his most severe look on both Heathers. His seat belt stopped him about halfway and the gesture came off more like petulant. "Nothing inappropriate about it at all. I been watchin' them reality cop shows on my satellite dish. You'd be surprised where perpetrators hide things."

"Snowballs? In her brassiere?" Two accused.

"Well, hey. It's not like I strip searched her. I just patted her down."

"Nah. You copped a feel, and since she was out after hours and didn't want her folks to know, she didn't say anything because you let her sneak in her house afterwards. She didn't tell her pa, who would likely come after you with an ax handle. And she didn't tell her boyfriend, who would probably punch your lights out and then get arrested for assaulting a law officer."

"So she told us," the Heather in the back seat continued, "'cause she thought we might hint to Dad that one of his deputies needed to learn to keep his hands to himself."

"Which we will, if we ever hear about you doing anything like that again," Two resumed. "Or might, anyway, if you don't keep your promise and teach us how to drive a standard shift."

"But why today?" Wynn complained.

Two practiced downshifting to third again, then back up to fourth. "'Cause Englishman says he'll start driving this cruiser more and leaving his truck for us once we learn how to handle a standard transmission. Only he's never got the time to teach us. And, 'cause you're actually a pretty sweet guy and would probably have done this out of the goodness of your heart if we'd only asked you nicely in the first place. Right, Heather?"

"Right, Heather."

"OK, OK. Only let's pull off on some back roads where you won't have to pass any more semis. And let's slow down, pretend there's a thirty mile speed limit."

"Sure," Two of Two agreed, swinging onto the first cross-road to the west. There was just enough patch ice in the intersection to let the back end go loose on her, only she steered into the skid and kept it on the road, managing a pretty smooth downshift into second in the process. "Is this better?"

"Gack!" she decided, was probably not an affirmative response.

◇◇◇

Judy was out of the door before the Taurus stopped rolling. The wind finished the job she hadn't completed with the brake pedal, bringing it to rest inches short of their front fence. The wind did its best to finish her, too, strafing her with snowflakes and tugging on her clothes as it resisted her frantic efforts to get to the front door.

Boris met her with a delighted bound into her arms that almost knocked her down but seemed gentle in comparison to the buffets dealt by the wind.

"Heathers!" Judy shouted. Relative silence was her only reply. Boris panted and tried to cover her with slobber. The house creaked and groaned as the storm probed it for weakness and rattled the windows. There was no sign of the girls, only the note on the dining room table. She had just finished reading it, crumpling it with rage, and was about to let loose a scream that would have been nearly as wild as her fears when the doorbell rang. Boris launched himself, madly barking, ready to battle the forces of darkness or welcome his wide circle of friends.

It was the nosy woman from next door, so wrapped up in her parka that it took Judy a moment to recognize her. Boris exchanged barking for tentative tail wagging. He knew her but she wasn't a dog person, not worth his time.

"Is everything all right, Judy?" the woman asked. "The way you drove in, and after all the excitement over here today, well, I'd begun to worry."

"Excitement?" Judy pictured a band of armed terrorists seizing her house. She could see the fire trucks, visualize the row of ambulances, hear Englishman directing his SWAT team. Too bad Buffalo Springs only had one volunteer fire truck, an ambulance would have had to come from outside the county, and Englishman didn't have enough deputies to police the roads, let alone put together a Special Weapons and Tactics unit.

"First the deputy came by in the patrol car and left with the girls. Then your husband drove up and was in and out in a minute. Now you. I mean, I was concerned, especially after I noticed the girls letting themselves into your house just before dawn. I couldn't imagine what they might have been up to."

Maybe her neighbor couldn't. Judy's imagination began selecting among a variety of disasters.

Mad Dog's Saab made it as far as the third bridge after the first turn south. Only the third bridge wasn't there anymore. Mad Dog spent a moment thanking *Maheo*, the Cheyenne All Father, for the Swedish engineers who'd designed the Saab's brake system. His tires were right at the edge, but on the right side of that edge.

When had the bridge washed out? He'd driven this road not long ago, well, maybe a couple of years. Whether last year's spring floods took it, or those of the year before, didn't matter. What mattered was his only options were abandoning the car or going back. His throbbing left ear convinced him. He threw open the door, stepped out, and squinted back up the road into the wind. There was too much snow in the air to see anything. Maybe, if the truck were some color other than white…

The nearest farmhouse was Tommie Irons', about half a mile distant. Any other choices were all more than two miles away.

Would whoever shot him know that? And, hell, who would want to kill him? Half the county was upset with his protest over the election's results, or his vociferous support for other unpopular political causes, but he couldn't imagine anyone actually shooting him because of that.

Some of Tommie's relatives might be ticked off. Not that any of them had cared enough to visit the old man while he was still alive. Again, Mad Dog couldn't picture them coming after him with a gun.

He slid into the ditch, climbed a barbed wire fence, and tested the ice on the stream. It was plenty solid, as well as plenty slick. He proved both, simultaneously, when his feet went out from under him and he slid all the way to the far bank. Hailey joined the game. She pounced on him, nuzzled him too close to his sore ear, then bounded into the under-brush beyond. Mad Dog thought he heard an engine coming down the road. He didn't bother to confirm it. He just grabbed a handful of frozen branches and hauled himself off the frozen stream and into the brush, hot on Hailey's trail.

Mad Dog pulled his parka up over his ears as he went. The left was already so numb from the cold that it hardly complained. He stuffed his bare and bleeding hand deep into a flannel-lined pocket. He found wolf prints and followed them. After a few yards of scrub and skeletal tree trunks he found himself on the edge of a pasture. Hailey's prints preceded him, already eroding to invisibility as the wind erased them. The Saab was a dark bruise back where the road should be. He thought he saw a truck-like shape behind it, then the wind and a fresh blast of driving snow made his eyes water and hid them from him. Mad Dog didn't complain. He stretched his legs and began to run.

He ran nearly every day, though usually not in heavy boots on frozen pasture. On the days when he didn't feel like running, he reminded himself he was nearing sixty and aerobic exercise might add to life's quality and quantity, then ran anyway. He liked to tell people he was running for his life. Now, suddenly, he really was.

Every school child has encountered, by whatever name and sex, a Simon Hornbaker of their very own. Simon was two years older than the sheriff. When the one-room school, where English attended his first five grades, finally closed and he and his schoolmates were packed off to immense Buffalo Springs Elementary, Simon was the first student he met.

Simon had been a scrawny, small-for-his-age, dull-normal sort—a natural target for the jokes and taunts of his own age group. But two years gave Simon a nice edge on a boy just entering sixth grade and without friends to offer the strength of numbers. On his first day, the boy who would be sheriff had approached the building overburdened by a load of books and anxieties. Simon picked young English out, recognized his fear, and struck, knocking everything from his hands as he fought through the crowded entrance. The sheriff still felt the humiliation, scrambling about on hands and knees, trying to rescue his belongings from beneath a stampede of students. Some had paused to smirk or giggle—maybe even grin a little wider because of the way Simon stood there and mocked him. One year was all it lasted. Less, really, because by the end English had friends. There wasn't a middle school at Buffalo Springs then. Next year, Simon was suffering his own humiliations as a mere freshman at the high school next door. Their paths seldom crossed again, until English became a freshman himself. By then, he was nearly Simon's size. Too near for the harassment to continue. But for one brief year, Becky Hornbaker's darling Simon was the sheriff's worst nightmare.

"Finally got here, eh, Sheriff. Took your sweet time. You find that thieving brother of yours yet?"

Simon was sorting through the contents of a dresser drawer he'd brought into the hall. Well, not really sorting, more like tossing, piece by piece, into a pile at his feet.

"Simon, what are you doing?"

"Looking for our family's property. Your nut-case brother made off with it."

"If Mad Dog took something, why search here?" He noticed the drawer contained women's lingerie. "And whose room did that stuff come from? That's not your uncle's."

"Any of them old biddies who helped Mad Dog cart Uncle Tommie off coulda stole it. When there ain't no law around, sometimes we gotta make our own."

Simon stirred the silks and satins with a foot, then turned toward the door. It led into Alice Burton's room.

"Simon. You don't have permission to search this room. Mrs. Martin and Mr. Deffenbach said they've asked you to leave. Now I'm doing the same."

Simon had put on weight and muscle over the years. He probably had twenty pounds on the sheriff, though most of it hung over his belt. He tried to suck it all back into his chest as he swung around.

"Who's gonna make me?"

The childishness of the remark took the sheriff right back to grade school. Hadn't Simon matured at all?

The sheriff edged to the side, getting a look around Simon and into the room, trying to reassure himself that Mrs. Burton was OK and Levi wasn't waiting just inside to back his father's play.

The old lady was in her rocking chair by the window, but someone had tied her hands to its arms. Her eyes met his. "Get these filthy Hornbakers away from me, Sheriff!" she yelled.

The sheriff let his hand drop near his holstered .38. "I want you to raise your hands, turn around, and put them on the wall."

"Like hell, you Englishman's bastard," Simon shot back, ever the master of juvenile repartee. His hand darted under his coat, like he was reaching for a gun of his own. The sheriff stepped in, pivoted, and kicked. Though the toe of his boot connected a foot lower than it would have when that sergeant taught him the move, the sheriff's Army training paid off perfectly. Simon Hornbaker folded in half and collapsed against the wall with a crash. He wasn't reaching for anything anymore, except maybe his breath. The sheriff stepped in, grabbed him by his hair, and straightened him out on the floor. A quick pat down revealed a cozy little 9 mm automatic. The sheriff dropped it in one of his own pockets and connected Hornbaker's right wrist and left ankle with handcuffs. Simon tried to say something. It didn't resemble any of the languages spoken in Benteen County.

The sheriff unsnapped his holster and pulled his Smith & Wesson. After Simon's attempt to draw a gun on him, he had no intention of giving Levi the same opportunity. The sheriff flattened his back to the wall beside Mrs. Burton's open door. "Benteen County Sheriff! Levi, come out with your hands up!"

No one came. No one answered. The sheriff gathered himself, silently counted down from three, and threw himself inside. As he cleared the door he found himself face to chest with the mountainous Hornbaker boy. That was when his radio squawked.

"Englishman!" it demanded in a tinny imitation of Judy's voice. "Where are the Heathers?"

It surprised the hell out of both the boy and the sheriff. They stood there, exchanging baffled looks, until something heavy popped the sheriff on the head and things went dark and dreamy inside.

◇◇◇

J udy tried again. "Englishman! Damn you! Answer me!"

Mrs. Kraus ran the sheriff's office with an iron hand. Nobody came behind her counter without an invitation. Nobody touched the department's radios without her say so. Nobody strode through her crowded reception room, filled with people demanding to know about a baby murderer on the loose, shoving them aside in single-minded determination to get an answer to her question…except Judy English.

Mrs. Kraus recognized the look in her eye and got out of the way.

Supervisor Bontrager, back with his followers for more, didn't. He got bumped. He'd been explaining to folks that Supervisor Hornbaker had already reported from his personal reconnaissance. He had shared knowledge about the case they couldn't release just yet, but that they had things under control. The collision knocked his hat off and Bontrager lost his balance and stepped on it. Bontrager's blood pressure spiked as he came around the counter and tried to take the radio away from Judy.

"You just hold on now, Ms. English. That's county property. Not for personal use. And you can't use language like that over the public airways."

Judy twisted away from his ineffectual grab for the radio.

"Englishman, damn it! Are you out there? Is anybody?"

Bontrager reached again. "Now see here, missy!" Mrs. Kraus could have told him not to do that, but, deep down, she thought she would enjoy the results more if she didn't interfere.

The radio made Rice Krispy noises as Bontrager got a hand on it, then found Judy English's face right in his. "Bontrager, you kumquat. You are a pompous, incompetent, bureaucratic joke. If you don't take your hands off me, I'll break them."

Mrs. Kraus smiled a little, even though she knew she could kiss one vote for the budget that might have funded her raise goodbye. That vote had been pretty unlikely anyway. A few of the folks crowding the sheriff's office nodded in agreement with Judy's outburst.

Mrs. Kraus didn't have any kids of her own, but she knew you put yourself at risk if you got between a worried mother and her children.

"Mr. Supervisor," Judy continued, backing Bontrager against the counter with the power of her maternal rage. "Unless you can tell me where my daughters are, you will stop bothering me and get out of my way."

"I don't know what's wrong with the radio, Judy," Mrs. Kraus said. "The sheriff was about to check on something over to the Sunshine Home, last he called in. That was just minutes ago. I'm sure he must still be there."

Judy turned her back on Bontrager. "The Sunshine Towers?"

"Yes ma'am."

"Thank you, Mrs. Kraus." Judy flipped the radio over her shoulder and Mrs. Kraus caught it just before it smacked Bontrager in the face. Judy headed for the exit. Everyone in the room scrambled to clear her a path.

"**O**h, oh!" the Heathers chorused.

"That's Mom," One of Two said.

"She knows," Two of Two agreed.

"Do you think we should answer?" Heather English's question was directed at Deputy Wynn. He was the adult. He was the responsible party, or so she suddenly hoped, given the tone of their mother's voice. Also, he had the radio. Or, rather, it was down on the floor between his feet where it had fallen when they spun around twice and ended up in the ditch, hood deep in a snowdrift.

Their father didn't reply to Judy's harangue. That surprised all three occupants of the immobile sheriff's department black and white.

"Maybe you better talk to her," the first Heather suggested to Wynn.

Wynn wanted to do no such thing. As he picked up the radio they heard Judy English clearly, though less distinctly, threaten the person of Supervisor Bontrager.

Wynn fumbled with the radio, passing it off, like it had suddenly turned molten, to Two behind the steering wheel. She declined, batting it back to One. By the time One worked up enough nerve to try a tentative "Uh, Mom?" Judy was no longer within hearing range.

Since, in the process of playing walkie-talkie volleyball, Wynn and the girls had accidentally changed frequencies, the small mob watching the door swing closed on Judy English's heels failed to hear either.

"Mom? Dad? Mrs. Kraus? Anybody there?"

Nobody was.

◇◇◇

"Are you all right, Sheriff?"

"Yeah. Sure. I'm fine," the sheriff lied, trying to remember where he was. He stood up and had to grab the edge of the doorway to keep from being thrown to the corner of the ceiling by the wildly spinning room. Gradually it slowed and he tried to figure out who had asked. It wasn't easy, because his eyes were having trouble getting just one image clear enough to recognize.

"Maybe you should lie down on the bed for a minute."

She was little, with chopped white hair and bright red tennis shoes. He should know her. Something about a baby.

"No, really. I'm fine. Uh, how about you?"

"Some of us locked ourselves in a room down the hall after Simon and Levi came in and started going crazy, searching rooms and threatening folks if they didn't give back what was stolen."

"Give what back?" His ears were ringing and his head felt like it was being used by the drummer for a heavy metal band.

"They never said what they wanted."

"Never said?"

Geez! He sure had a knack for law enforcement. Such a snappy interrogation technique. It was working though.

"Nope. They just demanded to know who was with Tommie before Mad Dog came and got him, then they started telling us to give it back. Not what, just it, though I'm sure it was that ring."

"Ring?"

"Big heavy silver-looking thing. Ugly, but Tommie wore it all the time until the last few days. Someone asked if he'd already given it to the family, but he said no. 'If I can't take it with me,' he said, 'then I'm not going.' Didn't make any sense, 'cause he already wasn't wearing it. But he was taking a lot of morphine then." She got a distant look in her eyes and sighed.

"Simon asked me what Tommie was wearing when we wrapped him up for Mad Dog and I said nothing, 'cause that's what we'd been told to do, just clean him up and wrap him naked in a blanket. I thought that might shock Simon, only it didn't. He just pointed at his finger and asked, 'Not even jewelry?' When I told him no, he didn't seem to believe me."

It was coming back. Mad Dog, of course, had started this whole crazy day by taking Tommie Irons' body out of here sometime before dawn. And then the old folks had decided to take a walk and came back with the baby and...

"Mrs. Burton. She was tied up in her chair."

"I undid her. She's in the bathroom, getting a damp cloth to clean up that nasty place on the back of your head. I'm sorry about that. I flung a silver hairbrush at Levi from down the hall, but it wasn't aerodynamic enough to fly true. Lucky you were wearing that hat, though it's gonna be hard to get a proper shape back into it." She reached down and picked up the sheriff's Stetson and handed it to him. Sure enough, the back had been flattened as effectively as if someone had put it between a hammer and anvil for a few hundred blows— much like his head.

Simon Hornbaker. He remembered now. "I handcuffed him. How'd they…"

"Levi just hefted him up." It was Alice Burton's voice as she came out of the bathroom. She hurried around the bed and handed him a damp washcloth and he experimentally dabbed it against the back of his head. He was surprised to discover a kind of a bloody lump there, instead of shattered pieces of skull and oozing brains.

"Picked Simon up and ran him down the stairs. From the sound of it, maybe dropped him a time or two on the way. They drove off just a minute before you started coming around again. Would you like me to get you some aspirin?"

"How many can you spare? No, wait," he said as she turned to go check. He had the feeling that no matter how many she found, it wouldn't be enough. The room listed to starboard again, then settled back into place. He turned until he could look Alice Burton in the eyes. Her memory was a lot better than most people thought. He believed she could tell him, so he asked.

"Mrs. Burton, where did you find that baby?"

She peered at him through long lashes. In spite of the deep lines that creased her face, she was still an attractive woman. She must have been spectacular once.

"May I have *my* baby back?" she asked. Her mind seemed to be going somewhere else again.

"I'll get him for you," the sheriff offered, "if you'll tell me where you left him."

"Klausen's," she said. "On the back stoop at Klausen's, where I got the other one."

It was manicured pasture, closely trimmed by Tommie Irons' herd of Brangus cattle. Under other circumstances, Mad Dog would have preferred more cover. Not today, though, since the wind and snow had picked up so much that he couldn't see either side of the field. There was no hint of his Saab back there, no sign of the white pickup he thought was following him, and no evidence he was being pursued. No proof he wasn't, either.

Conditions were deteriorating, approaching white-out. Somewhere ahead, he knew, there was a hedgerow that separated this pasture from an adjacent wheat field, and, at the south end, a cluster of trees and outbuildings around the Irons' farmhouse. Mad Dog couldn't see any of it. No sign of the cattle either, which was just as well. The herd bull was pure Brahma and pure meanness. Mad Dog just pumped his legs and fought for balance and tried to guide himself toward where he thought the house would be. Occasionally, he found some of Hailey's tracks to follow. Even a tundra wolf, he figured, would be looking for shelter on a day like this.

Mad Dog was breathing hard, harder than his exertions explained. He tried to analyze it, and was surprised to discover it wasn't because he was afraid of another bullet. No one back at the road could see him. Unless they could run, blinded by a blizzard and across a frozen pasture, a lot faster than he could, they weren't going to catch him or come in range of a good shot. No, it was that very absence of road behind him and of trees ahead that bothered him. The wind and the snow were closing him in, shutting down the kind of view he was accustomed to—horizons that reached from here to forever, flat earth stretching to infinity and arguing against the possibility that the world was round. What it was, Mad Dog finally realized, was claustrophobia.

And then there was something, looming behind the swirling snow. The shadows of trees appeared, naked branches reaching to snag the sky and tear it open, and behind them something big, something boxy. A tool shed, maybe, or a chicken coop. He was a lot closer before he realized there were more shadows beneath the trees. Cattle. The biggest stepped out into the wind to stand between his harem and whatever threat Mad Dog might constitute. It was the Brahma bull Tommie was said to have named, on account of its color and disposition, Black Death.

Supervisor Bontrager was stumbling around the sheriff's office in search of his lost dignity when the telephone rang. It had been ringing pretty regularly all morning.

"Ms. Kraus?"

The voice was faint and distant, the connection a shade worse than you could get by attaching a couple of tin cans to a long piece of string.

"Yes?"

"Ms. Kraus, it's me." Mrs. Kraus knew a lot of people called "me." Most of them had voices she recognized. She was inclined to say so, but there was a crowd there with Supervisor Bontrager listening in on everything. She controlled herself and settled on polite.

"Me who?" Well, semi-polite. Polite wasn't her strong suit.

"Me, Hank Wilson. Benteen County Deputy Sheriff. I'da used the radio, only my batteries are dead."

"Where the hell are you?" Mrs. Kraus rasped. Bontrager went into conference with some of his cronies over near the door. She could hear something about gathering the rest of the county supervisors for a special session.

"What we got here ain't law enforcement, it's fascist, God-less communism," Bontrager said, working his way around the political spectrum. "The sheriff is out of control," he continued, getting further and further out of control himself, "and his wife…"

"I could use a deputy right here in this office at the moment," Mrs. Kraus continued. "Shouldn't you be here by now?"

"You looked outside lately?" Wilson's voice was not only distant, it was beginning to snivel. "There's a damn blizzard out there. I'm stuck out to Fred and Virginia Miller's place, about twelve miles out. I don't see how I can get through unless a snowplow happens along for me to follow, or someone with a four-wheel drive comes and brings me in. Can you send anybody?"

Mrs. Kraus probably couldn't even send someone for hot coffee and a sandwich, and Bertha's was just across the park from the courthouse, not two hundred yards away. Bontrager was leading his mob toward the foyer, on the way back to the county supervisor's offices again. Mrs. Kraus gave the mob a thorough once over. She didn't see anyone with a four-wheel drive, or much sympathy for the sheriff.

"Not likely," she said. "You make some calls from there, I'll see what I can do from here. I'll let you know if I find someone. You do the same."

"What's that?" Wilson's voice barely emerged through a burst of static. "Ms. Kraus? You still there? Can you hear…" And then she couldn't, except for a hollow kind of silence that made her suspect a phone line had gone down somewhere between the Miller's place and town. She picked up her cellular and tried calling Wilson back. Nothing. She tried the sheriff's cell phone. Nothing. She tried the radio. Three strikes and she was out.

She could hear Bontrager's voice echoing down the hall—something about impeachment proceedings. She wondered what to do next. Using the Glock had a certain appeal, but was probably an overreaction. She would do all she could, Mrs. Kraus promised herself.

But a chill walked up her spine. Someone just stepped on my grave, she thought. It scared her, because all she could do might not be enough.

◇◇◇

The massive bull would have stood out like the central figure in a black and white negative, only he'd been plastered with so much snow that his onyx coat had acquired an icy patina. He had faded into the landscape, like those missing horizons, but Mad Dog's precipitous arrival brought him back—ghostly but real.

The Brahma snorted and stomped and Mad Dog stopped in mid-stride. The bull stood directly between him and the fence. While Mad Dog wouldn't object to going around to get where he wanted, the bull seemed to prefer that he go back the way he'd come—just a little faster than its hooves and horns could direct him.

"Easy big fellow," Mad Dog soothed. "I'll bet you're actually a softy like my Buffalo Bob." The Brahma shook his head and snorted in what seemed to be clear denial. It edged sideways and cocked its horns. No one had ever blunted those horns. They looked sharp enough for surgical work, which seemed to be what the animal had in mind.

Cattle exploded from the fence line and the inadequate protection of the scraggly tree row, scattering as if they'd spotted a buyer from Burger King pulling into the farm. The bull spun, searching for the new threat behind him. And then Hailey was there, darting in and nipping his heels. The bull jumped and whirled, like he was coming out of a rodeo gate, bucking and kicking, only Hailey was at his heels again.

Mad Dog dashed for the fence, scrambled over the strands of barbed wire and between the thorny limbs of Osage orange trees. He had reached his destination, but he hadn't thought about what to do once he got here. Back on that road, after the gunshot, there hadn't been time for planning.

Hailey cleared the fence and joined him. What he could see of the pasture was now empty of cattle. Mad Dog led the way to the leeward side of a shed. The farmhouse huddled in the midst of its outbuildings, just beyond. Fresh snow was beginning to pile up on all the structures' south sides, not deep yet, but not without promise.

It was a big house, a boxy two-story frame with a porch that stretched around the sides toward the front. An upstairs sleeping porch hung over the back, an area currently better suited for additional freezer space.

Mad Dog surveyed the place with interest. He'd never been here before. Few people had. Folks got along all right with Tommie Irons, but they'd done that on his trips to town. He never invited visitors here on account of his sister, Becky Hornbaker.

A gust of wind sneaked in the hood of Mad Dog's parka, past his collar, and down his spine. He would have to find someplace warmer soon, but he didn't want Tommie's relatives knowing where he'd left the body. He didn't want to get shot by whoever was in the white pickup, either.

Tommie Irons had been born here almost seventy years ago. He and Becky grew up on this farm until Tommie started first grade. Then something happened.

One of the joys of living in a place like Benteen County was that everyone knew everybody else's business. They shared your joys, and gossiped about your tragedies. That's what had happened then, a tragedy. A child died. It happened a few years before Mad Dog was born. Tommie and Becky had wandered off from a Sunday school picnic with another boy. The boy drowned, and Tommie and Becky got blamed. Feelings in the community ran so high that the Irons children were shipped off to Oklahoma and raised by family down there. They hadn't come home again for years. When they did, people remembered. Especially after word of what they'd left behind in Oklahoma filtered into the county. And hard on the heels of that news, their parents and sister died in a car crash. Tommie lived with it. Becky didn't. She never forgave those she thought had whispered behind her back.

The Irons children had been sent to live with a well-to-do uncle in Oklahoma, Abel Hornbaker, who had three boys of his own. Abel got himself murdered just before the pair returned to Kansas—killed by his own sons, some hinted maybe with the help of their cousins.

Strange, Mad Dog thought, that Becky was the one to get upset by the whispers. She'd had an alibi. Tommie had been accused of committing the crime. Only he'd come back to Kansas and, with the help of a former Benteen County sheriff, cleared himself.

Maybe Becky's reaction was because of Ezekiel. She and Zeke, Abel's oldest, were married with a boy of their own at the time. Zeke did fifteen years in prison for the murder before a governor examined the evidence, determined justice hadn't been served, and granted him a pardon. He'd come up to Kansas then, and reconciled with Becky. That was almost thirty years ago. Time enough, Mad Dog thought, for Becky to come to terms with the county she lived in. But it hadn't happened.

Simon Hornbaker and his twins lived here too. Simon was Zeke and Becky's son, younger than Mad Dog, and, like his own boys, a bit simple. Something in the genes. Maybe that was why Tommie never married.

It was in the seventies when Zeke Hornbaker, now Benteen County's most conservative supervisor, reappeared. Mad Dog couldn't remember ever seeing him on a tractor or otherwise involved in the labor of farming.

If that was Zeke…Mad Dog recalled the bones and the ID in his pocket.

Simon and his sons farmed the place these days, though everybody knew Becky was the one making the decisions.

There was smoke coming from the chimney, but Mad Dog wasn't sure what that meant. The place was heated with propane. There was a tank on the west side of the house. Someone must have been home to light the fire, but that didn't mean they were still here. No fresh tracks marred the circular driveway. Again, it was meaningless. Too much wind, too much fresh snow. The landscape was changing even as he watched.

Mad Dog decided to start with the barn. It was worth checking, and it would be a step removed from the elements, a little warmer than standing in a snow drift, waiting for someone with a rifle to come along and try for his other ear.

It had been a red barn once. The north face looked salt-and-pepper gray, speckled with fresh patches of snow that had begun catching on the weathered wood. Mad Dog kept the irregular row of evergreens along the north side of the driveway between himself and the house, then closed the last fifty yards with a sprint. Hailey stayed with him all the way. Maybe she was ready to get out of the storm, too.

The barn door wasn't latched. That was no surprise. Folks in Benteen County didn't lock their houses, much less their barns, not unless they planned to be away for a long time. Of course, Tommie had planned to be away forever.

The door slid smoothly on rollers hanging from a rail above. Mad Dog slipped through and closed it behind Hailey. It was dark inside, heavy with the rich aromas of hay and manure and grain. The wind didn't howl in the ear he might or might not have anymore. Instead it rattled shuttered windows and tugged at the great sloped roof, eliciting tired groans from the timbers supporting it.

There was a vehicle just inside the doors. A green Chevy Blazer. Mad Dog recognized it as Tommie's.

Mad Dog opened the driver's door and the dome light came on. The keys were in the ignition. That was the Benteen County norm. Hailey jumped aboard, bounced in and out of the back seat, then placed herself in her favorite position by the passenger's window. She seemed to think they would borrow it. Mad Dog decided he was willing to argue a little grand-theft-auto with his brother, considering what was in his pockets and what had happened to his cell phone.

He got in and tried the key. The Blazer started right up. Mad Dog ran back to the doors, pushed them wide, backed the Blazer into the storm, then closed the doors to make it less obvious in case no one had seen him in the act. The doors to the house stayed closed. No one ran into the yard to protest. He couldn't even see anyone peering out a window. Mad Dog engaged the four-wheel drive and pulled out of the yard and onto the road.

When he got to the blacktop it was clear. The highway ran almost as purely north/south as the wind and snow blew, so it wasn't collecting drifts. He didn't see any white pickups. He didn't see any traffic whatsoever, not that that was unusual. As he passed the first mile line he considered driving back to get his Saab. The wind tried to tear the Blazer off the road and set it in a ditch and he decided this wasn't the time. Buffalo Springs was straight ahead. Just a few miles and he was home free.

"Hey, Mister!" The little-girl voice came from the back seat. "When we get where we're goin', can I have some candy?"

Three steps out the front door of the Sunshine Towers, the wind snatched the sheriff's Stetson and launched it toward Oklahoma. He hardly noticed. He was feeling distinctly rocky, having trouble keeping the world lined up the way it was supposed to be. Besides, the hat didn't fit that well anymore. Its new shape failed to conform to the new shape of his head. He tucked his chin into his wool collar and concentrated on putting one foot ahead of the other, and staying off the ice. The sidewalk tended to tilt occasionally. By the time he made the parking lot, things were stabilizing again. His pickup only shifted when the wind buffeted it.

He aimed himself back toward Klausen's, concentrating on keeping track of the edge of the streets. They were beginning to disappear under drifting snow and diminishing visibility. He didn't notice Judy's Taurus doing a one-eighty at the corner of Main and Adams as he crossed the latter a block south on Pear. He thought the ringing in his ears got worse once, then wondered if it might be his cell phone. It was buried so deep under his jacket he didn't bother digging for it. He remembered turning it on before he left Alice Burton's room. He'd started to make a call, then couldn't recall who he was dialing, or why. His radio crackled at him too, but it was only static, at least to his ears. He couldn't hear that well over the roar of the blower that was keeping his windshield from frosting up and letting him see just enough to navigate into Klausen's parking lot.

He was relieved to find Doc's Buick still there and realized it would have been smart to call ahead to be sure. Maybe that was what he'd planned for the cell phone.

He parked alongside Doc's station wagon and made his way to Klausen's back door with the same sure and certain steps of the final customer to heed last call at the nearby Bisonte Bar. The door was on the south side, out of the wind, collecting snow. The sheriff leaned against it for a moment, briefly confused about what he was doing here. He needed to get Doc to look at his head, but there was something else. Something about a baby doll. Maybe Doc would know.

He let himself in and the long white corridor corkscrewed toward the front of the building in a totally unfamiliar manner. By leaning against the wall, the sheriff made it to Doc's door. He didn't bother to knock.

"Where's the doll?" he demanded. It would have been more impressive if he'd managed to stay on his feet. Better yet, if Doc had been in the room.

"We can't make it," Wynn shouted. "We'll have to go back to the cruiser." The wind snatched his voice and muffled it in a garment woven of snowflakes. The Heathers managed to hear him anyway.

"Sure we can." Heather English grabbed his shoulder and pointed with the other hand at the intersecting dirt roads just ahead. "That's Uncle Mad Dog's place right there. His driveway's only another quarter mile, just the other side of the pasture. It must be farther than that back to the patrol car. We'd just have to sit and wait there, hope somebody finds us before it runs out of gas and we freeze to death."

"We should go back. That radio will start to work again pretty soon. You wait and see."

"We tried it," the other Heather said. "I wish you hadn't forgotten to bring your cell phone today, Deputy."

It was a wish he shared, but it reminded him of another "Lose Some" moment and made him feel contrary. "I vote we go back."

"Don't be scared. Uncle Mad Dog's only got a couple of wolves left, and they're penned up in the barn. They can't get out...except maybe Hailey, but she's just a big sweet puppy. She wouldn't hurt you."

"What about that buffalo?"

"Bob? That's his pasture, right there," Heather One said. "But with weather like this, he'll probably be holed up in his shed near the house. Uncle Mad Dog has done a lot of work on that fence. He can't get out, and he'd just stay away from us even if he did. He's shy, not dangerous."

Wynn peered toward the pasture. Sometimes Buffalo Bob liked to wait behind the evergreens near the road and watch for Mad Dog when he was away from home.

"There was more than a quarter tank of gas in that cruiser."

"And it burns gas faster than any other car in the county. Go back if you want to," Two said. "I'm going to Mad Dog's."

As she trudged into the intersection, One made another plea to the Deputy. "This storm is getting worse. There might not be anybody driving this road again till it's over. Even if Uncle Mad Dog's power and phone should go down and we end up stuck there, he's got a fireplace and a big woodpile. He keeps a lot of canned goods in his larder in case of days like this. I'm going with Heather. You don't want to go back to the black and white alone, do you?"

Wynn didn't, but he didn't have to admit it, or even agree to accompany them. Two had turned around and was shouting something at them. The wind whipped her hair into her eyes and her voice toward the gulf coast. She pointed. He tried to see at what. The snow slackened for just a moment and he noticed an unlikely patch of color in Mad Dog's pasture. Near the evergreens there seemed to be a splash of red, then it was gone and Heather was shouting in his ear again. "Look! A truck."

He forced himself to face the wind and there it was, just before his eyes began to tear up enough to temporarily blind him. An old white Dodge stood just beyond the intersection. He stumbled toward it.

"Hot damn! Girls, we're saved."

An apoplectic Stan Deffenbach stormed into the lobby of the Sunshine Towers. "Mrs. Kraus just hung up on me," he complained to Judy English. "She can't do that. She's a public servant and I'm the public. We need an armed guard over here and she says there's no one to send. How can that be? Where's your husband? He should be here. He shouldn't have left without even a word to me."

Judy wasn't as concerned about Stan Deffenbach's security problems as she was that Englishman had gone.

"Englishman left?"

"At least he chased off those Hornbakers, but then he just marched out of here. Wouldn't tell me what was going on or where he was headed or when he was going to get a deputy over here in case they come back."

"Might he have told someone else?"

Deffenbach continued punching numbers on the phone at the front desk. He ignored her and said to the phone,

"Now don't you hang up on me again, Mrs. Kraus," and then: "Oh damn! She did."

Judy looked around for someone else to ask. Lucille Martin ducked her head into the lobby. "Mr. Deffenbach," she said. "You need to speak to a couple of the ladies. They're packing clothes and threatening to call their families and move out of here this very afternoon."

"Mrs. Martin," Judy interrupted. "Do you know where Englishman's gone?"

Lucille Martin shrugged shoulders that slumped more deeply than Judy remembered. "No, I'm sorry, Judy." She aimed Stan back into the building and fell in step behind him. Judy found herself alone in the lobby with a giant cage of songbirds, several of them chirping almost as wildly as Deffenbach before he disappeared.

"You're Mrs. English?" The voice came from the direction of the birds. A tiny woman with short white hair rose from a high-backed chair that had hidden her. She was wearing sweats that looked more appropriate for the gym than the lobby of the Sunshine Towers Retirement Home. She had on bright red tennies, too, so bright Judy thought they might glow in the dark.

"Yes?"

"I'm not sure where your husband went, but you should know the sheriff got clonked on the head."

"What?" Judy was too focused on her daughters to take it in at first.

"He was still pretty wobbly when he went out to his truck."

"Englishman's hurt?"

"Not too bad, I think, but I doubt if he should be driving." She paused for a moment while Judy absorbed this fresh catastrophe and tried to prioritize it. A brilliant orange and black bird at the end of the room broke into a song that hinted at tropical rain forests as a blinding gyre of snow briefly hid the parking lot from view.

"Mrs. English. Maybe I do know where he's gone. I'll tell you. Only, first, there's something else I found out that he needs to know. Promise you'll tell him?"

"Sure."

"Do you know about Tommie Irons?"

"I do."

"He had a big clubby silver ring. Didn't look like it could be worth that much, but he said they'd come pry it off his dead hand. He didn't want that. Said he had a plan to take it with him. He's been swallowing it. I saw him gagging on it once. I think it must have passed through him several times. Then, finally, at the end, he just couldn't force it down. He gave it to one of the ladies to hide. Then I think he forgot, what with all the morphine. I didn't know until just after your Englishman left. It was Alice Burton he asked to hide that ring. She did. She hid it under the diaper of that dolly she carried, the one she traded for the dead baby last night. Sheriff needs to know that. If he finds what the Hornbakers want, maybe he can work out how to stop these troubles."

"Where is he?"

"Gone to be with the dead, I think. Alice told him she found the dead baby on the back porch at Klausen's."

"**F**ollow my finger, not the light."

The sheriff was having trouble with complex instructions like that. Especially since Doc had him holding a cold pack against the sore spot on the back of his head at the same time.

"Umm hmm," Doc said, switching off the pen light and stepping back to sit on the edge of his desk.

"You know I don't understand technical medical jargon like that, Doc. Just tell me if I'll live."

"Not long, if you continue letting folks strike you on the head with blunt objects."

"I wasn't planning on the first time."

The sheriff experimentally pulled the cold pack away and explored the bump with his other hand. It didn't seem quite as big as a baseball anymore, but it still hurt like sin.

"Are you going to prescribe anything?"

Doc put the little flashlight back in his shirt pocket beside a collection of ballpoints. "Bed rest and observation. You should go spend a night in a hospital where someone who's qualified can keep an eye on you."

"Nearest hospital's in the next county."

"You didn't ask me what I expected you to do. That's just what you should do. You've got a mild concussion. The bump will go down. You aren't cut badly and the bleeding's pretty much stopped. People who've suffered a blow to the head shouldn't lie down and sleep it off unmonitored. Somebody should check on them regularly to be sure their cognitive functions are still within a normal range. You shouldn't drive, drink alcoholic beverages, or go chasing Hornbakers. I assume you're not going to take my advice about any of that, except maybe the booze, so I'll offer an alternative therapy. Take two aspirins and call me in the morning."

The sheriff pushed himself up off the couch onto which Doc had helped him after coming to investigate the noise in his office. The effort made the sheriff's head pound, but the room stayed steady and the pain went back to bearable quick enough.

"You're a very funny man, Doc."

"Actually, I'm serious. That's the best I can do for you, Sheriff. I'd offer you a stronger painkiller, but not if you're going to be out there driving in this storm. Your coordination is going to be off a little anyway. You'll get steadily better, unless you form a blood clot on the brain and collapse with a stroke. Or, if I give you too many blood thinners, maybe it could be an aneurysm instead."

"But neither, I gather, is likely."

"No, not likely. But don't get hit over the head anymore for a few days."

"Thanks, Doc. I appreciate the advice. Now I've got to get back to work."

Doc stepped over and opened the door for him. "Don't let me keep you."

The sheriff approached Doc instead of the door. "OK, then. Tell me about the baby, Doc. Alice Burton got it from here."

Mad Dog somehow managed to keep the Blazer out of a ditch. He was coming up on a mile line, so he pulled off at the crossroads to turn around and see who was in the back seat. This wasn't going the way he'd planned. Grand theft auto was one thing. Kidnapping, quite another.

She was brunette and pretty, but with a thin, sallow face. Young, too, in her teens, he guessed. Young enough to be clutching a diaper-clad plastic doll. Mad Dog wondered if that made it even worse.

"Hi," she said. "Who're you?"

Mad Dog felt like asking the same question. He pretty much knew everybody in Benteen County, though he had trouble keeping up with the kids. They looked different from one day to the next, or whenever he saw them.

"I'm Mad Dog." He wondered if he should be using his real name, but he couldn't imagine her being unable to identify him. There weren't many adult men who shaved their heads in this county, fewer still who'd just been shot in the left ear.

One of the first things Mad Dog had done when he got in the Blazer was pull back the hood on his parka and examine his ear in the mirror. He couldn't get the best of angles on it, of course, but from what he could tell, most of his ear was still there. Bloody, but intact.

"I'm Mary. Are you the Mad Dog who's an Indian?" Her eyes were big with wonder. "Are you gonna scalp me?"

"No." He ran a hand over his bald head. "I have enough trouble scalping myself, and your hair looks pretty right where it's at."

When he didn't recognize kids, he could sometimes figure out who they were by who they looked like, especially since he could remember the faces of so many parents when they would have been about the same age. This one seemed familiar, but not familiar enough.

"I should know who you are," he said, "but I can't place you. Who're your folks?"

"I don't have folks. Just Gran." She smiled, like it had been a trick question and she'd been too clever for him to catch her. The way she spoke, her attitude, even her voice, was too childlike, far younger than she looked. Of course, it was hard to tell much because of her heavy jacket and all the thick blankets she'd wrapped herself in.

"What were you doing in the barn in the back seat of this truck on such a rotten day?"

The smile went away. "I have to go to the barn when I'm bad. Gran leaves me blankets and puts the keys in the ignition so I can run the heater when it's real cold, like today. You don't think I'll get in trouble for leaving the barn, do you? I couldn't help it if a wild Indian came and stole me away. You'll explain that, won't you?"

Mad Dog ran his hands through nonexistent hair. She was acting like a little girl. Considering where he'd found her, and the fact that she seemed to suffer the malady that occurred too frequently among them, he figured she might be a Hornbaker. Only there weren't any Hornbaker females he knew of except Becky.

"Oh, look. There's Uncle Simon," the girl in the back seat said. "You can explain it to him."

Mad Dog followed her finger. A white pickup was coming down the blacktop from Buffalo Springs.

Uncle Simon was a Hornbaker. He was a bad-tempered oaf about Englishman's age who helped on the farm with his twin boys. Mad Dog couldn't remember his wife. She must have left him years ago.

Mad Dog knew Simon always carried a couple of rifles with scopes in the gun rack against the back window of his Dodge Ram. Mad Dog didn't want to explain the Blazer and the girl to such a heavily armed uncle.

The driver of the Dodge had spotted them. He was slowing, acting like he planned to pull in alongside for a friendly chat.

"Boy, is Uncle Simon gonna be surprised to see you," the girl said. Mad Dog thought that was an understatement.

"Lord Almighty!" Becky Hornbaker exclaimed. "What're you and these children doing out here in the middle of this blizzard, Deputy Wynn? You all climb inside this cab with me right now."

Becky loomed behind the wheel of an elderly Dodge Power Wagon. Its white paint was camouflaged with rusty dents and patches of mud from seasons past. Her grandson occupied the seat next to her. They both wore heavy jackets that were unbuttoned—evidence that the truck's heater was fully functional.

"Judah," she told the boy. "You take a blanket out from behind the seat and get back there in the bed. Gonna be hard enough crowding all these poor frozen souls inside here with me."

"What're you doing out here?" Heather English asked, wondering if she knew. Probably not. None of her plans for this day were working out the way she'd expected.

Wynn cut off a response. "You're just in time, Ms. Hornbaker," he said. Heather English knew Wynn didn't use the term *Ms.* to be politically correct. That just happened to be the way most Kansans pronounced either Miss or Mrs. It was a regionalism that had briefly put them ahead of the curve, regardless of personal inclination.

"I wasn't sure we were gonna make it." The deputy was already trading places with Judah and crowding the heater. One of Two had been in a couple of classes with Judah and his twin brother Levi. She'd known them nearly all of her life. But not well. They were older, still in high school because they'd been held back. Levi and Judah Hornbaker were big and dull and sullen, and had never shown any interest in her sister or her, other than an obsessive tendency to stare at their tits.

One of Two looked around for alternatives. She didn't see any. "We just want to get to Uncle Mad Dog's," she explained. "Judah can stay up front with you. Heather and I'll be fine in the back. It's only a quarter mile."

"No, child. We can't take you there. Your Uncle's not home. We were in there looking for him only minutes ago. Besides, somebody vandalized his place. Lord, would you believe it? The times we live in. His windows are all busted out, doors kicked in. You'd freeze in there.

"You girls climb in here with the Deputy and me and we'll run on down to the home place. You can call your folks from there, or we can get warmed up a bit and then one of the boys or I can run you back home."

That was odd. One knew Becky never welcomed company to her farm. The Heathers remained beside Becky's door. "Somebody knocked out Uncle Mad Dog's windows?" One asked. "Why would anyone do that?"

The question was echoed by her look-alike. "What about his wolves? What about Buffalo Bob? Are they all right?"

"You two look enough alike to be twins," Becky said. "And sound alike too. Climb on in. Let me close this window and keep some heat in here. I don't know much, but I'll tell you what I do along the way."

One was reluctant to obey. She didn't want to go to Becky's place, but she could appreciate the impracticality of going to Mad Dog's if he wasn't there and the house couldn't be sealed and heated. She'd be happier if Becky would just point the Dodge toward town, but Judah was going to be pretty uncomfortable in the bed of the pickup and she and Heather weren't dressed warmly enough for that long a ride.

"Come on now, before you catch your deaths."

They obeyed hesitantly, one Heather sitting on the lap of the other as the truck lurched through the intersection and headed toward the blacktop. Heather English turned and looked back toward her uncle's place. Her imagination was running wild about what might have happened there. Judah had hunkered down near the rear window, in front of which hung a pair of rifles.

There was a second figure wrapped in blankets back beside Judah. It was long and slender and Judah didn't seem to want to get too near it. A deer, Heather thought, taken out of season.

"You been hunting, Mrs. Hornbaker?" Heather asked.

"In a manner of speaking, child," Becky replied.

Something about the answer troubled the sheriff's daughter, but then Wynn launched into his version of how the girls had put the patrol car in the ditch and she felt compelled to join her sister's defense.

Neither Heather noticed when Judah leaned over and readjusted the blankets around the bundle beside him to hide the naked toes the wind had briefly uncovered.

Doc put a hand to his chin and massaged it, as if that would somehow cancel out the sheriff's question and the sheriff would then leave while Doc got on with his day.

"Doc, you told me Alice Burton's faculties weren't that far gone. You were right. Turns out she remembered where she found the baby. What was it doing here?"

Doc leaned his head around the door into the hall to reassure himself that it was vacant, then went back and sat behind his desk.

"She found it just outside the back door?" Doc asked.

"That where you found her doll?"

"Yeah. That's where it was."

"Talk to me, Doc. I've got more headaches than the one I got from being popped on the noggin. Mad Dog's made off with Tommie Irons' body. Some valuable heirloom Tommie owned has disappeared, along with him, and that's turned the Hornbakers into crazed vigilantes. You've got a dead baby in the freezer next door and I've got no idea where it came from. There may be more dead bodies in this county. My daughters are missing. And, on top of all that, I can't find a deputy to help out. I don't have time to run back and forth between the Sunshine Towers and here, Doc. You need to be straight with me. Where'd that baby come from? Who's the mother?"

Doc appeared to shrink in on himself. He looked older and smaller than he had in his role of medical authority.

"We already had part of this conversation, Sheriff. No matter what good friends we are or how completely I trust you, there are still things I can't tell you."

The sheriff opened his mouth to protest but Doc waved him off. "Hear me out, now. Let me see what I *can* tell you."

Doc pulled one of the ballpoints out of his pocket and stuck it in the corner of his mouth while he stared at the ceiling and considered what he was going to say.

"Like I said," Doc began, "I don't do abortions. Not even sometimes, when I think they should be done. That's what this was. One of those times when it would have been better for that baby never to be born.

"I can't tell you who the mother is, but maybe I can relieve you a little. Your Heathers aren't involved. Wherever they are, it's got nothing to do with the baby next door."

The sheriff felt a wave of relief buoy him. He trusted his girls, but it was amazing how much that trust had eroded under even the slightest doubt. Of course, they were still missing in the middle of a classic Plains blizzard. His relief washed back out on the same wave.

"The mother in this case shouldn't have a baby. She's got genetic problems of her own. On top of that, she's too immature to have given informed consent. In essence, she was raped. By a relative.

"I've been aware of this pregnancy from early on. Though I didn't offer to abort the foetus, this time I suggested the family take her someplace where that could be done. They chose not to. Even when I could pretty much guarantee this baby wasn't going to be healthy."

Doc paused to suck on the ballpoint. He didn't smoke, but he must have once. The sheriff recognized the signs. Doc was stressed and in need of something to occupy his hands, something to put in his mouth. Freud would have had some interesting things to say about that. Wrong, maybe, but interesting.

"The family didn't want anyone to know about the pregnancy. They hid it. They wouldn't take her to a hospital for the delivery. They intended to handle it themselves, only there were complications. They called me early this morning. It sounded like a breech birth. I told them to meet me at the clinic, only they wouldn't because the community might notice. They wanted to come to my house, but that would have taken too long. We compromised. They were supposed to meet me here.

"When I arrived, I found bloodstains and a plastic doll on the back porch. No sign of anybody. I brought the doll inside and tried calling them. No answer. I almost called you. Then one of them came and knocked on the door. Said the baby was born dead. They were afraid they would be discovered because people were wandering around near here. Some teenagers and some old folks. They got nervous. They left the baby by the back door, knowing I'd be here soon, and drove off until things settled down. I persuaded them to let me check the mother. She was in remarkably good shape for what she'd been through.

"That's it, Sheriff. I don't think I can tell you more."

"You've just added rape and incest to the list of things I should be looking into and you can't tell me more? Doc, what's to keep it from happening again?"

The ballpoint snapped between Doc's fingers. "Don't appoint yourself my conscience, and don't think that doesn't worry me. But I took a vow, and I renewed it quite specifically to these people so I could treat that girl. Besides, I don't know for sure who the father is, and I'm not sure she could tell you."

The sheriff shook his head. "I don't know if that's enough. Can you guarantee the girl is safe? Not just from whoever did this to her, but from the crazies in this community who will want to punish her for intentionally disposing of her baby?"

"I don't guarantee sunrises, let alone human behavior. But I doubt they'll find her. I can't tell you why, because that would help you figure out who she is."

"Well, I've got plenty to occupy myself, but you and I have more to talk about. This isn't over, Doc."

"Yes it is," Doc said.

The argument ended there. The back door to Klausen's flew opened on howling winds, then crashed shut. Both men turned in its direction.

"Englishman!" Judy shouted. "Where are my daughters?"

Mad Dog decided not to wait for Uncle Simon's Dodge Ram. He put the Blazer back in gear and floored it. Even with four-wheel drive it went all squirrely getting back onto the blacktop, extensive patches of which were now frosted and white.

Mad Dog flashed his headlights and made all sorts of waving motions, like he was indicating something important somewhere behind him as he went past the Dodge. Simon wasn't behind the wheel. It was one of his boys—Levi, Mad Dog thought. It looked like a hand and a foot were sticking up out of the back seat of the crew cab, just in front of the gun rack in the back window. The guns persuaded Mad Dog to keep his foot on the Blazer's accelerator in spite of the wind-shield wipers' inability to clear the front glass of snow and his capacity to be sure where the edges of the highway had gone.

The Dodge pulled over at the intersection where Mad Dog had been parked and a puzzled face turned to watch them fly into the teeth of the storm. It didn't take long for swirling snow to swallow the glow of the Dodge's brake lights.

Mad Dog didn't think they were following him. He let the speedometer drop back to something that was merely irrational instead of insane.

About two miles south of Buffalo Springs, the highway and Adams forked, each jogging away from the other to become two avenues into town. Mad Dog took Adams, but just far enough to realize how hard it was going to be to follow the street. He felt less likely to run into another Horn-baker this way, but it also looked like it might be tricky to navigate, even in a four-wheel drive.

Mad Dog stopped to consider his options while Hailey fogged the passenger's window and the girl in the back seat leaned forward and peered over his shoulder.

"Where we going, Mr. Mad Dog?"

And that, Mad Dog realized, was exactly the question. Where did you go in a stolen car with a kidnapped child? To jail, his conscience answered, and most likely for a very long time.

The Dodge Ram streaked through his rearview mirrors and passed the intersection with Adams going even faster than Mad Dog had been willing to risk. Too fast to stop when the driver saw the Blazer. The Ram's brake lights came on as it disappeared behind a stand of evergreens that separated the roads.

Where no longer mattered so much as going. If the Dodge didn't end up in a ditch it would be back, bringing an armed and angry Hornbaker, with maybe a rope necktie to offer him a similar fate to Uncle Tommie. The Blazer went, and, to his surprise, Mad Dog decided he finally knew where.

◇◇◇

B ut for the sound of the wind ripping at shutters, testing
windows, and banging on doors, the big house was silent.
"Hello?" Becky called again, and again her echo was the
only response.

Judah, Deputy Wynn, and the Heathers crowded the dim
kitchen. It had a simple, functional look to it. A man's
kitchen, Heather English thought. A stack of dirty dishes in
the sink indicated heavy use.

"That's peculiar," Becky said. "I thought Simon and Levi
would be here. Judah, didn't I tell them to hurry on home?"

Judah wasn't chatty. He just blinked piggy little eyes and
nodded.

"Deputy, you take these children into the living room.
We left a fire in the hearth. Even if it's gone out, you can toss
some fresh logs on the coals and warm yourselves. I'll heat
up a pot of coffee, and make some hot chocolate for the
girls. Judah, you go check the barn and the garage. See if
someone's out there."

Heather English was tired of being called a child. She and
Heather were both sixteen. Two of Two was only three months
shy of her seventeenth birthday, though One would have to
wait till fall. Still, they were both too old to be referred to as
children. She looked over her shoulder at Mrs. Hornbaker as
they paraded through a swinging door and into the living
room. Judah shuffled back outside with an obvious lack of
enthusiasm.

Heather wasn't good at estimating the ages of old people.
Once they got gray and their skin began to crinkle, they were
just old. Becky Hornbaker qualified, though she didn't look
nearly as ancient as her brother, Tommie Irons, had the last
time Heather saw him. In spite of gray hair and weathered
skin that had faced into lots of years of Kansas wind, the
woman was handsome in a rugged kind of way. She was tall
and the lean-hard cut of her was especially noticeable as she
shed her coat and reached up into a cupboard for cups and

saucers. She couldn't compete with the Heathers for perky, but she sure didn't have the traditional old lady figure.

The living room was a mess. Someone had taken books off of shelves and stacked them at random on the floor. Cushions were tossed helter-skelter from the sofa and the easy chair. Only the TV and the recliner—remote control sitting on its arm—looked to be where they belonged. The fireplace held nothing but coals. Heather thought that was just as well since an occasional gust whistled down the chimney and might have scattered sparks onto the worn carpet or the combustible piles of books and cushions lying too near a screen that looked anything but effective. Wynn selected some logs from a pile that had been stacked right on the carpet, without even putting down something to catch the bark and sawdust. A man, she figured again, though probably not Mr. Irons. He'd been in the nursing home for months.

"Should we try to call Mom or Dad?" Heather whispered to her sister as Becky rattled pots and pans in the kitchen and Wynn kneeled to blow on the coals and raised a fine cloud of ash that settled over his face and hair.

"Yeah, you go ahead," Two of Two replied, suddenly finding a need to busy herself rearranging cushions onto furniture. Heather had been hoping for a reason not to make the call, or for her sister to volunteer for the hazardous duty. Mom had sounded seriously pissed on the radio. She must have discovered they weren't home. They were going to be in big trouble for skipping school, and then skipping out without telling anyone where they'd gone. Deputy Wynn's involvement might have some mollifying effect, but Heather thought they were probably grounded for life, and maybe about to be packed off to a nunnery. Still, the longer their parents worried, the angrier they'd be. There was a phone by the recliner and Heather went over and picked it up. She managed to dial her mother's office and let it ring twice before it occurred to her that Dad was the softhearted one. If she could explain to him first, find a way to make it sound like a teen-age adventure instead of the crime of the century, Dad might calm Mom before she handed out penalties she'd have a hard time backing away from. Heather put the phone back in its cradle and went over to whisper in the other Heather's ear.

"I think I'll call Dad first. You got any ideas how to minimize this so he doesn't lock us in our rooms until we're thirty?"

Two didn't get a chance to answer. The fire ignited with a poof and smoke began to billow into the room from under the mantel as Wynn frantically tried to wave it back inside the chimney. Becky Hornbaker came through the door with a tray of steaming mugs and a plate filled with cookies, set them calmly on an end table, and stepped over to adjust the flue. The chimney immediately began to draw properly.

"Oh my, that's a lovely fire, dears," she said, passing around steaming mugs of coffee and chocolate. "And a good thing, too. I think we should stay here for a little. That storm's getting nasty and our old Power Wagon has seen better days. I'd hate to find us stranded somewhere between here and town. Simon and Levi should be back any time. They're in a more reliable vehicle, and roomier too.

"Oh, and I'm so sorry, dears," she said, turning to the Heathers. "But we won't be able to call your parents. My cell phone's not working and now the regular phone is out too. A line probably blew down or a tree limb fell and knocked us off."

Heather's jaw dropped before she managed to catch it and stick it back where it belonged. Becky Hornbaker and Deputy Wynn didn't seem to notice but Two gave her the raised eyebrows.

The phone had been working only moments before. Would Becky lie about that?

Mrs. Kraus was on the line to Bertha's trying to talk someone into bringing a sandwich and a piece of butterscotch pie across the park to the courthouse when the phone went dead. All of a sudden there was only silence, not even a dial tone.

Mrs. Kraus buttoned another button on her outer sweater. She was wearing two. In weather like this, it never got much above sixty in the courthouse. Too much space for the old furnace, and too many cracks between the bricks that let cold in and heat out. The place would have been condemned years ago if the county could afford a replacement.

It looked fine from the outside—quaint, kind of picturesque. It was one of those old red-brick Victorian-era courthouses that sprouted all over the United States around the turn of the preceding century and looked, but for variations in gingerbread, pretty much alike. Two extra-tall stories were set atop a six-foot-above-ground "ground floor." Above that, peaked roofs filled with cracked dormer windows and chimneys that were long since clogged and dysfunctional covered an unfinished attic. And finally, like the figures atop a wedding cake, a tower, built for sightseeing and now only occasionally used by adventurous couples willing to ignore DANGER and NO TRESPASSING signs to admire the view.

The building looked romantic. Lost tourists were known to stop and take photos. Sitting at the west end of Veteran's Memorial Park, it had the comforting look of a place where government and justice would be meted out in the idyllic fashion the founding fathers had in mind—until you got close enough to see the flaws.

There was a crowd with one of those flaws down the hall in the supervisors' offices, arguing about what should be done. Their raised voices echoed through the building all the way into the sheriff's office. Mrs. Kraus gathered removing the sheriff was foremost on their agenda. That probably meant they intended to sweep her out the door with the same broom. She considered her Glock and wondered if she had the authority to accuse them of plotting a mutiny, and what would happen if she went down and arrested everybody and stuck them back behind the wall to the jail where it was more than ten degrees colder and she wouldn't have to listen to them anymore.

She tried the cell phone. No signal, it told her. The damn transmitter up by the interstate in the next county was probably down again. It could be counted on to fail whenever it got real windy. In central Kansas, that happened about fifty-one weeks out of the year. It was the reason Mrs. Kraus hadn't let herself be conned into getting one of the fool contraptions yet. Neither had most county residents. Cell phones were more status symbols than reliable forms of communication around Buffalo Springs.

That left the radio. She wasn't sure whether she should bother Englishman. No question he had his hands full out there, but it had been a long time since he'd checked in. She was having trouble containing her curiosity. It hadn't been a problem when the phone was ringing off the hook and the office was filled with critics and gossips. Now, with phones out and a band of revolutionaries down the hall, she felt abandoned. She wanted to know what had been going on over at the Sunshine Towers. She wondered what Doc had told Englishman. She wondered if Judy had found Englishman yet, and just how much that might have complicated his life. And, most of all, she wondered if there was any reason for her to sit here and keep an office open that nobody but the sheriff and any deputies within radio range were likely to contact in the midst of a full-fledged blizzard. Maybe Englishman could use her help in the field. Maybe he wouldn't mind if she stopped by Bertha's for some lunch on the way...

And then she wasn't alone anymore. He came in the door, bundled in a snowsuit that made him look like the Michelin Man. Only he was covered in mud and blood, and even his friendly smile wasn't enough to keep her from picking up her Glock and putting a couple of extra steps between herself and the apparition on the far side of the counter.

"Hey, Mrs. Kraus. It's only me," Mad Dog said.

◇◇◇

"Judy, Doc reassured me our girls have nothing to do with that baby. Even so, you have to go home and wait for them, just in case."

"In case of what? The phones are out, both regular and cellular. The girls can't get in touch with me there, no matter how hard they try."

"No, but they can come home. They might even be there now. And we don't know why they left. They might need us. But I've got things I have to do. Now! I don't have time to sit here in Klausen's parking lot arguing with you."

"Then take me along. You need a deputy and can't find one. Use me."

"You can help most by waiting at home so I know the girls have a safe place to go."

The wind rocked the Taurus and momentarily hid his Chevy, only a couple of spaces away, behind a billowing curtain of snow.

"Englishman. If I go home and wait by myself, I'll go crazy. If the girls are there or they turn up and we need you, we aren't going to be able to get in touch with you. Sticking me at home, out of the way, doesn't make sense. Use me like you would a deputy. You know I'd be better than Wynn Some."

"I sent Wynn home."

"Look. I can go to the courthouse and pick up a couple of spare radios. I can take one home and check to see if they're there. I'll let you know either way. If they aren't, I'll leave a radio with a note to call us the minute they come in the door. Then you can use me. I know which girls might be worth checking on about the abandoned baby. They're more likely to tell me than you, if there's anything to tell. And I can look for our daughters. Ask at their friends' homes, at least the ones in town. That would free you up to look for Mad Dog or arrest some Hornbakers. What do you say?"

"Weather like this, I'm not even sure we can count on the radios," the sheriff said. Only they could.

"Five-hundred to 501," Mrs. Kraus muttered from under the sheriff's coat.

◇◇◇

"Five-oh-one." Englishman's voice sounded like he was speaking into a Geiger counter just downwind of Chernobyl, but for all the clicks and pops, he was easy enough to understand.

Mrs. Kraus was holding the radio in her left hand. She wasn't ready to put down her Glock yet.

"Thought you might want to know your wacky brother is here at the courthouse. He just came in the office, all covered with blood, wanting to know where he could find you. Went over and stole a candy bar from out of your desk, then said he'd go clean up some, but for me not to go nowhere. Says he's got some questions for me."

"Has he got Tommie Irons with him, or this other body he called you about?"

"He don't seem to be carting any carcasses around. But he had enough blood on him to double donate if he happens on a Red Cross blood drive."

"Is he hurt?"

"Don't know if any of that blood was his. If he's hurt, it can't be serious. But he's got opportunities to remedy that. Some hotheads are down the hall making plans with Bontrager to run you out of town on a rail. I'm sure they'd be proud to practice on Mad Dog."

"Keep him away from the supervisors and their friends. I'll be right over. Don't let Mad Dog leave before I get there."

Mrs. Kraus glanced at her pistol. "That mean I can wing him if I need to?"

Mad Dog was delighted. His ear was still there. All of it, so far as he could tell from the mirror in the courthouse restroom. He'd caught some shrapnel in it, and in his hand when the bullet disintegrated his cell phone, but none of his ear seemed to be missing or even badly shredded. He picked out a couple of pieces of plastic and that set the ear to bleeding again. No big deal. He held a paper towel to it as he went back across the foyer and into the sheriff's office.

Mrs. Kraus was sitting at her desk. Its top was cleared of paperwork and her pistol occupied the place of honor between her phone and one of the department's walkie-talkies.

Mad Dog nodded his head back toward the voices that echoed down the hallway. "What's going on?"

"Some fans of yours are discussing this morning's events and deciding what to do about them. I'd say they're about equally split between tar and feathers or a hemp necktie."

"What's everybody so upset about? Becky Hornbaker and her family never visited Tommie at the Towers. Why make a big deal of him after he's dead?"

"Rumor is Tommie had something valuable and it's missing too."

"I don't know about that. I took him out of this world the way he came into it—naked. Whatever they're looking for, Tommie didn't have it and neither do I."

"Well, that's not what most folks are all het up about. It's the dead baby, and the way Englishman and Judy have failed to placate some egos."

"Dead baby?" Mad Dog didn't know about the baby so Mrs. Kraus filled him in.

"Well, at least that's not something they can blame on me."

Mrs. Kraus shook her head. "Plenty of folks in Benteen County would believe someone crazy enough to steal and dispose of an old man's body might be capable of doing the same with an infant's."

Mad Dog sighed. He was used to being misunderstood. Besides, he had problems of his own to solve, including a little girl who was eating Englishman's candy bar and waiting for him back in the jail.

"Mrs. Kraus, you've lived in Benteen County all your life. Can you help me understand all this?"

Mrs. Kraus watched him like she expected he might reach in his jacket and start pulling out dead babies, which, Mad Dog recalled, he could do. He still had the skull in a pocket.

"Come on. Help me here. What happened to sour relations between Tommie and Becky? Or don't you know either?"

That turned the trick. Mrs. Kraus prided herself on knowing everything that went on in Benteen County.

"Well, you know about the murders?"

"Yeah. That kid when they were little, then their uncle, just before they came home."

"The kid died when the Reverend Irons arranged a picnic for the children at his Sunday School."

"Reverend Irons?" Mad Dog said. "That's right. The old man was some kind of preacher, wasn't he? I'd forgotten."

"Fundamentalist fanatic kind. Church of Christ Coming Now. Never had much following. What few there were abandoned him after that boy died when Becky and Tommie christened him in Calf Creek. Full immersion, baptized to death."

"Intentional?"

"Sure, only…Well, Momma always said they were too young to understand what they were doing. Others said they were too smart not to know."

"Smart? Tommie wasn't any dim bulb, but I never thought of him as having any extra wattage."

"More Becky," Mrs. Kraus said. "And maybe they seemed brighter because the Ironses had another daughter who wasn't right. The Reverend probably wasn't all there either. Momma said he fell straight off the turnip truck. Sure didn't have no common sense, and there ain't hardly been a Hornbaker who wasn't a little dull. Only one in the family showed any brains, before Tommie and Becky, was their mother. She was something else, what they used to call a witchy woman. She was a healer who, some said, made a pact with the devil and paid it with the souls of her children. That was supposed to be why they killed that boy."

"They've been close to a lot of violent death."

"Real close. Becky had an alibi for when their uncle, Abel Hornbaker, was murdered, but Tommie didn't. He was a prime suspect for a while, until he turned himself in up here. Proved his fingerprints didn't match those on the murder weapon.

"That was just days after their parents and sister died in that terrible wreck. Car hit a bridge abutment and ended up in the Kansaw. Not much left of the car, or the Ironses."

Mad Dog remembered seeing the crumpled remains after the car was pulled from the river. "Tommie and Becky stayed on the farm after," he said. "I guess they were still close then."

"Who knows. Becky never tolerated visitors. Had to guess, I'd say they were going their own routes already, or not long after."

"So why'd both stay on the home place?"

"Well, the inheritance for one. Abel Hornbaker left everything to Becky. Not that his boys would have got it anyway. Two of them convicted of his murder, and the other missing and presumed guilty. And not Tommie, either. Just Becky. Tommie inherited half their family's farm after the wreck, but Becky got the other half and she had the money to keep it going, and probably needed help raising that worthless Simon."

"Then Supervisor Hornbaker got pardoned," Mad Dog said.

"Fifteen years later. Freed because he was impregnating somebody else when his father was murdered. Always surprised me Becky took Zeke back. Especially since he brought that woman and his daughter along when he first turned up. But Becky had the money. Maybe that made the difference. He does like spending it. His other family was into some kind of radical politics. Not hardly our Zeke's style. I think he preferred rich and conservative, and Becky maybe thought her boy needed a daddy."

"Didn't Zeke's truck blow up?" Mad Dog reached into his pocket and fingered the ID he'd found with the bones. "Were any of them hurt?"

"No. Zeke and them had engine trouble. Left the truck where they'd been camped out and borrowed Tommie's car. They were gone, long before the explosion. About a month later Zeke came back, alone this time, and patched things up with Becky. After that, Tommie seemed to stay out of the house as much as he could. But he was the one made that farm work. So, I guess Becky and Tommie put up with each other on account of convenience. And Becky with Zeke, on account of Simon. There's more'n a few relationships based on less that go on for years."

Too many possibilities, Mad Dog thought. And there was still the question of who Mary was. He reached in his pocket and pulled out the battered ID card he'd found with the bones. Mrs. Kraus raised a curious eyebrow. He would have shown it to her but Supervisor Bontrager burst through the door, a busy man in too much of a hurry to pay attention to what was happening around him. He went right past Mad Dog without noticing.

"My phone's out of order, Ms. Kraus. I'm gonna have to borrow one of yours."

Mad Dog put a finger to his lips and slipped silently out the door behind the supervisor as Mrs. Kraus' second eyebrow rushed to join the first.

◇◇◇

They were watching *The Lion King*. Becky Hornbaker had selected the tape and fed it into the VCR after discovering nearly as much snow on the regular channels as was falling outside. The wind must have twisted the satellite dish, she explained. She didn't ask what any of them wanted to watch, apparently choosing something appropriate for the "children," Heather English thought. It had been a favorite for her and Two only a few years ago, and remained a staple they used when babysitting. She and her sister were paying more attention to what was going on outside the windows, and to Becky Hornbaker's distracted tapping of her steepled fingers as she sat in the chair nearest the phone.

Wynn, on the other hand, was completely absorbed by the movie. "This is a good part," he told them, often enough to establish his familiarity with the latter-day Disney classic. He had a kindergartner at home as an excuse, but Heather was willing to bet the deputy was more addicted to the movie than was his progeny.

Maybe she should be protesting the delay, doing something about getting them pointed back toward Buffalo Springs or finding a way to communicate with Mom and Dad. Two appeared equally concerned, but Becky Hornbaker's presumption of absolute authority was more than a pair of sixteen-year-olds was prepared to challenge.

The back door crashed opened and, though the door between the living room and the kitchen was closed, a breath of frozen air licked the back of their necks.

"You all stay put," Becky told them, halfway to the kitchen. "I'll see what Judah's found."

Heather wasn't interested in sharing Judah's discoveries, but Judah picked the moment to turn loudly informative.

"Nobody here," he shouted. "Simon's truck's gone. So's Uncle Tommie's Blazer, and Mary along with it."

"Who's Mary?" Two of Two whispered, receiving a puzzled shrug of One's shoulders in return.

The instant Becky disappeared through the kitchen door, Heather grabbed the telephone. There was no dial tone. Had the line really gone down? Could Becky have known that when she said so, or had she simply pulled a plug somewhere to make it so?

"What now?" One inquired of her companions. Wynn was the only one to offer a suggestion.

"Wait for this part. This is great."

It was hard to tell where the parking lot and the driveway were anymore, though Mad Dog decided it probably didn't matter much. Street, park, yard—they were all flat and they were all covered with snow. Mad Dog drove around the north side of Veteran's Memorial Park. The trees and shrubs there were farther from the edge of the street so the drifts weren't quite so deep. He decided he'd made a good decision when he glanced across the park and saw someone trying to maneuver a Taurus station wagon out of a drift across from Bertha's. It looked like Judy's car, but Mad Dog didn't turn down the street to help. Judy wasn't someone he wanted to run into just now. Besides, she could get plenty of volunteers to push from Bertha's lunch crowd.

He almost collided with the Cadillac Escalade that came plowing through a drift and skidded wide through the turn from Adams onto Cherry. Fortunately, he'd been slowing to make the turn south when the Chairman of the Benteen County Board of Supervisors missed his front fender by a distance that could be measured in snowflakes. Wynn Senior whipped over into his tracks and sped toward the courthouse. If Supervisor Bontrager had managed to persuade Chairman Wynn to come in on a day like this, Mad Dog thought, both he and Englishman would be better off somewhere far away. And, if Zeke Hornbaker showed up again, they would have a quorum and present a threat to every resident of the county. Mad Dog had signs in the trunk of his Saab stating his opinion of the current board. BENTEEN BOARD OF SUPERVISORS: OF THE PEOPLE, BY THE PEOPLE, FOR RENT!

The Blazer did more than its share of slipping, but he kept it slow and easy and steered for the shallowest part of every drift. He glanced down Oak as he headed south. Sure enough, that was Englishman out there, jumping up and down on the bumper of the Taurus, trying to give it a little extra traction. That meant Judy was most likely at the wheel and both of them were probably stressed, by events and by each other. Mad Dog kept going.

He put the Blazer in a parking spot behind the Bisonte Bar, just down the street from Klausen's. He carried the girl and she hugged her naked doll. She wasn't much of a burden and she seemed too weak to wade through drifts. Hailey reluctantly followed them out of the Blazer. It had a good heater and the passenger seat fit her better than the one in his Saab. They made an interesting procession, had there been anyone to see them, like something out of one of those old Hollywood B movies—the monster, the werewolf, and their innocent victim. They followed the alley south of Main and crossed Klausen's parking lot to the funeral parlor. It seemed an appropriate destination.

Mad Dog had to scrape snow away from the back door with his foot in order to get it open. The long white hall was surprisingly quiet once the door closed behind them.

"I don't like this place," Mary complained. Hailey whined agreement. Mad Dog knew how they felt, but he needed a medical opinion.

Doc's office was empty. Mad Dog put the girl on a sofa and helped her rearrange her blankets. Hailey joined her, resting her head in the girl's lap and competing for attention with her battered dolly.

"I'll be right back," Mad Dog promised.

"Yes please." she seemed frightened, but she took courage from the presence of her new friend with the big teeth.

Doc wasn't in the embalming lab. That surprised Mad Dog since Doc's Buick was still in the parking lot and it didn't seem likely he'd gone for a walk. Mad Dog followed the hall toward the front of the building, exchanging antiseptic simplicity for plush elegance at a pair of swinging doors wide enough for even the most luxurious coffin. Dull light streamed through the stained glass windows that flanked the front doors and transmogrified a dull beige carpet into something magically Persian, perhaps, and surely capable of flight. Whether by design or by accident, the pattern thus applied to the carpet led to the mortuary chapel. Mad Dog followed. Only a few wall sconces, tastefully hidden behind lush bouquets of silk flowers, glowed dully in the chapel, along with the spotlights that highlighted a simple wooden cross

on the back wall. The cross could come down to be replaced
with a menorah for those few residents of Benteen County
whose messiah was yet to come. Or the wall could be left
empty for the rare atheist brave enough to face eternity without hedging a few bets. So far as Mad Dog knew, no symbols
of other religious creeds had ever been requested here.

Doc sat in one of the pews about midway down the aisle.
It was hardly a place Mad Dog would have expected to find
someone so adamantly agnostic. Mad Dog hated to interrupt
anyone who might be communicating with their god, or
goddess, or even just contemplating their spiritual navel. All
the same, someone had tried to blow his ear off today. And
someone still prowled the streets of Buffalo Springs, seemingly
more intent on introducing Mad Dog to eternity than letting
him consider it. That played hell with his patience.

He cleared his throat, and Doc cleared the bench and
whirled toward the entry. "Christ!" he said. It almost sounded
like a question.

"This is too weird," Heather English told her sibling. They
were peering through the drapes of the living room's
north window into the teeth of the storm. Becky Hornbaker
was out there, crawling behind the wheel of her old Dodge
Powerwagon while her grandson, Judah, rode shotgun.

"Yeah, this part is kind of scary," Wynn agreed from where
he sat on the rug with his nose glued to the TV.

"What's going on?" Heather Lane wondered. "If it's safe
enough for them to drive over to the highway, why can't they
take us along?"

"Yeah, and what's all this about staying in the living room
or the kitchen? I mean, what does she think we are, some
kind of snoops?"

The truck pulled slowly out of the back yard and disappeared behind a building that stood between the house and
the barn. The girls followed it, going through the door to

the kitchen so they could see it dig its way to the road and turn cautiously into an alien landscape of undulating white that reshaped itself and continued a southward migration while the girls watched.

The truck disappeared behind a row of lilac bushes. It was impossible to tell whether it emerged on the other side because the horizon no longer extended that far.

"That wasn't very polite of her. 'You all just wait here while we go see to our family and when we get back we'll see about your family.' Ours is as important as hers. And then telling us not to stray from the living room and the kitchen because the rest of the place is such a mess and it's all locked up besides."

"Yeah, who'd want to look around their old house anyway?" There was a little hall at the south end of the kitchen with a small bathroom on the side. One of those doors they'd been prohibited to pass through stood at the end of it.

"You think it's really locked?" One wondered.

"Of course," Two replied, testing her opinion. It was an old door in an old house and it was solid and sealed, but the lock was one of those keyhole shaped things through which some dim light could be seen, especially if you got down on your hands and knees and put your eyeball right to the opening.

"Anything?"

"Not really," Two admitted, "but I bet this would be easy to open."

"Looks pretty stout to me."

"I didn't mean we should break it down." Heather Lane fished through her pockets. She didn't produce a skeleton key, but she did find a paper clip which she inserted in the keyhole and began twisting experimentally.

"You're gonna get it now, Scar," Wynn howled from the living room. The wind was louder, but both were behind walls and too busy to notice a bit of teen-age testing of limits.

"We shouldn't do this," One of Two objected, so she could say she'd warned her sister if it ended up getting them in trouble.

"I'm just showing you how easy it would be. It's not like I care what's on the other side," Two protested, and then they were.

It was a man's den, wood paneled with most of its shelves empty of anything but dust. An unoccupied gun rack stood against one wall. A desk was beneath the room's only window, its drawers having been dumped on the floor. Evidently there hadn't been much in them, and what was apparently hadn't mattered to whoever searched them.

"The movie's almost over. Wynn's gonna come looking for us in a minute," One cautioned. There were two other doors leading from the room. The other Heather was trying the one opposite the window. It wasn't locked. The door swung open on a staircase that climbed to a dimly lit hall above.

"You don't suppose they have something to hide, do you?" Two offered a justification for further exploration. A chorus of animals were singing something cheerful in the living room and Wynn had joined in.

"I don't think we should go up there," One said. "The way my day's going…"

"Hey," Two gave her sister a quick hug. "It's no big deal. We got called on account of weather. We'll just try again tomorrow."

One wasn't sure they'd get the chance, but something else was competing for her attention. "What's that?" she asked.

A soft voice tumbled down the stairs. A breathy *a capella*, hardly understandable. The tune sounded familiar. There was a sad, lonely quality to it, and it drew the Heathers up the stairs like tourists to the world's largest ball of twine, to be found just a few counties away.

The words grew clearer as they advanced.

"Somewhere, over the rainbow…"

"**G**eez. I'm sorry, Doc, I didn't mean to startle you."

Doc smiled and did a kind of a self-deprecating shrug. "Not your fault, Mad Dog. I was a million miles away. I spend too much time around this place. And it's been one of those days that leads me to wonder how I'll be judged when my own time comes, if there's anybody to do the judging. Or, perhaps worse yet, how I'll judge myself."

"You'll come out fine," Mad Dog reassured. "You're one of maybe half a dozen folks in this county who can be trusted with anything."

Doc tried to brush the compliment off. "That's about how many people still live here."

His attempt at humor sounded forced. "Sorry, guess I'm trying to laugh my way out of a personal graveyard and," he waved, a gesture that encompassed Klausen's Funeral Parlor, "I picked the right place for it."

"Doc, I hate to bother you but I've got a problem."

Doc stepped out of the pew and gestured for Mad Dog to lead the way. As they turned toward the back of the building, Doc threw an arm around Mad Dog's shoulder. It was an uncharacteristic act between men in Benteen County, but it made Mad Dog feel good. Kansans didn't go in for the touchy-feely stuff. Men shook each other's hands, but they didn't hold on long and seldom hugged and never shed a public tear. Mad Dog had cut through Doc's shell with his remark about trust. But it was true. Otherwise he wouldn't be here.

"I've already heard a little about your problem. Come on back to my office and we'll talk about it. But first, humor me. I've got a question for a long-time resident."

"What's that, Doc?"

"There are some brass plaques on the pews. I was sitting there, staring at one. LOUIS HENRY SILVERSTEIN, GUARDIAN OF THE WORDS. I don't think I've heard of him. Who was Silverstein? What words did he guard?"

"He was a librarian, Doc. That abandoned sandstone building just down the street—you know the one—it used to be the Benteen County Public Library. Silverstein was a scholar from somewhere back east, Ivy League school I think. He was headed west to retire, only he happened through Buffalo Springs on a day they were having a book sale, culling the collections to raise enough money to keep the place open. Silverstein bought every book and donated them all back to the library. Then he stuck around and started volunteering his time. Before long, he and his retirement funds were all that kept the library going. Somewhere along the line he acquired an old printing press and started putting out a weekly newspaper. Only paper we've had since the Depression. *The Times of Buffalo Springs*. Both the paper and the library closed when he died. Would have been a better memorial if folks found a way to keep them going, but all they managed was that plaque."

"Somebody cared, though. Thanks, Mad Dog. Silverstein meant enough for them to put up that little monument. Sitting there, I came to think I owed it to him, and me, to find out who he was. I hope one day someone cares enough to ask a similar question about me."

Doc pushed through the double doors that separated the public portion of Klausen's from the work area, two very different sides of one universal coin. "Excuse me. I don't know why I'm being so maudlin. What brought you here?"

Mad Dog reached in his pocket and removed the answer, setting the skull gently into Doc's outstretched palms.

Doc's head rocked slowly from side to side. Mad Dog thought it was out of sadness more than denial.

"You're in luck, old friend," Doc said, shell suddenly back in place as he hid behind the cynical humor for which he was known. "Seems I'm having a special on dead babies today."

When Judy's Taurus slid past the drive to the parking lot behind the courthouse and went nose first into the shallow ditch, the sheriff decided that was as good a parking spot for it as any. He pulled his Chevy up beside her and left it on more solid footing. Even with the bags of concrete he was carting in the bed to weigh down the rear end and give it traction, the truck was proving to be marginal transportation. Better, he decided, not to pit it against the drifts building up in the lot, even if there were fresh tracks through them.

He helped Judy from the Taurus and, together, they waded across the lawn and up the steps to the front doors. They were hard to open under the best of circumstances. Damned near impossible on icy footing as gale-force winds threatened to give free hang-gliding lessons. The sheriff wedged the south door open an inch or two, then the wind shifted and slammed it open the rest of the way. He reached back and pulled Judy in after him. She continued through the inner doors on her own as he tried, without success, to close what had been nearly impossible to open. When he gave up and followed her, Judy was just inside. Not far beyond her, near the foot of the staircase that led to the courtrooms on the second floor, stood a small crowd of spectators. They included Supervisors Wynn, Hornbaker, and Bontrager. Mad Dog wasn't there.

"Mrs. Kraus?" the sheriff called, making a raised eyebrow do in place of what he wanted to ask her about Mad Dog.

She stuck her head around the corner of the door to his office, read the eyebrow and answered it with a shrug. "Communications are all out, Sheriff," she told him. "Not much goin' on here, 'cept this lynch mob."

Mad Dog was gone, or out of the way someplace. The sheriff wanted to talk to his brother, but not in front of this crowd.

"Something I can do for you?" They didn't show any signs of going on about their business. That probably mean *he* was their business. Just what he needed. One more impediment to finding his daughters, the body of Tommie Irons, and the mother of the baby at Klausen's.

Supervisor Bontrager decided to act as spokesman. That didn't surprise the sheriff much.

"You're just in time, Sheriff. Supervisor Hornbaker was just explaining what he's discovered about this morning's events. I was about to suggest that we discuss relieving you of your duties, pending an investigation into the manner in which your office has operated, or failed to operate, during this crisis."

Zeke Hornbaker nodded in agreement. "Yes. With your brother involved, that would seem appropriate. Perhaps Deputy Wynn should assume temporary control."

"What the hell are you two babbling about?" Wynn Senior demanded. "Even I know my boy can't be trusted to enforce the law without careful supervision. Kid can hardly pour piss out of a boot when the instructions are printed on the heel. I don't know what's going on between you all and the sheriff, or you and Mad Dog, but I'm not about to interfere with the best law enforcement officer this county's had in my lifetime, even if he is registered to the wrong party."

The sheriff wanted to ask everyone to hold it while he got the chairman's statement typed up and had them sign as witnesses. He couldn't remember Papa Wynn ever passing him a compliment, beyond once, a few years ago, a brief hint he appreciated the sheriff maybe saving his son's life.

"Sheriff," the chairman continued, "actually I'm here for your help. I guess I don't know half of what's caused this dust up. I do know you've got your hands full looking for old Tommie Irons and the mother of some abandoned baby. But now my boy's missing too. Told his wife last night he'd be home after his shift this morning. Mrs. Kraus says he went off duty hours ago. Well, he's still not home. With this weather, I thought he might have got stuck someplace. I've been cruising the back roads. Sheriff, I found the Benteen County patrol car in a ditch about half a mile from your brother's place. Nobody in it, though his radio and this notebook were on the back seat."

Chairman Wynn held up a spiral notebook with unlikely bright-pink pages. That made it instantly recognizable, as did the florid script on its cover proclaiming it as the property of One of Two, aka Heather English.

"What would our girls be doing at Mad Dog's with Deputy Wynn?" Judy didn't seem to know whether to be relieved or even more concerned by this revelation. The chairman proceeded to point them in the latter direction.

"I naturally figured they'd go to Mad Dog's from there, what with the weather and all. Sheriff, your brother's place is a mess. Somebody went in there and knocked out his windows and kicked in his doors. Worse yet, they took a gun to that buffalo of his, and then they went back to where he's got those wolves penned..."

"**Y**ou girls missed the best part."

Wynn Some wandered into the kitchen. Heather English stood with her back to the door her sister had opened a few moments before.

"Where's Heather?" Wynn asked.

"Uhh, in the bathroom." She hurried across the kitchen and took him by the arm. "Let's give her some privacy. Didn't I see *The Little Mermaid* in their tape collection?"

Two listened as her coconspirator bought a little time. Maybe even enough.

Her head cleared the level of the floor above. It was quiet up here now. No voice. Just the singing of the wind, and the creaking of old boards responding to its relentless pressure. Unless some of those creaks were footsteps...

She wasn't going to creep herself out. Not with a genuine mystery to solve. The stairs opened onto a thickly carpeted central hallway, a dusky place with heavy curtains over the windows at each end of the house. Three pairs of doors stood along a hall that stretched the length of the building. All were closed. More than that, she discovered as her eyes adjusted to the gloom. The three doors along the south wall had devices to lock them from the outside. That sent a chill up her spine. This felt like a scene out of one of those slaughter-the-teenagers movies.

The first door had a hinged metal strap and a ring for a padlock, though there was no padlock on it. The center door had a modern keyed lock, as well as a dead bolt. The third and last was encaged behind a metal grill. It looked like something you might find in a zoo, not in a farmhouse in the heart of a Great Plains tamed of virtually every beast but the weather.

"I don't like this," Two admitted to herself.

Like it or not, she was an explorer by nature. She tried the first of the externally locked doors. There was a bedroom inside. It looked like a museum, like a place no one had been in for a long time.

It was lit well enough. Curtains at windows looking south and west were drawn back, giving a view of swirling snow thick enough to argue against global warming. The room was feminine, lots of lace and frills. And there was a collection of Judy Garland pictures. One showed her on the yellow brick road in the company of Scarecrow, Lion, and Woodsman. Judy had sung "Over the Rainbow" in that film and forever tied the tune to Kansas. The room called out for further investigation but even Wynn would start to wonder if she supposedly spent half an hour in the bathroom. And who knew when Becky Hornbaker or her family would be back.

The carpet absorbed the sound of her footsteps. It absorbed sounds from downstairs as well. If Heather and Wynn had fired up a second movie on the VCR, she couldn't hear it. The second door was beside a banister that guarded the drop into the stairwell. She put her head to its cool wood surface and listened. With the sounds the storm continued to make, about all she could be sure of was that there wasn't a party going on inside. She twisted the dead bolt. If the modern door handle was locked, her skill with a paper clip wasn't going to do any good.

The door swung open the moment she twisted the knob. This room was feminine as well, though not so elaborately decorated, nor so long abandoned as the first. A paper shade hung half way down from its roller, allowing plenty of light from the snow-filled front yard. The bed was unmade, as if it had only been abandoned a few hours ago. A conservative flannel nightie lay across a padded rocker as if someone had gotten up and left in a hurry. There was nothing personal about the room. Heather thought she'd have to sort through drawers and dig into the closet to find even a hint of the person who lived here. She didn't have the time.

The third door drew and frightened her. Cages were meant to keep something in…or out. The door to this cage appeared homemade. It looked like someone had taken pieces of rebar and cut and welded them into shape, then housed them in a metal frame that ran a few inches on either side of the wooden door behind. It looked solid enough, but what about the windows within, what about the walls and floor and ceiling? If a solid wooden door wasn't enough, how could glass and wood and plaster be trusted?

Heather couldn't decide whether she was relieved or disappointed to discover that the metal door was firmly secured. The gaps between the bars, however, were large enough for her to reach through. She tried the handle to the regular door within and it turned. She pushed gently. The knob was ripped from her fingers. She backpedaled across the hall as something threw itself against the iron grate and taloned claws raked her wrist.

And then she was running, bolting for the other end of the hall and the staircase and the safety of a sister and a deputy. She was almost down the stairs before she realized the thing hadn't followed her.

She managed to stop her headlong flight and look back. No terrible beast trailed her down that dusky hall, only a soft voice she could barely hear.

"The only thing we have to fear is fear itself."

◇◇◇

"**R**aise your right hand."

Chairman Wynn did. So did Judy.

"Do you swear to uphold the laws of the United States, the state of Kansas, and Benteen County?"

"I do," they chorused.

"Consider yourselves deputized. Mrs. Kraus, we got any extra badges?"

"Badges," Judy whispered. "We don't need no stinkin' badges." The sheriff thought she was maybe a little hysterical. He still wanted to deposit her at home with a spare radio, but there would be no keeping her from joining a search for the Heathers now, not after what Chairman Wynn had told them.

"Badges? On our budget?" Mrs. Kraus took advantage of the situation to do a little lobbying.

The sheriff pulled out a key chain and unlocked his bottom desk drawer. There were a pair of old revolvers in there in holsters designed to clip onto a belt. He offered one to the chairman.

Chairman Wynn shook his head and opened his jacket. "I've already got something a little more modern."

The sheriff decided this wasn't the time to discuss illegally concealed weapons. "Judy?" he asked.

"I'll pass," she said.

"You hear from anybody who knows anything," the sheriff ordered Mrs. Kraus, "let us know. We'll check in every ten minutes. If you lose track of us, call the state troopers, soon as you get a phone line or a cell back up. Tell them we got two dead bodies so far. You don't have to mention they died of natural causes. Suggest they start rounding up Hornbakers and asking questions till they find our kids. Got it?"

Mrs. Kraus nodded, head snapping with the precision of a military salute. The only Hornbaker in the vicinity had slunk back with Bontrager and their followers to the Board of Supervisors' offices. To lick their wounds, the sheriff thought, or maybe plot an alternate strategy.

"Lock yourself in here after we're gone, Mrs. Kraus. Just in case. Don't let anybody in you aren't sure of. Use the Glock if you have to, only fire a warning shot first. All right?"

Her head snapped again. The sheriff hoped no one did anything foolish while he was gone.

"We're taking your Cadillac, Mr. Wynn. We need your four-wheel drive. I don't think my truck will make it through these drifts. We'll go by the house first. Drop a radio on the off chance the girls show up. Then go to the squad car and Mad Dog's."

"No problem."

"And you've no idea where Mad Dog went?" the sheriff asked, turning to Mrs. Kraus again.

"No sir." She'd turned into a crisp model of precise efficiency in the crisis. "He was asking about Tommie and Becky, the family's history. When they came back to Benteen County. When they stopped being close to each other and whether I remembered anything about it. We just got to when Zeke arrived and the time that truck blew up when Supervisor Bontrager came in and Mad Dog slipped out."

"I remember that truck," Chairman Wynn said. "Lord, what was that, early seventies? I was with the volunteer fire department then. Wasn't hardly a thing left by the time we got organized and drove out there. Pieces of it all over that pasture.

"The crater was already filling with spring water before we left. Wasn't a day later that Tommie Irons was out there grading up a dam and turning the thing into a pond. I went back out with the fire chief the next day. Remember seeing Tommie blade pieces of that truck right into the walls of his dam. Told me he was building a burial mound."

"Burial mound?" The sheriff swung on the new and improved version of Deputy Wynn. "He called it a burial mound?"

Wynn Senior rubbed his chin and nodded his head. "Yeah. That's what he called it."

"We've still got to check out the black and white and take a closer look at Mad Dog's," the sheriff said, "but now I know where we're going after that."

"**D**o not forsake me, oh my darling."

The figure was hard to make out. There was no light in the room with the barred door. Two of Two thought it was human, sort of, with long, scraggly-gray hair that hung over its face. Scrawny arms clasped a shaggy blanket about shoulders as thin as its voice.

Heather went cautiously back down the hall. It was frightening, but hardly terrifying. She stopped a few paces shy of the door and listened as it babbled softly into its hands. It was hard to hear and harder to understand, but she didn't let its whispers draw her back within reach, not with that line of fresh scratches running across her wrist.

Still, she was close enough to make out a little. "We have to distrust each other. It's our only defense against betrayal."

The figure blocked most of her view of the room behind, but what she could see answered her questions about the practicality of a barred door in a normal room. Bars continued on the other side covering every inch of floor. A matching web hung well short of the ceiling. There wasn't even the outline of windows in there. They had been more than just boarded up, she assumed.

"Who are you?" she asked. Heather couldn't even tell what gender the prisoner was.

It raised its face just enough to peer over clutched hands. Pale, bloodshot eyes looked her up and down.

"I'm nobody! Who are you? Are you nobody, too? Then there's a pair of us—don't tell! They'd banish us, you know."

The eyes darted down the hall, then flashed back to Heather. There was nothing dull in the way they appraised her. "Childe Roland to the dark tower came—" it whispered again. "Easy is the descent to Hell; night and day the gates stand open; but to reclimb the slope, and escape to the outer air, this indeed is a task."

"Are you asking for help?" Heather wondered aloud. She was sure she couldn't break through those bars or open the lock without a key. "I suppose I could try."

She would tell Englishman. He was the sheriff. He'd know what to do. "But who are you? Why are you a prisoner?"

"Self is the only prison that can ever bind the soul," it said, then giggled softly. "So little time, so little to do."

"Do you know where the key is?"

"A zealous Lock-Smith Dyed of late, and did arrive at heaven's gate, he stood without and would not knock, because he meant to pick the lock."

Heather was getting frustrated. "I can't help if you keep spouting nonsense. I'll just have to leave you to your fate."

"I am the master of my fate; I am the captain of my soul."

Some of this sounded familiar, literary quotes, she thought, and snatches of songs. Heather grabbed one out of thin air and tossed it back. "Friends, Romans, countrymen, lend me your ears; I come to bury Caesar, not to praise him."

The figure smiled. "The reports of my death are greatly exaggerated."

"You've switched," she said. "Yours was Mark Twain. Mine was Mark Anthony."

The smile faded, became a grimace, perhaps a cringe. "By the pricking of my thumbs, something wicked this way comes." The figure melted back into the darkness and the door swung gently shut.

Heather turned and found herself face to face with hulking Levi Hornbaker. "Shit," he said. "Now I suppose we'll have to kill you all."

◇◇◇

They took the skull into the mortuary room where there was good lighting, as well as access to a number of magnifying devices.

"Where'd you get this one?" Doc put it on the stainless-steel table where he'd earlier conducted an autopsy on the dead baby from the Sunshine Towers.

"I don't think I can tell you yet, Doc. I'm sure it's Cheyenne, but I need you to tell me more—when it died, and how—before I decide whether anyone should know where it came from."

"Cheyenne? What? Did you divine that somehow? Give me a break, Mad Dog, I'm a coroner, not a witch doctor."

"But there are things you can tell, aren't there?" Mad Dog pleaded. "I mean like, is it ancient? Could it have been in the ground a century or more? And maybe how it died? Was it natural? Hell, Doc, I'm just trying to figure out whether this is Englishman's business. If it isn't, he's got his hands full already. If it is, well, here's one more thing I gotta dump on him."

Doc chewed his lip. Mad Dog was an eminently reasonable human being, only sometimes you had to figure out his starting point and follow the path his mental processes had taken. Then you could debate him logically. Sometimes you could get a healthy dialog flowing, occasionally even persuade him to re-examine the point he was trying to defend and maybe modify it. Sometimes he forced the same of you.

"Look, Mad Dog," Doc said, leveling a finger at the big man in the filthy snowsuit. "Everyone in the county knows you went off to dispose of Tommie Irons in some appropriately Native American fashion this morning. Now, you're back here with somebody else's bones. It's not hard to work out that you don't want to tell me where you got these because it's where you left Tommie and you don't want him disturbed. Right?"

"Sort of," Mad Dog hedged.

"So let's leave out the specific part of where, and move to the general. Tell me that and maybe I can answer some of those questions of yours. Did you find this in the ground?"

Mad Dog shuffled his feet. "Not exactly, though it probably eroded out of what looked like a grave."

"And this wasn't out at Southlawn or some other organized cemetery? Some place you might expect to find human remains?"

"No."

"What makes you think it's Cheyenne?"

"I can just tell. I could tell the minute I touched her."

"Her?"

Mad Dog shook his head. "Now that surprised me. I didn't know she was a girl until just this minute."

Doc chewed his lip some more. He wasn't sure he had the energy for a theological exchange with Mad Dog based in Cheyenne shamanism. Most locals thought Mad Dog's career as Benteen County's only born-again Cheyenne shaman was a phase. Doc wasn't a local and didn't agree. He'd only lived in the county some twenty-odd years. That made him an outsider. Mad Dog had had to work all his life to achieve outsider status. He was native to the county, but he'd spent significant portions of his life here as a hippie, an atheist, a Buddhist, and even a Rastafarian. That had been after his Black Power days and shortly before his Chicano period. Oh, folks knew, Mad Dog had always been Cheyenne, and proud of it, but until a few years ago, Mad Dog hadn't understood what that meant.

The mother he and Englishman shared had claimed to be half Cheyenne, but she hadn't practiced the culture. There was nobody in the county to practice it with, so it wasn't until Mad Dog started researching his heritage that he learned enough to latch onto. And he'd latched on hard, especially when his first vision quest corresponded with a murder. Mad Dog had convinced himself he was a natural shaman, and the murder was his fault because he'd somehow released ancient evil spirits. When he managed to land square in the middle of the action that did in a pair of lunatic killers, it further established his bona fides. At least in his own mind.

It made Doc uncomfortable to think about it, but he had to admit Mad Dog's interpretation of those events made more sense than his own—that it was all a series of incredible coincidences. Still, he wasn't going to get into a philosophical debate with Mad Dog now.

"Well," Doc allowed. "You may be right. This may be a girl. But I can't tell you that, not at this age. Sex characteristics in the skeletons of infants are virtually non-existent." He reached up and turned on the light over the worktable, picked out a magnifying glass and bent to give the little skull a closer look. "You could even be right about this being an Indian," he continued, more surprised than he let on. "Skull shape's right. That wouldn't mean much, since a baby's skull can be badly deformed after passing through the birth canal. But I don't think this one did that. And look at this incisor. It wouldn't have erupted through a gum yet, but it's got that classic shovel shape and that makes this kid most likely either American Indian or Asian."

Mad Dog didn't look as pleased as Doc might have expected.

"Doc, can you tell how old this baby was. Months, weeks?"

"No, no," Doc corrected. "Look at the way the sutures between the occipital and the parietals are still open. I don't think this kid had been born yet. If it was, it was a preemie and delivered by C-section."

"Aw, geez. But what about the other bodies?"

Doc rolled his eyes, patience gone. "You found more bodies? Mad Dog, are you insane? Of course Englishman's got to be told. And he and I should see what's out there in situ. This skull's a little stained like you'd expect of bones that have been in the earth for a while. There's no soft tissue left, and no evidence that it was taken by scavengers, so we're talking years here, but there's nothing to indicate these bones are old in the sense you mean. Not unless you found something buried with them to tell us when they went in the ground. That's what Englishman and I need to look for. Artifacts, clothing, something to give us a hint who's in there and how it happened."

Mad Dog looked embarrassed. "You mean like, if an identification card had been found with the bones?" He reached into another pocket and produced a battered plastic ID. "I didn't have my reading glasses with me so I'm not sure what this proves."

Doc took the ID and held it under the light and a magnifying glass. "Jesus H. Christ!" he whispered. "This looks like Supervisor Hornbaker, brother-in-law to the corpse you stole."

"But for the nose," Mad Dog replied.

The two men looked at each other and back at the photo. Doc nodded. "I suppose he could have gotten a nose job…" He handed the card and the magnifying glass to Mad Dog. "Say, how'd you get blood all over your jacket?"

"Oh yeah," Mad Dog replied. "I meant to ask you to take a look. Somebody tried to shoot my ear off."

Boris the German Shepherd took advantage of their visit for a quick dash into the yard and the chance to write his name in the snow. He settled on the canine spelling, a series of yellow dots and dashes, in his effort to hurry and get back inside the warm house.

"Mrs. Kraus." The sheriff wasn't bothering with codes. "This is the radio we're going to leave here in case the girls come home. Judy's writing them a no-nonsense note, explaining that they'd better use it to check in the moment they get here. Can you hear it OK?"

"Perfect," she responded.

"And I got you loud and clear out here in the street," Chairman Wynn chipped in.

"Then we're on our way to where the black and white got stuck, then to Mad Dog's. Let us know if my brother puts in another appearance, or if the crowd in the back of the courthouse makes any trouble."

"You can count on me, sheriff." The sheriff knew he could.

He and Judy gave Boris apologetic pats as they abandoned him to his own devices for another stretch of the day, closed up the house, and joined the chairman in the Cadillac. It felt strange to lower your butt into a heated leather seat while a CD serenaded and the wind gusts that whipped the branches of the trees beside the street hardly affected those within the sumptuous interior of the upscale SUV.

Years ago, the sheriff had been bounced into first class when the airline he was flying oversold tourist. They took pity on a poor soldier, desperate to get home on leave. Only the hearts of palm salad and the filet mignon he'd been served in that plush seat kept it a notch above the Caddy's bucket. He half expected a flight attendant to materialize out of the rear compartment to take their drink orders.

Chairman Wynn's SUV was several levels of pretention beyond what the sheriff would look for in a new vehicle— assuming he and Judy could justify shopping for one instead of putting away for the Heathers' college funds—but it was a marvelously efficient means of getting about in the middle of a Blue Norther. The Caddy dug through drifts up to two feet deep on its way down Cherry, then back south to Main.

"Can't we hurry more?" Judy complained from the back seat.

The sheriff was about to tell her they couldn't, only the chairman proved him wrong. They plowed west on Main, toward the intersection with the north/south blacktop.

"I wish I could have talked to Mad Dog," the sheriff muttered. "I'd sure like to know what he was doing back in the office, and what kind of trouble he's gotten into."

"He's probably halfway across the county by now," Judy said.

"Or gone back to his farm," Wynn Senior offered. "Good chance we'll find him there."

They went by Klausen's, throwing a bow wave of snow that the wind turned into a rolling breaker in which the sheriff surfed, nestled in luxury.

"I don't know," he said, glancing back to where Doc's station wagon was rapidly being drifted in. "Somehow I've got the feeling he's a lot closer."

"What're we gonna do with them?" Levi asked. He had found Two of Two upstairs—almost literally with the skeleton in the Hornbaker closet.

Simon Hornbaker wasn't in the best position to consider the big oaf's question. He was awkwardly perched on a butcher block while Judah tried to cut a pair of handcuffs off his wrist and ankle with kitchen tools. Heather thought she recognized the cuffs as her dad's. Englishman must have come in contact with them, then they'd gotten away. She hoped he was looking for Simon and his boys, and not lying in a ditch somewhere, the victim of their escape attempt.

Everyone was crowded in the kitchen. It was roomy enough, though the deer rifle that Levi kept aimed in the direction of Deputy Wynn and the Heathers made it feel more confined.

"You shouldn't have gone off and left them," Simon said.

"*She* made me go with her. You didn't argue none when she sent us all back to get you freed up." Judah's butcher knife and meat cleaver were seriously the worse for wear. Simon kept flinching whenever Judah swung. There had been more misses than hits to the chrome chain that kept him bound like a calf in the roping event at the annual Pretty Prairie Rodeo. Chunks were missing from the meat cleaver, but the chain showed no damage.

"Probably ought to let that Heather pick these for us, since she's already shown a knack for it," Levi suggested. He was the smart twin, though smart was measured on a different scale for them. He was the smaller one too, huge, but not as enormous as Judah.

"The door was unlocked, honest," Two protested. Actually, anyone in the room could probably pick the lock on the cuffs, One knew. If those were Dad's, that's how he opened them, with the blade of his pocketknife or a handy screwdriver. They were for show, or the occasional violent drunk down at the Bisonte Bar. She didn't tell the Hornbakers, though. Somehow, she didn't think friendly gestures were going to buy them off, especially not after what Levi had threatened when they found Two upstairs.

"There's bolt cutters in the tool box on the porch," Levi said. He set down the rifle and went out the door and got them. "We need someplace safe to stick these three until *she* gets back," he said as he came in again. *"She'll* know what's to be done."

"Why not just kill them?" Judah wondered.

"We could lock 'em in with the witch," Levi countered, applying the tool to the chain. Suddenly Simon was mobile again, though still wearing a shiny bracelet and anklet.

"No. We won't do either," Simon said, stretching his arm and hopping around on a leg that had gone numb in its awkward position. He was about her dad's size, with a beer belly tacked on, but his twins dwarfed him. "I got me a idea. Judah, get the rifle and keep them covered. You three, you wanted to see the house. OK, follow me. There's more you haven't seen."

He led the way through the door Two had picked, into the office, and up the stairs to the second floor. The door behind the cage cracked open and a thin voice gibbered at them.

"The game's afoot…"

Neither Simon nor the parade of Hornbakers paid attention. Heather found herself wondering why a deputy sheriff was allowing himself, and his employer's daughters, to be ordered about so cavalierly. There was only one armed Hornbaker. Surely Wynn Some had been trained to disarm a dumb farm kid with a deer gun following too closely up a set of dark stairs.

Judah tripped and went to one knee. Sure enough, Wynn was on him in a flash, offering a hand and helping him back to his feet. Heather slammed a mental hand against her forehead and decided his training ran more to helping serial killers cross the street.

They went into a room on the north side of the house. A couple of unmade beds lined one wall. There was another door on the far side of the room. Simon opened it onto the ice-cold sleeping porch. A pair of mattress-less bunks and some snow-covered metal chairs stood along its length. Most of the wire mesh that screened occupants from mosquitoes on summer nights was clogged with snow, but there were still enough holes for the wind to remind Heather of every inadequacy in the outfit she'd chosen for their jaunt with Wynn.

"You can't leave us out here," the deputy said, finally speaking up. Only he was wrong. They could. He was addressing a solid oak door, behind which a latch was being thrown.

◇ ◇ ◇

"I think we can save your ear."

Using a cotton swab and alcohol, Doc cleaned the dried blood, along with fabric from Mad Dog's parka, that clung to the wound. Wounds, actually. There were half a dozen places where shattered plastic had encountered flesh and pierced it. None of them were very significant.

"If you've ever thought about an earring, this might be the time. There's gonna be a little notch in here, but a nice thick ring would hide it completely. You say somebody shot a phone out of your hand?"

Mad Dog nodded, and winced when the action caused the alcohol swab to rub against a raw spot. "Yeah. Somebody shooting from a white pickup truck. I couldn't see who, or tell much about the truck. It was already snowing pretty good, and, once the phone exploded, I didn't spend much time trying for a better look."

"But why?"

"That's what I was planning to ask you, Doc. I figure it was probably a Hornbaker, considering where I was and what I was up to. But I don't know that. And I don't know who this skull or those other bones belong to. Zeke Hornbaker's not in that hole. Not the Zeke I know. But it might be about whoever is, and not about what I was doing with Tommie. Though how would some outsider associated with the skeletons know I was there or what I'd found?"

"Maybe they just knew it, same as you." Doc regretted the wise-ass remark, but not enough to apologize. He moved his attentions to Mad Dog's hand. It had a few scrapes and scratches too, though the mitten he'd been wearing appeared to have absorbed most of the damage. "Hell of a shot, especially under those conditions."

"I don't think they were aiming for the phone."

Doc poured a little alcohol onto the deepest scrape and Mad Dog yanked his hand back and shook it while he sucked air and tried to act manly about something Doc knew hurt way out of proportion to the size of the wound.

"I just can't make sense of it, Doc. I guess the Hornbakers are looking for that ugly old ring of Tommie's. But why not just go take it off him before he died? It's not like he had anybody else to leave anything to, or like it could be worth enough for a shooting. And this girl's skull, those other bones, that ID... I keep thinking there must be something else. All I can come up with is that dead baby Englishman found over at the Towers after I left. Maybe somebody thinks I had something to do with that. What do you think? You know anything about that mess?"

"I can't tell you that, Mad Dog. Even if I knew something, hell, even if the mother of that baby were to come through that door over there right now and..."

Doc stopped dead in the middle of his speech. The mother of that baby was coming through the door trailing a naked plastic dolly from one hand. She looked as pale as a ghost, and as scared as Doc suddenly felt.

"Mary," Doc whispered. "What on earth are you doing here? Are you all right?"

She stood peering around the doorway into the mortuary lab from the hall, and, if the scene wasn't already surrealistic enough, Mad Dog's wolf peeked into the room beside her.

"I got scared," she said, offering an excuse. Then she focused on Doc. Her eyes began to glisten. "Doctor Jones. I changed my mind. I'd like to keep my baby after all."

One memorable spring evening some twenty-five years before, a tornado had passed this way. Not just any tornado. This had been one of those behemoths that occasionally roam the plains. It was what they now term a force five event, with wind speeds exceeding 260 mph. Back then it was just a big mother, half a mile wide on the ground. At the crossroads, where you turned off the blacktop to go to Mad Dog's, there had been lines of hedge trees, traps to catch the wind and deter it. And there had been a pair of farms, big two-story homes with a collection of outlying buildings and picturesque barns, one red, one white. Had been. The monster devoured them.

After the storm passed, none of it remained. Every tree in those windrows was gone. Every building had disappeared; nothing but concrete slabs and basements were left to mark where they'd been. Shrubs, bushes, flowers, trees from which ropes with tire swings hung. All gone. One of the families had been at a funeral in Hays. The other was home, heard the warnings, saw it coming, and fled to their basement. They were joined there, during the terrifying moments it took the vortex to pass, by a tractor that had been parked in a field several miles away. After it was lifted out, the owner was able to drive it home. It didn't even have a flat tire. The family came out virtually unscratched as well. Tornadoes were capricious. That titan of destruction was a master of property damage, but it hadn't claimed a single human life. The county had known many smaller ones that reversed that profile.

Tornadoes are a fact of life if you live in Kansas. Maybe that's why Kansans tend to have a conversational relationship with their god. Watching a spinning serpent descend from heaven to strike at your home and family has a way of eliciting requests of the almighty. Some hear answers, others think the tornadoes *are* God's response. This was, apparently, the opinion of the families whose homes once stood here. Neither rebuilt. Not that this location was any more likely than any other part of Benteen County to suffer cyclonic winds, or heavenly whims, again. One family moved to California, the other to Utah. They felt distance improved their odds.

No one else built here afterwards, nor did the farmers who followed replant the windrows. In fact, they tore out the occasional volunteer that sprouted along their fence lines. That made this spot a peculiarly open one. The place drew tourists. The sheriff had discovered them, stopped alongside the road here, on several occasions. He remembered the first ones best. Their tags were from Pennsylvania, a land of mountains and forests. Even though vast numbers of people packed together there, sometimes neighbors couldn't see each other because of a sudden change in elevation or a brief profusion of trees. This couple had pulled their car off the highway at the intersection. They were standing beside it, clinging to each other. The sheriff stopped and got out to ask if they needed help. The man hadn't been able to answer. His wife waved her free hand in a gesture that took in everything around her, or more accurately, the absence of things.

"We didn't know it was so big," she said. There were tears on her face. There were tears on her husband's, as well. "We didn't realize…how insignificant we are."

From this corner, there was virtually nothing to block the horizon in any direction. The only rise in elevation was so slight it wasn't noticeable, and this corner was its peak. A few grain elevators, baby teeth, nibbled at the vault of heaven. Sky couldn't get bigger than this. To those who weren't accustomed to it, it could induce a kind of reverse claustrophobia, a sense of how small they were and, perhaps, how meaningless. Visitors sometimes stopped here at night as well, when a profusion of stars glowed bright enough to demonstrate the depth of that expanse of emptiness. They stopped, they marveled—they were afraid.

The view was very different today, but the sheriff thought he could finally appreciate what strangers to this open country felt when they paused here. There were no horizons today. The Cadillac seemed to drift on an infinite sea of tumultuous gray and white. Nothing outside the SUV looked real, not even the fence posts and phone poles that faded in and out of existence as thick flurries of snow slalomed between them. This view might be similar to what a sailor would see in a heavy fog—sea blending into sky, an infinity of nothingness into which one might slip and never be found again. This mist was white and swirled madly, but it felt equally bottomless. The sheriff had to reach back and pull his soul into that warmed-leather bucket seat when Chairman Wynn slowed to a stop and suggested they install his chains.

The road to Mad Dog's wasn't there anymore. Just two lines of fence posts on the far sides of ditches. The edges would be a guess.

The sheriff opened his door to help. The wind tore it out of his hands and he had to struggle to get it closed. Wind and snow stung his eyes. That must have been the cause of his freezing tears when he met the chairman at the back hatch.

◇◇◇

"You better let us back in," Wynn threatened, without specifying what the consequences would be if the Hornbakers failed to comply. The door remained closed, and continued to do so even when the deputy backed up, got a run, and slammed his shoulder against it. Solid core in a well-made frame, evidently. It held up, but Wynn sort of oozed down to the floor and lay there, ineffectively beating it with his fists.

"There'll be other doors," Heather English suggested. She and Two checked them, and both proved locked and as solidly built as the one by which they'd entered the porch. Equally impenetrable shutters covered windows and were bolted from the inside.

Heather was already starting to shake from the cold. Neither she nor her sister had dressed warmly enough to be outside today, and Wynn's parka was still in the living room. At least he had a thick wool sweater.

"I guess we go out the hard way." Heather English picked up a chair, stepped to the west end of the porch, and swung it against the screen. The sleeping porch was better con-structed than she'd thought, but when Two added her efforts with the aid of a handy end table, it didn't take long for them to open a tear in the mesh big enough to fit through.

"They've got to know we can get out this way," Heather Lane said.

One agreed.

"Maybe this is what they want us to do, but I can't see that it matters. If we stay out here, we're goners."

One stuck her head through the hole they'd made and surveyed the ground below. "Nobody down there." She had to pull her head back inside to make herself heard. "Though they could be sitting behind the windows, watching for us. But there aren't enough of them to watch all the windows. I've got an idea. If we make the hole a little bigger, we can stand on this ledge and jump over onto the roof of the side porch. It'll be slick, but we might be able to follow it around to the front of the house, maybe come down someplace they aren't watching."

Two nodded. "Sounds good. Then what?"

"Then it's your turn for ideas."

"I was afraid of that."

"Don't worry," the first Heather reassured the second. "We probably won't get that far anyway."

"**S**he's Mary Hornbaker," Doc explained. The girl had been soothed, her vitals taken, and she'd been returned to Doc's office, where he dug through his desk until he found a comic book to keep her occupied. She and Hailey were curled back up on the couch and Doc and Mad Dog stood just outside his closed door in the sterile hallway where they could respond if she needed.

"She's the mother of the dead baby?" Mad Dog thought the possibility should have occurred to him when he found a pale, confused teen locked in a barn in the middle of a blizzard as if she were being punished for some awful transgression. But it hadn't. She seemed too young, too innocent. And he had troubles of his own.

"She was out in the barn?" Doc heaved a sigh worthy of Atlas. "Well, you heard what she said. I don't suppose I can claim the confidentiality of a doctor/patient relationship, not entirely anyway."

Mad Dog nodded and Doc sighed again. Mad Dog supposed doctors ran into a lot of strange human behavior, but, from the look of it, Doc was venturing into places seldom traveled.

"She's a Hornbaker?" Mad Dog asked, trying to recall any Hornbaker girls. "Who are her parents?"

"I don't know. This kid's kind of a mystery. Last summer Simon Hornbaker caught me as I pulled into my driveway one night. He had Mary with him. Wanted me to confirm that she was pregnant. Up to then I didn't know she existed. There's no record of her birth that I can find. She's never been in the school system."

"You're kidding," Mad Dog said, though he knew Doc wasn't.

"Simon didn't want to explain her, but she was pregnant. When I confirmed that, he asked me to do an abortion."

"The son of our county's foremost champion of the pro-life cause asked that?"

"Maybe your values shift when it's your own family."

Mad Dog didn't argue. Long ago when he and Janie Jorgenson were the sweethearts of Buffalo Springs High by day, and studying comparative anatomy by Braille in the back seat of Mad Dog's Chevy by night, Mad Dog had made that very choice. Worse, he'd just come up with the cash, then let Janie handle the then illegal solution to their problem all alone. It was not one of his prouder moments.

"Well," Doc continued, "you know I don't do abortions. I refused, till he told me who the father was. I don't guess it matters now. Simon said it was Tommie Irons. That Mary was his daughter and Tommie's grand niece, and mentally retarded. Struck me as an interesting observation, coming from Simon. Plenty of folks would say the same of him. He told me Becky had a premonition there would be something wrong with the girl, so they hid her. Becky delivered her at home so the child wouldn't have to be born at a hospital or known to the community."

"It can't be true." Mad Dog was sure that, as a natural born shaman, he would have felt the evil radiating from Tommie Irons. Then he remembered the bones in Tommie's burial mound and didn't feel sure of anything anymore. Not even his abilities as a shaman, which, come to think of it, weren't proving very consistent.

"So I said I'd do it."

"Jesus, Doc!" Without thinking, Mad Dog addressed a deity other than the one he favored. "Really?"

"Rape and incest. Powerful arguments."

Most residents of Benteen County would have been surprised to learn Mad Dog was opposed to abortions. Not that they knew his history of involvement with the subject. Janie never spoke about it, then she left Buffalo Springs and never spoke to him again.

Since rural Kansas was a conservative place, if you wanted to be an oddball and hold views contrary to the majority, you had to lean toward the liberal. Mad Dog did that, pretty near all the way to Commie Pinko, at least so the gossips down at Bertha's would tell you over a cup of coffee, a piece of pie, and a raised and disapproving eyebrow.

Along with civil rights, women's rights, arms control, gun control, welfare, and other definingly liberal issues, Mad Dog had been a stout proponent of a woman's right to choose, and not just Janie's—until he became a born-again Cheyenne.

This was one of the tenets of Cheyenne faith that he had the most trouble with, but he didn't think you got to pick and choose if you were going to be Cheyenne. It was like converting to Catholicism and then denying the Pope's infallibility. It didn't work.

Mad Dog's inclination was to believe a woman's body was her own. What she wanted to do with it was up to her, not him, nor some group of mostly white males gathered in the District of Columbia. He'd never been a fan of abortion as birth control, but he'd preferred it to unwanted children. Then he started learning the Cheyenne way.

People—Cheyennes—recycled. Those who had once been Cheyenne would be again. After they died, their souls went to wait among other Cheyenne souls until it was time for them to come back. Every Cheyenne baby contained the soul of a Cheyenne who had lived before, returning to earth to complete another cycle. There were no new people. Though eggs and sperm might meet to create a new physical form, it housed an old soul. That made abortion murder, plain and simple. Only, of course, nothing is ever simple.

The Cheyenne don't proselytize their religion to outsiders because outsiders aren't people. Well, there were exceptions. They were willing to concede that other Native Americans were people, a little different and maybe just a tiny bit inferior, but people, also capable of recycling. But Earth's teeming billions, the population rapidly filling the globe, the endless supply of whites who had come west and destroyed the buffalo and stolen their lands, those weren't people. Those were spiders, a term of contempt. Worse, they had bodies, they occupied space, they could fight and kill and steal what belonged to people even though they weren't people themselves. They had no souls. They were just beasts. Walking, talking meat. The Cheyenne didn't care whether spiders aborted their foetuses, except that, occasionally, people didn't come back as Cheyenne or other Native Americans. Occasionally, a soul appeared among the meat. Since you couldn't tell whether someone had a soul until they were born and grew up enough to demonstrate personhood, Cheyennes, such as Mad Dog, opposed abortions under any circumstances.

Mad Dog rubbed his fingers through nonexistent hair and pondered. Surely this was an exception. And then he let himself relax because Doc hadn't done it. He might have planned to, but he hadn't. The baby had been left in the womb until it arrived, stillborn. *Maheo*, or perhaps another of the pantheon of spirits who ruled over such things, had taken care of this abomination without Doc's intervention.

"But you didn't do it, obviously."

"Well." Doc didn't look comfortable. "I didn't do anything surgical, but I saw to it that she got something that should have terminated her pregnancy. I thought it had. I told Simon I'd have to see her again. He agreed, only then he told me it had worked and she was fine and he couldn't chance bringing her back. I went by the farm a few times. It was hard to catch Simon alone, but I used reporting on Tommie's condition as an excuse to be there. Simon said they'd sent her away. I don't know that I believed him. The only way I could have forced the issue was to make it public. I let it go.

"Then, last night, Becky called. Told me she had a girl there in labor, only the baby wouldn't come. They wouldn't meet me at the clinic so I persuaded them to come here. It was Mary."

"Yeah," Mad Dog said. "I know the rest. Mrs. Kraus filled me in on what you told Englishman. How they were already gone by the time you got here and there was just a little blood and a doll on the back porch of the funeral parlor."

Doc looked toward the door to the mortuary. He swung his hands in a gesture of helplessness.

"I lied," Doc said.

Mrs. Kraus was listening to a weather update on the radio. A freight train was stuck in a massive snowdrift on the old Santa Fe line that cut across the southern edge of the county. There was a local rash of downed phone and power lines. Things were a mess, but they were pretty much normal once you got a few miles from Benteen County. Forecasters predicted the storm would blow itself out by nightfall. The announcer was in the middle of a list of helpful suggestions, such as staying indoors, when the power went off, taking his reassuring voice with it.

It didn't get much darker in the sheriff's office. There were only a couple of sixty-watt bulbs in the overhead lights and, with no phones to answer and no messages to transcribe, Mrs. Kraus hadn't turned on her desk lamp. The office was just a wing off the south side of the main building. The room had tall windows facing front and rear. The sky was low and dull enough to diminish the illumination they normally provided, but with everything underneath that sky coated in reflective white, it wasn't much dimmer than normal in the office.

It was uncomfortably quiet, though, except for those groaning noises the old building made as the storm tried to shove it to the other side of town. And it was lonely. Mrs. Kraus thought about picking up the radio to check in with Englishman's posse, only it hadn't really been that long since they'd called. She didn't want to start pestering them like some nervous old woman.

She didn't recognize the knock on the door to the sheriff's office at first because of all the other noises the building was making. When she did, it was with relief. She walked over to the door and shouted, "Who's there?" Ezekiel Hornbaker identified himself and she unlocked it and let him in. He entered, wide-eyed and cautious, as if he expected her to use him for target practice. She went over and put the Glock back on her desk. He wasn't the company she wanted, but, any port...this sure qualified as a storm.

"Your lights out too? Mine just went off and I thought I'd check. Make sure it wasn't just one of the circuits that was out."

He appeared to take her silence for, if not a welcome, at least a truce. He edged a little farther into the room.

"You heard from Englishman? Seen anything of Mad Dog?"

"The sheriff will inform you about this investigation when he has time." She didn't really know anything, and wasn't inclined to share what she did, including Mad Dog's visit.

"Look," he said. "I'm sorry. I guess I've made an ass of myself this morning."

Lord have mercy, an apology from Zeke Hornbaker.

"It's just that some issues rile me. Like abortion. It's the same as infanticide, which it looked like this might be for awhile."

Infanticide. Zeke had a wider vocabulary than Mrs. Kraus would have given him credit for. He ambled over to the counter, looking less sheepish and more relaxed.

"I didn't mean any harm. There are things a man's gotta stand up for."

Not a woman, of course. Only place a woman should stand was firmly behind her husband. Mrs. Kraus allowed herself a "harumph" that let Zeke know all was not forgiven.

"Look here. I got carried away. I admit it. But it seemed like Englishman was too caught up in family matters and not paying proper attention to his job. Mad Dog's sure got my dander up. And I'm concerned about where that baby came from. Who the mother might be and whether she may have contributed to its death."

Mrs. Kraus could contain herself no longer. "What about the father? If you're gonna hand out blame, how about his share?"

"Oh sure," Hornbaker admitted. "The father's to blame too, only he might not have known what was happening. Hell, sometimes the fathers don't ever know there's a pregnancy."

Maybe she was too young and ashamed to understand and tell anyone what was happening to her. Ignorance was no excuse in the eyes of the law, but if an unwilling mother's inability to face reality was to be punished, how about the father's unwillingness to bother finding out whether his seed sprouted after he planted it. Mrs. Kraus tossed in a "Pshaw." There was no point in this argument anyway. They didn't know the facts. They were just supposing. Only he was ready to blame and punish the woman, and Mrs. Kraus was inclined to defend her own sex. Sexists, that's what they both were.

Mrs. Kraus was no feminist. She hadn't burned her bra or argued for the Equal Rights Amendment, wouldn't be forced to share one of those unisex bathrooms like had turned up on Ally McBeal (not that she would admit watching the show). And she didn't favor abortion, though there were times…What bothered her most was that the people kicking up the biggest fuss about it seemed to be men, like Zeke Hornbaker, with not the slightest clue of what it meant to carry a child and deliver it. Them and the women who bought into that stand-*behind*-your-man bullcrap.

"But you're right," Zeke was saying. "I hear Doc says the baby was a stillborn. Everyone seems to agree, especially with the storm and all, there's no rush to follow up on this. Everybody went home after Chairman Wynn left with the sheriff. Even Bontrager." He shook his head as he leaned over and put his elbows on the counter. "I still feel like we should be doing more to find out," he said.

"Englishman's doing all that's possible."

"Oh, I know. He's limited by the weather, and there wasn't anything about that baby to give him a clue."

"There was the mark." Mrs. Kraus regretted her words the moment they were out. She'd let herself grab a chance to show Hornbaker he didn't know all he thought he knew.

He leaned over the counter. "The mark?" He had turned wild eyed and peculiar looking. "What was it?"

"Just that. A mark, like from an ink pen. Just a stupid offensive symbol, that's all."

His eyes got big and his pupils looked hollow. "A swastika?" he whispered.

It was Mrs. Kraus' turn to be astonished. "How'd you know that?"

There wasn't anyone there to answer. She heard his footsteps pound across the foyer, down the back hall, and out toward the rear exit.

She was alone in the courthouse. It wasn't a comfortable feeling, especially after the odd way in which Zeke Hornbaker had left, as if he'd just seen a ghost.

A moment later, the supervisor came spinning out of the parking lot in the family's old Dodge Powerwagon. He was going faster than he should. He swerved to avoid Judy's Taurus and caught a front wheel in the edge of the ditch. The truck went in a circle and ended up passenger side down at a forty-five degree angle to the road.

Hornbaker spun his wheels, forward and backward, and never moved an inch. She watched him kick open his door and go plowing through the drifts in Veteran's Memorial Park, headed in the general direction of Bertha's. He hadn't even paused to take his coat. It was eerie.

Mrs. Kraus didn't believe in ghosts, though if any place in Benteen County was haunted, this should be it. Pretty much all the evil in the county passed through here. And there were those two accused murderers who'd committed suicide by hanging themselves back in their cells about a century ago. The noises the old building made in the wind suddenly sounded more ominous. She relocked the door.

A shadow seemed to flit by the windows. Just a low cloud, she reassured herself. A distant rafter—surely it was only a rafter—moaned. Boards creaked. It sounded like footsteps, like someone coming across the foyer from the entrance to the jail. She backed up against her desk and watched the door, expecting the knob to begin to turn. A disembodied voice whispered her name behind her.

After Mrs. Kraus came down from the ceiling—where she was sure you could find the marks her fingernails had made as she sought to suspend herself there in sheer, unmitigated terror—she realized it had only been the radio. She had trouble finding the breath with which to answer it.

"**M**rs. Kraus?" the sheriff asked again.

"Yes sir." It was hard to hear her over the wind and the efforts of the Caddy's defroster to keep the windshield clear.

"We found the cruiser. It's nearly buried in snow, but we dug down to one of the back doors and confirmed that no one came back to it. No people, no messages. Anything at your end?"

"Power's off. Supervisor Hornbaker…came in." Her voice sounded breathless, like she'd just run a hard 10K. "Everybody's gone. Even Hornbaker. Sheriff, he…seemed to know… about the swastika."

"How could he? And what makes you think so?"

"He was being a know-it-all." She was getting her breath back, or maybe she'd just been having trouble with her radio. "Said something about there being no way to identify the baby. I had to open my big trap. I told him there was a mark, a symbol. He turned seven shades of pale and said 'A swastika,' and then he ran out of here like the devil himself was nipping at his heels. Didn't even stop for his coat."

Hornbakers kept popping up to cause him trouble, the sheriff thought. But how could the supervisor know what had been on the infant's forehead? Was there some sort of neo-Nazi gang operating in Benteen County? Could bumbling Zeke Hornbaker be a member of a white supremacist group trafficking in deceased infants? Not possible, the sheriff told himself.

"Where'd he go?"

"Last I saw, he was on foot and crossing the park toward Bertha's."

The sheriff exchanged puzzled frowns with his companions in the Cadillac. No one offered any opinions.

"Mrs. Kraus. You got a clue what this is about?"

"Nary a one, Sheriff."

"Anybody?" The sheriff offered Judy and Wynn the elder a chance to contribute to the conversation. They were too busy shivering, recovering from the chilling effort of checking the cruiser.

"OK. We're on our way to Mad Dog's. We'll call from there."

"Or sooner if you like. It's frustrating, sitting here in the cold and dark, all alone, not knowing what's going on."

The sheriff understood. It was every bit as frustrating from where he sat.

"**Y**ou know what a breech birth is?" Doc asked.

Mad Dog knew, but not exactly. "Sort of."

"The baby doesn't turn the way it's supposed to for a normal delivery. It tries to come feet or butt first. Things get all twisted up. It's no big deal anymore, if you're in a maternity ward or a good clinic. There are techniques to turn the baby, or you can just do a C-section. Problem is, nobody saw this girl during her pregnancy but me, and then just to confirm it. Nobody with any real training was there when she went into labor. They let it go on too long. By the time Becky Hornbaker got Mary here, she was exhausted from hours of contractions. I was going to do a Caesarian, but Becky wouldn't hear of it. We tried some other techniques. They worked, much to my surprise. I got the baby turned and coming the right way, only it was a slow delivery because Mary didn't have it in her to push very hard. When we finally got the baby's head out, the umbilical cord was twisted around its neck. Blood wasn't flowing through the cord the way it's supposed to."

Mad Dog nodded, sympathetically. "So that's why it was born dead."

"No. The baby was alive. There was a pulse."

"But you said…"

"I told you, Mad Dog. I lied. I delivered that baby in a hurry then. All I needed to do was clear its windpipe, get it breathing on its own. Only this was a baby Simon Hornbaker persuaded me should never have been born. Rape and incest. And the child's mother is retarded. This baby had all kinds of chances for birth defects and brain damage. I looked at this infant and saw what I wanted to see. Head shape was wrong. Color wasn't good. It had been without proper oxygen flow for a while. Too long, maybe. I played God. Oh, it was stillborn, but only because I didn't prevent that."

"No!" Mad Dog couldn't imagine Doc doing that. It was like finding out Santa brought cancer instead of toys.

"What I did was worse than an abortion," Doc confessed. Mad Dog wasn't qualified to hear one, though he was a priest of sorts, and probably the only one in Benteen County to whom Doc would tell all this. "I pulled a Kevorkian. Some might call it a mercy killing, a kindness, considering all that child had going against him, but I'm not sure I can go hide there. Mad Dog, I murdered that child."

◇◇◇

Wynn Some, Lose Some didn't exactly leap from the roof. He hadn't been all that keen on leaving the sleeping porch. It had a wall that stood about three feet above its floor. If you hunkered down it kept you out of the worst of the storm's fury. Only the girls shamed him into leaving. They weren't going to let Becky and the Hornbakers cage them out here where they'd slowly freeze to death. They punched a hole in the screen on the west side, then hopped across and tested the roof above the wrap-around exterior porch. It held, and one of them came back to argue that they could crawl under a window or two and pick a place to get down where they wouldn't be easy to see from inside. She made him feel like a wimp for not leading the escape effort. Besides, he didn't want to stay behind alone.

The gap the Heathers hopped with ease looked like an immense chasm from the edge of the porch.

"Don't look down," One hollered, so he did. It was hard to believe he was only on the second story. The ground at the edge of the house looked far enough below to kill the man unlucky enough to plunge to its depths. It took him several tries to work up his nerve. He got one hand on the side of the house to help pull, used the other to push off from one of the uprights that supported the porch roof, then kicked off with every ounce of his strength.

It was more than enough. He landed two feet beyond the edge he'd been concerned with. He also landed closer to the downhill edge, where the roof drained into a series of gutters that fed the shrubbery below. And, he landed on his heels. Normally, they would have bit into the shingles and he would have stopped abruptly, maybe even stumbled back into the edge of the house behind him. Today did not qualify for normally. It was a snow-slick slope and he hit it with force and velocity. His feet went out from under him, his arms windmilled past a pair of girls frantically trying to grab him, and he did a backward somersault while proceeding inexorably toward the brink. He got back onto his hands and knees in time to see it coming and pushed off hard enough to delay the inevitable. If ever a man positioned himself with the maximum potential to fly as he launched into the abyss, it was Wynn. The deputy wasn't wearing a cape and tights with a scarlet S emblazoned on his chest. Ultimately, he flew about as well as the laws of physics predicted.

He glanced off a branch on the way down. That helped him straighten out and get his feet under him for a landing that was a lot softer than it should have been because the snow was beginning to drift over the shrub where he hit. Judges at some extreme sporting event would have given him high scores, especially if they, like the Hornbakers, were unable to hear over the storm as his terrified scream trailed him to the ground.

The Heathers dropped on either side of him.

"You OK?" One asked.

"'Cause we'd better run!" Two explained.

Wynn was fine, and scared enough to turn in a dash time that would have impressed an NFL scout. He left the girls behind, but not the blizzard.

Except for where it was drifting behind the evergreens, the pasture hadn't accumulated much snow. The winter-stunted grass wouldn't hold more. The wind took the rest and went searching for a snow bank to invest in that might keep it safely deposited until spring.

The sheriff had lived at or regularly visited Mad Dog's place all his life. He knew it in all its aspects, even smudged by a driving snowstorm. He'd noticed the drift that didn't belong in his brother's pasture. They were missing three people, and the drift's size was too close to human for him to ignore, even though the chairman had told him what was there. He left the chairman and Judy in the car, just short of Mad Dog's driveway, while he went to check. He'd expected an argument from Judy. He'd thought he might have to take her along, only the lump in the pasture was so obviously not alive that she'd stayed behind, uncharacteristically silent and obedient.

The snowdrift wasn't human. It had hooves, and, when he brushed at it, revealed a great rusty stain where blood had gushed, thickened, then frozen, from the bullet wound that had killed the last buffalo in Benteen County.

"It's Buffalo Bob," the sheriff told the radio.

"Who would kill Mad Dog's hand-raised pet?" The walkie-talkie was hard to hear over the wind. He couldn't tell, though he thought the comment came from Mrs. Kraus. He'd used the radio to alert the office to this extra-vehicular activity.

"Mr. Chairman," the sheriff continued. "Get your gun out and ready. Let Judy drive so your hands are free. We know this didn't happen recently. All the same, somebody with a high-powered rifle could be waiting up at the house. I'll circle around to the barn, come on the house from the back while you drive in from the front. I'll call you again when I'm in position."

"Understood," the chairman answered.

The sheriff let the wind shove him toward the barn. Mad Dog's house was hardly visible behind a screen of snow-capped lilacs and forsythia.

The drifts near the barn were deep enough to cause problems. The sheriff finally reached its back door by circling some and wading through others. He was breathing as hard as if he'd finished his usual four-mile run when he slid one side open and stepped into the relative stillness of the barn's dark interior.

It wasn't any warmer inside, except for wind chill. Temperatures far below freezing weren't ideal for olfactory impressions, but the sheriff recognized the coppery scent the moment he closed the door. Mad Dog had turned the stalls along the south wall into pens for his rescue wolves. Someone else had turned them into an abattoir. It was hard to take, even though he had known what to expect.

The sheriff knew several ranchers who feared those wolves enough to react this violently if their stock had been slaughtered by loose dogs or coyotes. He couldn't imagine even one of them taking Mad Dog's buffalo too. This had a taste of personal vengeance to it, or maybe madness.

The sheriff made his way to the other end of the barn. The yard behind Mad Dog's house was as empty of life, but less violently so. No bodies, living or dead. No vehicles. No indication anyone was home.

"I'm going in," he told the radio. "You too, but come ready."

Judy came like one of those stunt car drivers at the fair, sliding the Cadillac to a stop by the walk to Mad Dog's front door so the bulk of the vehicle was between the house and Chairman Wynn as he jumped out and leveled his pistol across the hood. It was a more impressive approach than the sheriff was accustomed to getting out of his deputies, but unnecessary.

The house was as empty as it looked, and it, too, was a victim of the sick violence that had visited Mad Dog's barn and pasture. Most of the windows were broken. The front door had been kicked to splinters. Furniture was overturned, appliances broken, bookcases toppled. Books had been hurled about as if they could feel the same emotions they might impart. It didn't make sense. Neither did the frozen red swastika someone had drawn on the kitchen floor. At least it wasn't blood, just the contents of a broken ketchup bottle.

"I had a bison calf," Mad Dog said. "There was something wrong with it. Back legs weren't right. It couldn't stand and it bawled all the time. I knew better, but I tried to nurse it, keep it alive. Finally, I had to do what I should have done at the start."

Doc Jones rolled his eyes. "You trying to equate putting down a calf with murdering a child? Jesus, Mad Dog! I'm not asking you for absolution. I know what I did and I'm past trying to hide or deny it. I'm ready to face up to it."

Mad Dog leaned down and put his face right in Doc's. It shut him up. "Enough *mea culpas*, already. You aren't listening to me. What I figured out, finally, was that calf's spirit wasn't right. It wasn't really a buffalo. Maybe it got crossbred with some beef cattle. Anyway, what I mercy killed never had the chance to be a buffalo. That's what happened with you, too, isn't it? You did an autopsy on that baby. What did you find? Was it normal?"

"Normal is a broad term…" Doc tried to back away but Mad Dog pinned him against the wall.

"Was it a person who could have lived?"

"There's no way I can be certain."

"Yes there is, Doc. Just like I know that skull I brought you is Cheyenne, you knew that baby wasn't right. You just won't let yourself admit your occasional insights are every bit as valid as your scientific tests. Psychic diagnosis isn't something you're ready to accept. I know you, Doc. You wouldn't have done whatever you did unless it was necessary. And I can tell. Call it Cheyenne mysticism or psychic mumbo jumbo from the local nut case, but I know you found something in that autopsy to justify it."

"But I couldn't have known then…"

"But you did. What was it, Doc. Tell me."

"It's rare. There were hardly any of the usual external indications."

"It had no soul, did it, Doc?"

"What's a soul? Where do I find it? Aw shit, Mad Dog. I don't know what to say. It was an anenceph baby. There was a brain stem that might have kept all the involuntary functions going if I'd let them get started, but not much else. The rest of the brain didn't develop properly. God! I suppose, if there is a soul, the brain is where it would live."

Mad Dog pushed himself back across the hall. Doc had his personal space again, except inside. It still felt like whatever was Mad Dog, his spirit maybe, was pushing that same part of Doc. Manipulating him.

"No human died here," Mad Dog said. "If someone had, I'd feel it. There would still be something left. You recognized that absence of humanity too."

"Maybe I knew," Doc admitted in a whisper, "but how can you?"

Not manipulating, Doc realized, guiding. With that under-standing, the pressure receded.

"Same as any shaman, Doc," Mad Dog smiled. "Same as you."

They ran west, because that was the way Wynn Some happened to be pointed, and it was away from the house.

A Hornbaker was in the driveway to their right. He fired a shot in the air. Wynn didn't seem to notice. The girls couldn't hear the report because of the wind. When he didn't aim at them, they stayed on course and followed the deputy.

He used the limb of a handy hedge tree to vault the fence and get into the pasture. Heather English followed suit, but she had to stop and help her sister disentangle her jeans from the top row of barbed wire. By then, Wynn was out of sight. But his tracks weren't, though the wind was trying to scrub them away.

The girls pursued them until the prints came to a skidding halt about a hundred yards from the fence, then changed direction, going southeast even faster. His new course was paralleled by the tracks of what must have caused his change of direction. Wynn had encountered something massive enough for its hooves to excavate chunks of snow and frozen earth.

"What do we do now?" Two asked One, who didn't know. All she knew was that they couldn't stay out in this weather long.

"We can't catch Wynn." She gestured at the hoof prints, "And I don't want to find what made those. Let's circle back toward the farm from the north. If that guy with the gun is following us, he'll have to make a choice. Maybe he'll follow Wynn instead of us. Whatever, we've got to find shelter, or transportation. It's miles to another farm. We've only been outside a few minutes and I'm already getting numb."

Heather Lane nodded. "You're the native. You lead, I'll follow."

"That could be a mistake," One muttered, but she turned into the wind, lowered her head, and started jogging.

"**W**here do you live, Mary?"

Mad Dog sat on the floor in a modified lotus position. He wasn't quite flexible enough to get both legs where they were supposed to be without cramping up. That sometimes hindered his efforts to meditate. Actually, it wasn't exactly meditation, since he'd switched from yoga to Cheyenne shamanism, but there were similarities. What he was usually trying to do from the position these days was relax, free his spirit from his body so it could travel through time and space and commune with other Cheyennes, past and present, or visit the pantheon of beings who saw to it that the universe remained in order and operated as it was meant to. It took a lot of patience, something Mad Dog was trying to acquire. Now he was only getting down to Mary's level.

"I dunno." She was kind of huddled up in the corner of the couch in Doc's office, half hiding under the blanket Doc had spread over her. She had one of those I-think-I'm-drowning grips on the rough of Hailey's neck. It wasn't something Mad Dog recommended with wolf hybrids, only Hailey seemed to recognize her need. It was like she had adopted the girl. When the grip threatened to get too tight, Hailey would just shift her head around and slather Mary's face with kisses until the girl calmed down and loosened it.

That was the kind of patience Mad Dog yearned for, and, he suspected, the kind he needed just now. Mary was very

young and her mind seemed even younger. There were a lot
of things Mad Dog wanted to know, things his brother needed
to know. Doc too. Doc had collapsed in the chair behind his
desk, swinging wildly on the pendulum of revelation between
guilt and relief and doubt and wonder.

"Do you live on the farm where I found you?"

"I 'spose."

"Who lives with you?"

She kneaded Hailey's fur. "It changes. Most times, Gran's
there. Sometimes Gramps. And Uncle Simon, and Levi and
Judah of course, and there's the witch at the end of the hall."

Witch at the end of the hall? What was real, what was
fantasy? Gran would be Becky, Gramps, Zeke, he supposed.

"What about your mom?"

She shrugged, like she wasn't sure what he meant.

"Where do you go to school?"

"I'd like to go to school."

"Mary," Doc interrupted. "Do you know a man named
Tommie? Tommie Irons?"

Mad Dog had been avoiding Tommie's name for a couple
of reasons. He didn't want to upset the girl, especially not
before he got some useful information. And, he didn't want
to talk about the man he'd befriended, not if Irons had done
to this girl the things he was accused of. Only she didn't react.

"They don't let me see anyone else."

Doc was as stunned as Mad Dog. "Honey. You must know
him. He lived there too."

She nodded her head. "I knew him. Don't tell, though,
'cause I wasn't supposed to. He was nice, then he went away."

Mad Dog wondered what nice meant.

"Who's the father of your child, Mary?" Doc persisted.
"Was it Tommie?"

She shrugged narrow shoulders and looked uncomfortable.
"I dunno."

Maybe Doc needed further evidence to support his waver-
ing self-justification. Whatever, he wouldn't let it alone.

"Honey. You've got to know. You remember where your baby came from. Somebody had to plant a seed in that same place before it could grow. It might have hurt when he did it. Surely you remember."

"Oh, that. Yeah, I remember."

"Then who was it?"

"Uncle Simon once. Then somebody else. A bunch of times. I thought I knew who it was then, but I wasn't sure. So, I asked Gran. Sure enough, she told me I was right." Mary beamed, delighted to be able to tell them what they wanted to know. "It was God."

"This is a Beretta." Englishman handed Judy the pistol he'd taken from Simon that morning.

"I don't need to know who made it to shoot it," she replied. She took it by the butt, dropped the magazine to ensure it was loaded, racked the slide, and dry fired it out one of Mad Dog's shattered windows. One look at Mad Dog's place and she was ready to carry a firearm after all.

"Stubby little cartridges," she observed.

"That's a 9 mm short." Chairman Wynn was pleased to demonstrate his knowledge of firearms. "It's not that potent. If you have to shoot somebody, do it more than once."

"Those hollow points will kill you quick enough at close range," Englishman said.

Judy nodded. She replaced the magazine and found a convenient pocket for the semiautomatic.

"What's all this about, Englishman?" Judy asked. "What are swastikas doing on a dead baby and Mad Dog's kitchen floor? And what the hell has it got to do with where our daughters and Deputy Wynn are?"

"You hear her, Mrs. Kraus?" Judy was surprised that Englishman had keyed the walkie talkie in time for her speech.

"Enough," the radio croaked.

"Chairman Wynn, Judy, and I are about the same age," Englishman told her. "We're post-war boomers. The people saluting swastikas had already surrendered before we were born. I know some racists in the county, but I'm damned if I know any Nazis or white supremacists. How about you, Mrs. Kraus? Can you tell us anything?"

"I ain't that much older'n you," she snapped, leading Judy to think she might be. This wasn't a moment for injured pride. Judy took the radio from her husband's hand.

"Mrs. Kraus," she pleaded. "Our kids are out there. Please help us if you can!"

"Well, hell, Judy. I remember some German POWs worked at the agricultural station near Hays. And families here worried about sending their sons off to kill their relations. But there weren't any Nazi sympathizers around Buffalo Springs. Not that I ever heard about."

"Any refugees come from Europe after the war?" Englishman wondered, taking the radio back. Judy found herself stumbling across the mess on Mad Dog's floor. She nearly fell and that focused her attention on the book that had caused her to trip.

"A Dutch family, real Dutch, from Holland," Mrs. Kraus said. The wind made her hard to hear and it made the book's dust jacket flutter.

Judy bent down and picked it up. It was a history of the Second World War. Its jacket was covered with the flags of the combatants. There was something about Germany's flag.

"Isn't Hornbaker a German name?" Mrs. Kraus asked.

Judy carried the book over to the door to the kitchen. The ketchup swastika was beginning to smudge beneath a collection of snowflakes, but it was still as brutally intrusive as she remembered. And the other part was as she remembered too.

"I think so," the chairman said, "but Zeke's no Nazi. He's a horse's ass sometimes, and he probably wouldn't eat anything kosher unless it was a pickle. Look, if Zeke's a racist, he's not an organized racist. He doesn't belong to anything more radical than the Farm Bureau."

"Englishman," Judy said.

He turned, but he didn't come join her in the doorway the way she expected. He didn't even ask what she wanted.

"Englishman. I think you should come look at this."

"I've seen it, Judy, and we're kind of busy right now."

He was being stubborn. It annoyed him when he thought she expected him to read her mind. And, she supposed, that was what she'd just asked of him.

"No really," she said. "This swastika. You need to look at it again."

Since their conversation with Mrs. Kraus was taking place on a mobile radio, there wasn't any reason he couldn't come. Englishman was stubborn, not stupid. And Chairman Wynn was curious enough to follow.

"What about it." Englishman was puzzled.

She showed him the book.

"The arms," she said. "The arms on this swastika. They're backwards."

"**I** can't go much farther."

Heather English understood Heather Lane's complaint. She couldn't feel her feet anymore. That made running a problem.

"You don't have to. Look, there's the fence."

And there it was, only a few feet away, hidden until that moment by swirling snow that only seemed to be getting thicker. Surely the storm would have to ease up soon. One snapped off a couple of branches to clear the way, then held the top strand of barbed wire while her sister scrambled over. A cluster of weathered outbuildings stood a few feet beyond the fence. They weren't nearly as far north as she'd thought. On the other hand, they hadn't been caught yet. That probably meant the Hornbaker with the rifle had followed Wynn's tracks.

"Which one?" Two asked, returning the favor with the fence.

"It doesn't matter. Any of them, just so we get out of this wind. We may have to try lots before we find a snug hiding place or a way out of here."

The nearest building was about a thirty foot square. Its windows had been boarded over. It had large swinging doors on the south end, big enough to drive a truck through, but impossible to open with more than three feet of snow drifted against them. There was a normal sized door on the north side. It opened out, against the wind. That made it difficult, but the wind had kept its approach swept clean. They forced it and found a room filled with dust-coated crates. The door slammed behind them, leaving them in dusky twilight.

"I can hardly feel my hands."

Heather English almost wished she couldn't feel hers. They ached from the cold. She was afraid that not feeling them, as was the case with her feet, might mean frostbite was near. She tried blowing on the former and stomping on the latter as she began exploring the interior of the building.

Her eyes were adjusting. There was a large, boxy form over near the other doors. It took a minute, but then the familiar green and yellow, and the massive lugged wheels, began to make sense. It was a tractor, an old John Deere with small, tricycle-type front wheels and a cab around the driver's seat. "Wow!" she said. Here was a possible means of escape, complete with weatherproofing.

"Can you drive it?"

One of Two was a town kid, but it wasn't a big town. She'd driven old tractors like this before. Well, steered.

"Of course I can drive it." She was pretty sure she could. It wasn't like you had to shift this manual transmission. You just found a gear going the direction you wanted and then let out the clutch.

She climbed into the cab. The key was in the ignition. She lowered herself in the seat and began examining the controls. She found neutral, pulled on the choke, and turned the key. It cranked over slow—on a day like this, the oil was probably thick and viscous—but it cranked over steady. What it didn't do was start, or even try.

"You're doing something wrong," Two complained.

She was pretty sure she wasn't. She climbed out of the cab and examined the metal casting that was the engine. There was no neat little screen to check for details about this operating system's fatal error.

Heather English was no mechanic, but she'd helped her dad do simple automotive chores for years. She knew the basic workings of an internal-combustion engine. "The gas goes through a carburetor or injector," she explained, "gets turned into mist, sucked into a cylinder and compressed by a piston, then a spark plug ignites an explosion that drives the piston down and turns the crank, and otherwise gets the show on the road."

"Like, what every girl needs to know."

The gas was there. She could smell the unburned fumes pumped from the exhaust stack. That left spark.

And then she saw it. The wire that went from the coil to the distributor cap was missing. Without it, they weren't going anywhere.

She went over and looked on top of a row of big crates. Maybe it had been set aside by someone interrupted in the middle of a tuneup. The crates were bare, except for simple labels. She bent and read one, curious. It didn't make sense. JESUS—AUTOGRAPHED PHOTOS. Before she could begin to react to that, the other Heather interrupted her.

"Uh, I think I found something." She didn't sound happy about it.

"What?" Heather English wondered, still curious how Jesus could have autographed his photos, much less posed for them.

"Here, wrapped in these blankets."

It looked like a rug. "Like that'll be more interesting than what I just found," One of Two countered, still peeved by her sister's comment about her internal combustion lecture.

Only it was. It was neatly packaged and propped in the corner, frozen solid as a popsicle. It was Tommie Irons.

"**M**aybe we got us a dyslexic Nazi," Chairman Wynn suggested.

"Or maybe it's that way on purpose." The sheriff threw an arm around Judy's shoulder and led her back into the living room. "Mad Dog had a shelf of old fiction and poetry over here somewhere. There were some Kipling books. You remember."

Judy did. "Yeah. *The Light That Failed*, a couple of collections of poetry. You're right, there were swastikas all over them."

The chairman was confused. "Rudyard Kipling was a Nazi?"

Judy found one. A piece of brittle leather had been torn off, but the crucial part was there. "These swastikas are the same as the Germans'." She sounded surprised and disappointed, but she handed the book to Chairman Wynn all the same.

"The bedroom," the sheriff said. He led the way down a hall strewn with towels and bedding.

The sheriff continued as they went, "Kipling was before the National Socialists. Look at the publication date. It's what, maybe First World War. I thought Kipling's swastikas might aim the other direction too, but that's not the point. They're proof that swastikas were around long before Hitler made them a symbol of evil. Kipling latched onto his in India— for good luck, I think."

Whoever had wrecked Mad Dog's house was running out of steam by the time they got to his bedroom. A lamp and a chair had been knocked over, and something had been thrown through the window. Otherwise, the only mess there could be blamed on live-alone bachelor Mad Dog.

"I don't see how this helps," Wynn said. "What's any of this got to do with India?"

The sheriff went to the cedar chest and opened the lid. It was right on top. He unfolded the blanket and spread it across the bed. It was red and black and gray and white in neat geometric patterns, and all four corners contained backward swastikas.

"Not India," the sheriff said. "This is a Navajo design from New Mexico. Native American—Indian—just like Mad Dog has decided to be."

"**I**t was God? What do you make of that?" Mad Dog asked Doc.

"Why don't you just touch her, the way you did that skull? Do your Cheyenne version of a Vulcan mind meld. Then you'll know."

Doc was being cynical again, but Mad Dog realized it was something he hadn't tried. He'd carried Mary in and out of the jail, and from the parking lot behind the Bisonte Bar to Doc's office, but both of them were so wrapped up in coats and blankets that he wasn't sure they'd made physical contact. Not that that should matter. He'd had a glove on when he *knew* the skull was Cheyenne. But he was still new at this. His powers weren't as controlled as they should be, and he wasn't that sure what he was doing. So, why not?

He reached out a bare hand and then he was lying back against Doc's desk while Hailey wiggled into his lap and nuzzled him with a cold, worried nose.

Doc was kneeling beside him and taking his pulse and Mary was looking at him with big, startled eyes. "Are you OK Mr. Mad Dog?"

"You had anything to eat today?" Doc did a touch and go on the other side of his desk and came back with a blood pressure cuff. "Might be your blood sugar."

"I'm fine," Mad Dog reassured them. Hailey was the only one to appear convinced, but he scrambled to his feet without wobbling and that counted for something in Doc's professional opinion. Something, but not enough.

"You passed out there for a second. Sit down somewhere and let me check you out. Any numbness on one side of your body?"

"I didn't pass out, Doc. I did what you suggested. I touched her with my *hematsooma*, my spirit."

Doc looked doubtful. "Now don't go all supernatural on me here, Mad Dog."

Mad Dog reached up and put his hand on his forehead. "I wasn't in here for a few seconds. I was…Well, I'm not sure where I was, but I've got to go. She's right, you know. There is a witch at the end of the hall."

"Why Tommie Irons' place?" Chairman Wynn wanted to know.

"You got a better suggestion?" The sheriff glanced into the pasture where the dead bison lay. It was nearly invisible, now, covered by a fresh coat of snow and smoothed into an Arctic landscape by the ceaseless wind.

"No, but…I mean, we're looking for our kids, right? What makes you think they might be there?"

The sheriff could feel Judy's eyes boring into the back of his neck as he considered the question. He wasn't sure he had a good answer. "I don't know where else to look. This is where they would have come after they ended up in that ditch. The girls would have known where they were and how far it is to anyplace else."

"But what the hell were they doing out here in the first place?" the chairman demanded, turning out of the driveway into the space that now required a bit of faith to be called a road.

The sheriff shrugged. Judy surprised him with an answer.

"I might know," she said. "Englishman, the girls have been pestering you for a car which, with their insurance rates, you said we can't afford right now. Only you said you'd let them have your truck some of the time, and you'd start driving the black and white once they learned how to handle a stick shift."

"Yeah, but…"

"But you never found the time to teach them. The Taurus is an automatic. They can drive it, only I'm always using it. Maybe they persuaded the deputy to give them a lesson in the cruiser. It's a four speed, the same shift pattern as your truck, less one gear."

It made sense, he thought. "Only why today?"

"Bad luck, maybe," she offered. "And they're sixteen. They're immortal. It's just snow. What kid doesn't like to play in the snow?"

"Could be," the chairman said, guiding them through the first intersection on the way back to the highway. As the crow flew, the Irons place was closer by another route, but crows, and everything else, were grounded for the duration. "My boy's a kid at heart too. It's just the sort of foolishness he might get involved in. Only I still don't get why the Irons place?"

"Mad Dog annoys lots of people," the sheriff said. "He gets a kick out of it. Some of them he annoys a lot. But I can't think of anyone who'd do that to his place and his animals, not without provocation.

"I don't know if it's a link or not, but Simon and Levi Hornbaker were at the Sunshine Towers as soon as they heard Tommie was dead, hunting for something they said had gone missing with Tommie's body. It was valuable enough for Simon to pull a pistol on me. And we've got a dead baby on Doc's doorstep. Benteen County, where nothing more serious than a little drunk driving ever happens, suddenly has all sorts of odd things going on."

"And Mad Dog's square in the middle of all of them," Judy said.

The sheriff nodded. "Not just Tommie's body and the missing heirloom. That backward swastika on Mad Dog's floor was a message to him. It links him to the dead baby, since it had a swastika on its forehead. Also backwards, if I remember right."

The chairman was too busy trying to find a safe path to argue, but the sheriff could see him shaking his head.

"I know," the sheriff said. "None of it proves anything, only everything seems to be linked to Mad Dog somehow, and Mad Dog's involvement started with Tommie Irons. So, we start there too, at Tommie's place. That's where Mad Dog took his body. I'd bet on it. Remember after the truck explosion, when he told you he was building a burial mound?"

The left side of the Cadillac dipped and Chairman Wynn had to fight to get it back out of the edge of the invisible ditch. "Makes sense, but there's no indication the kids ever got to Mad Dog's. The storm's bad enough, maybe they tried a short cut and…"

The chairman trailed off and Judy turned away to stare into the storm. The sheriff didn't say anything. He didn't want to follow that thought to its obvious conclusion.

It didn't help when they barely managed to spot the cruiser on their way back to the highway. It was nearly hidden, just one more snowdrift among many.

Swavastika! That's what the design was called when the arms were reversed, Mrs. Kraus remembered. What she couldn't recall was why she knew that. It was sort of a backwards senior moment. This time she had the answer but couldn't remember the question.

She'd only been six when Germany surrendered. And it wasn't like any of her family had served. Her dad was too old and her brother was just a baby. Her cousins were all girls.

Floyd was old enough to have served, though. Floyd Kraus, her dear departed husband, had been 4-F because of the heart problem he never thought was all that serious until the day it killed him. She'd married Floyd before she turned twenty. She'd felt so grown up, hooking a guy more than twice her age. And it turned out to be a pretty good marriage for the eleven years he lasted. Sometimes at night she still rolled over and reached for him.

Floyd! That was it. That was where she'd learned the term. It was when he'd brought that awful thing home after one of his sales trips. Floyd always brought her something. Usually, it was lingerie. The kind she couldn't hang on the line in a community like Buffalo Springs unless she wanted to be taken for a scarlet woman. In fact, she recalled fondly, most of the presents Floyd brought her were blatantly sexual. In a twisted way, so was the thing with the swavastikas on it.

He'd brought it home as a joke, he'd said, after she got so upset by it. He'd run into a man down in Oklahoma who traded in exotic collectibles. The man offered to sell it for some scandalous price, then made the mistake of playing poker with Floyd Kraus. Because it tickled Floyd's funny bone, he'd held the thing as a guarantee against the man's debt.

It was a battered old wooden container, a hand-carved box not much bigger than your fist. The swavastikas had been prominent among the faded symbols decorating it. She remembered now. That's when Floyd told her, when she first saw the thing and asked why he'd brought her some Nazi trinket. Not Nazi, he'd said. Older. The symbols went way back and were associated with lots of religions. These swavastikas were early Christian, as was the cross on top of the box, and the line of Latin script that had nearly worn away.

It wasn't a handsome thing, but the box wasn't the prize. It was what was within, Floyd told her. At his prompting, she'd opened it. Carefully affixed to a bed of silk had been something small and brown and leathery.

And what was that, she'd asked, not all that sure she wanted to know. The holiest of relics, he explained. Something that belonged to Jesus himself.

That was intriguing, even though what it looked like was the desiccated remains of some tiny rodent after an owl made a meal of the rest.

He'd toyed with her for a while before he finally told her what it was. And even then she hadn't known. The Holy Prepuce, he said. The one and only, or at least one of several claimed to be authentic. Most were held in a variety of church sanctuaries throughout the world.

She'd heard of pieces of the true cross. Seen the movie *The Robe*. The idea of holy relics was familiar, but she hadn't known what a prepuce was, not until she dragged out her dictionary and discovered that this was, supposedly, what remained after the Son of God was circumcised.

Floyd hadn't just laughed at her reaction. He'd howled. He'd fallen down on the floor and held his sides and roared until he cried. And she'd hurled the damn thing out the door in the direction of the trashcan. And not forgiven him until he stopped giggling long enough to show her that silk chemise she'd tried on for him for a few minutes late that same evening.

Later, when she'd gone looking for the box to be sure it was truly disposed of, it was gone. And not long after that, Floyd came into some real money and they'd taken that vacation to Havana. The Prepuce had been paid off, he said. Gone home to Oklahoma. Gone back to a fellow whose name suddenly rang a rusty bell. Hornbaker! His name had been Abel Hornbaker.

◇ ◇ ◇

"**S**top!"

Supervisor Wynn stomped the brake pedal. But for the Cadillac's sophisticated anti-lock brakes, they would have begun spinning, maybe ended up in a ditch like the county's black and white.

"There's a flower in the cemetery," Judy said. It sounded almost as odd to her as it must to them.

"Cemetery?" the chairman inquired gently, as if he understood how the stress of searching for their missing children during the worst weather the county had known in decades might have caused her mind to snap.

"Back there," Judy gestured. "Maybe a hundred yards this side of where they left the cruiser in the ditch. You remember it, Englishman. There's that little family cemetery along the edge of the road. Two or three trees, lots of weeds, maybe a dozen headstones."

"Mostly kids claimed by a cholera epidemic in the early twentieth century," Englishman recalled. "The family died out or left years ago. I can't remember anybody tending the graves. You sure, Judy? Who would leave a flower there?"

"Look," Judy urged. Occasionally, the wind ebbed enough so that she could still see the outline of the trees and maybe one of the bigger stones. A tiny patch of color, too, or so she tried to convince herself.

"Can't hardly see the trees," the chairman said, humoring her.

"Back up," Judy commanded. "I've got to check."

The chairman carefully reversed, back toward the carnage at Mad Dog's, the buried black and white, and the abandoned cemetery in which she was sure she'd seen a rose.

Judy threw open her door as they pulled up beside the little plot. "Ask Mrs. Kraus," Judy called over her shoulder. She was sure of it now. There was a single rose standing in a weighted can beside one of the stones. Artificial, she was sure, but a recent decoration. "If she doesn't know, I'll explain when I get back."

Judy couldn't remember what the name on the grave was supposed to be. She remembered the rest, though. It was the only stone on which an angel was engraved, the infant in its arms on the verge of being carried to paradise.

HARRIET MAE KENNEDY, DECEMBER 3, 1907, MAY 12, 1909. Judy remembered, now. The tombstone was for the youngest of six Kennedy children, the first carried off over the course of the spring and summer of a catastrophic year. Each stone that followed was a little smaller, a bit less elegant—

a testament to the failing resources, economic and emotional, of a decimated family.

The can was so badly weathered it was impossible to tell what it might once have contained. There were nails through its base, spikes really, she recalled, to hold it in place in spite of the Kansas wind. Rocks inside anchored the cheap plastic imitation of a single long-stemmed rose. Under the first of the rocks was a message, and a thick black hood. The note was short and to the point, a computer print out that would lend no clue to who wrote it. It spelled out today's date and a time. Beyond that, there were only brief instructions: "Remove flower. Sit out of sight of road. Cover and wait. If not contacted in thirty minutes, return same time tomorrow."

Mad Dog hardly recognized Main Street. It looked like something plucked out of a Currier and Ives print as interpreted by Hieronymus Bosch. Most of the curbs along the north side of the street were buried under drifts, some extending all the way across the street. An abandoned city was being swallowed by frozen white dunes. Though he picked his way carefully, avoiding deep snow, the Blazer slipped and skidded. In a couple of spots, he had to stop and rock it back out, then try again before plowing through. If it was this bad in town, Mad Dog didn't think he could make it down some of those country roads. He needed chains, so he headed for the Texaco.

Mad Dog hadn't known whether Hailey would come. Mary begged him to let her stay. He'd had to explain it didn't work that way with wolves, or at least not with this one. She went where she wanted. Hailey was obviously fond of the girl, though, and had made it clear she wasn't crazy about the storm. Just the same, when Mad Dog left, Hailey pranced out beside him.

Mary wasn't shedding tears when he looked back to where she and Doc stood in the door, but the expression on her face was nearly enough to make him do it for her. Clearly, she'd been abandoned and abused by people she trusted. She wasn't surprised that it was happening again, but it still hurt.

"I left some good luck behind for you and Hailey," she'd called. He had waved, and promised they'd see her again soon. He hoped it would really happen.

Hailey whined and fussed at Mad Dog when a white pickup pulled out from a side street and followed them. The wolf might have gotten his attention but the truck was in such a hurry that it slid into a monster drift that had already claimed an Oldsmobile. It was spinning all four wheels when the storm hid it from view.

Mad Dog expected the Texaco would be closed. Everything else appeared to be. No lights, no signs of life anywhere. Not that there weren't moments when Main Street in Buffalo Springs was equally empty any day, but not like this.

Mad Dog couldn't remember a storm this bad since the fifties. He'd been a kid and the thing had proved a pure joy for him. The school bus never got there to pick him up. It was an unexpected holiday. Englishman was just a toddler, too young to be a source of entertainment or distraction. His baby brother stayed close to their mother while she baked them cookies and made a pot of hot chocolate. Mad Dog spent the day of the storm at the windows, caught in the delight of watching the world reshape itself into something alien, or in an easy chair near the fire, deep in a good book— *The Swiss Family Robinson*—so he could transport himself to a warmer climate whenever he wanted.

He enjoyed the days after the storm most. He was old enough that their mother let him go exploring those strange new hills on the south side of every building and windbreak. He'd made himself a sled out of an old inner tube. His favorite slope included part of the barn's roof. He crawled through snow caves deep under the lilac bushes that filled the yard. If she'd known even half his adventures, she wouldn't have allowed them. His solution had been simple. He didn't tell her.

It took three days for the snowplow to reconnect them to the rest of the county. Every minute was magical. Now, fighting drifts just to get to the Texaco, it was hard to imagine he'd ever been so innocent.

There were lights in the Texaco. Mad Dog pulled as close to the front door as he could without blocking it or getting into the drift that was forming near the repair bays. Hailey followed him in. The woman behind the counter was the same one he'd seen before dawn that morning.

"Isn't your shift over yet?" he greeted her.

"Nobody came to replace me." She put down the book she was reading, a new one, Elizabeth Gunn this time. "And I can't get out of here to go home."

"Your power hasn't gone off?" Mad Dog gestured to indicate the flickering TV across the room and the bright neons overhead.

"Oh yeah. It's off, only we've got a generator on account of our food products have to be refrigerated. Not a problem today, of course. But since I'm the only one here to make management decisions, and they're not gonna pay me overtime anyway, I decided to fire it up and keep myself comfortable while I wait this thing out. You and Hailey are welcome to join me. All the comforts of home. More, if you like junk food."

"Actually, I was just looking for tire chains. Any left?"

"Yeah, couple of sets, I think. Over by the window, the other side of the jumper cables."

Mad Dog found what he wanted, though he would have preferred something heavy-duty to the one-size-fits-all (before they fall off because they didn't fit right to begin with) convenience-store specials.

"You really want to go back out there?" she asked, ringing him up at the register. "I haven't seen anything go by in the last hour, not even an eighteen-wheeler."

"Oh, it's not that bad." Mad Dog was trying to convince himself more than her.

"Not according to those TV weather folks. This thing's really localized, but it's powerful. You sure you and Hailey don't want to grab a couple of hot dogs and a good paperback and waste the afternoon?" She sounded a little lonely. Probably worried about the family she couldn't get to, or even phone, until this thing was over.

What would it have been like for Sadie Maddox, alone out there with a baby and a kid and no phone or electricity? How much butane had they had in the tank? How much firewood, in case that gave out? How much food in the pantry? His adventure must have been his mother's nightmare, though she never let on.

"What are the forecasters saying? How long's this thing supposed to last?" On the TV, a buxom blond was gesturing at a weather map on which a bright white swatch was centered over Benteen County.

"Should ease up by dark, start to clear around midnight, and then get really cold. Lows around zero. Mad Dog, I wouldn't go out there if I were you. You get in trouble, even right on the highway, it could be a long time before anybody comes along to help."

Her argument made uncommonly good sense and Mad Dog knew he better not think about it or he'd talk himself out of the demands of the "vision" he'd had at the mortuary. Those hot dogs smelled awfully good.

"I expect you're right, but there's something I've got to do. You mind if I leave Hailey in here while I put the chains on? She eats anything, I'll pay for it when I come back in."

"Glad for the company," the woman said.

Mad Dog ducked through the door and found himself face to face with a tiny woman bundled in sweatshirts and jackets and scarves, and the brightest red tennis shoes Mad Dog had ever seen.

"Hi," she said.

"Dorothy, what are you doing out in this?"

"Looking for you, of course. Took me awhile to work out who you really are."

"I'm Mad Dog, remember?"

"'Course. That's not what I mean."

He was honestly puzzled. "What then?"

"The Wizard," she said. "You know." She must have seen the confusion in his face. "That's who you really are, isn't it?"

He shrugged. In a peculiar way, he supposed, she was right.

"The Kennedy Cemetery?" Mrs. Kraus asked. "Just east of Mad Dog's place?"

"That's right," Englishman said. "There's a flower by one of the graves. Judy said to ask you. What's this all about, Mrs. Kraus?"

Mrs. Kraus sank into her chair in the dusky office and forgot all about swavastikas and prepuces. She hadn't thought about Harriet Kennedy's grave in years. Hadn't thought it still served that same purpose. And, even so, didn't want to talk about it with Englishman.

"You there, Mrs. Kraus?"

"Wish I wasn't," she muttered.

"Talk to me, Mrs. Kraus. What's a flower in an abandoned cemetery have to do with any of the shit going on today?"

Englishman didn't use words like that often.

"I thought that was over a long time ago."

"What was over?"

"You know how all those pro-life signs line the blacktops just outside Buffalo Springs? Well, abortion's never been an acceptable alternative in this part of the state. Not even since it got legal."

"What're you telling me, Mrs. Kraus?"

"Hold on, Englishman. I'll get there." Mrs. Kraus never talked back to her boss, either. Well, hardly ever. Stress, it seemed, was a two-way street.

"Long as I can remember, Sheriff, birth control has been a woman's responsibility. She didn't want a child, she better be prepared to say no or be on the pill or otherwise provide her own protection. Main reason is, she's the one gets stuck if there's a mistake. Women who live here, they know that. They talk to each other and remind themselves. But mistakes happen, and when they do there's always been a backup."

"You telling me someone's doing clandestine abortions in Benteen County?"

"Won't none of the doctors here do the other kind. Even Doc Jones is afraid he'll end up in the sights of some born-again sniper convinced he's doing the Lord's work and killing a killer.

"Back in my day, hell, some of yours too, abortions weren't legal. I never made use of this back-up system, you understand, but when I was a girl it was common knowledge you could get your pregnancy taken care of if you needed. Price was what you could afford. Way I heard it, nobody got turned down, even when they only had a few dollars to spare.

"What you did was you drove out to the Kennedy grave-yard. You needed help, you left your money and a note with a couple of days and times that were acceptable to you in the can beside Harriet Mae's grave. You left a purple flower in there too, so's whoever picked up your money and arranged things would know they had a customer. Your answer came back to the same spot, along with a red flower. That was how you knew to find out when and where to go."

"Who?" There was an edge to Englishman's voice that even the radio couldn't disguise.

"I don't know. Girls I knew who took advantage of the service said they never knew either. A hood got left in the can along with your instructions. You didn't wear it, you didn't get your abortion. Once you put it on you couldn't see a thing. Then somebody came and picked you up. Your only communication was in whispers. They drove you somewhere. Sometimes it seemed far, sometimes it didn't, but there were always lots of turns and twists and none of the ones I talked to ever had a clue where they ended up. It was a slick process, Englishman. The job got handled by someone who knew what they were doing, too. I never heard of any complications. No one ever got an infection or hemorrhaged badly. But, swear to God, Englishman, I had no idea it was still happening."

"Who, Mrs. Kraus? You may not know, but you have some idea."

"For a long time, I thought it was one of the doctors. Then I thought maybe it was Mrs. Irons, Tommie and Becky's ma. She had a reputation for practicing folk medicine. Hell, Englishman. I really don't know."

"You're holding back on me."

Mrs. Kraus was almost as angry as the sheriff. "You really want to know who I thought it was?" she demanded of the radio.

"That's why I'm asking."

"OK then. Them others, I suspected. But this was always too well organized and too attentive to what the desperate women of this county needed. Hell, Englishman. I was sure it was Sadie, your mother, yours and Mad Dog's, who was doing it."

Two deserted chicken coops and a tool shed yielded the Heathers nothing more valuable than a rusty scythe and a hoe with spear-like potential. They'd also found more curiously labeled boxes. In one chicken coop were six original shrouds of Turin. The shed held fourteen hat-size boxes, each containing a skull of St. John the Baptist. And there was a stack of five cases of TNT.

"I am getting seriously weirded out," One of Two told her sister. "And so cold I can hardly think."

Two nodded agreement.

"We've got to find some place to warm up," One said through chattering teeth. "I think that's the barn. There should be hay up in the loft. We ought to be able to burrow in there and warm up, only…"

"Only I don't care anymore," Two countered. "So it's an obvious place for them to look. I'm fresh out of alternatives and I can't go much farther anyway."

They headed for the barn. The girls knew they were being hunted. The effort was seriously disorganized, though, with armed Hornbakers poking here and there according to no apparent plan. That made it less likely anyone would recognize their tracks, since others were being randomly laid down and then blurred by the wind. But it made it more likely they'd eventually be spotted. Actually, they'd been seen once, but the ill-defined figure just waved, and then plodded on toward a building the Heathers immediately scratched from their next-to-visit list.

One pushed the barn door open just long enough for them to slip through. She pointed at the stairs. "Hayloft. We go up there and snuggle under some hay. If we burrow deep enough, maybe they won't find us."

Two was shivering too violently to answer, but she managed to start up the stairs.

Heather English realized she should go back and look out, assure herself they hadn't been followed. She couldn't find the energy. It didn't matter. If they didn't warm up soon, they might as well lie down in the snow and wait for the inevitable.

"Look out!" Judy screamed. She never would have seen it if she hadn't been staring mindlessly out the window. Her Heathers had been at that cemetery, or near it, and near the time on the note. On purpose?

Facing into the storm was like looking at that computer screensaver where you were flying in space and stars came hurtling out of the dark at you. Only there wasn't any dark out her window. She was in the heart of the galaxy and the stars were everywhere and, all of them, coming right at her. It made her feel queasy, like riding a roller coaster. She would have looked away, but mindless and queasy were better than thinking about Harriet and her daughters.

And then there was something else out there, materializing, becoming solid, like a Romulan Bird of Prey lowering its cloaking device. She'd been watching too many reruns with her Trekkie daughters. Only this was no TV starship. It was a truck painted garish yellow, the Benteen County snow plow, hurtling along with its blade raised and headed straight for where Chairman Wynn was piloting the Cadillac.

The chairman's head swiveled toward her scream. She saw him react, throw the steering wheel all the way to the right. She felt the big V8 lunge, heard wheels spin. The blade was coming and she knew they were dead.

The Caddy grabbed macadam, dug through snow, clenched frozen soil, and propelled itself into the ditch. They were going to make it.

She felt the impact. Felt herself thrown across the seat. Heard something pop and watched the world spin. And then they were still, facing into the ditch, the plow gone, rolling south, not even delayed by the contact.

Judy picked herself up off the floor. There was moisture in her eyes. Blood. She'd banged her forehead.

The chairman had a hand to his nose, testing it like it hurt. His air bag was draped over the steering wheel. Maybe that was what had hit his nose.

Englishman was holding his head, pushing his own airbag out of the way, fumbling for the radio that was somewhere on the floor now because it was crackling something at them— Mrs. Kraus's voice.

"I hate to bother you with anything else, only Supervisor Bontrager just came in. Says the county snowplow has been stolen. You may want to keep an eye out. Never know where you might run into it."

◇◇◇

Mad Dog bought Dorothy a cup of coffee. She chose the Sinnamon, which didn't surprise him. He got her a package of cheese-flavored chips, too, which she shared with Hailey while he went out and put the chains on the Blazer.

"We're ready to go," Dorothy said. They were waiting by the door as he came back in.

"Go where?" Mad Dog couldn't imagine where Dorothy expected to be taken.

"You're going to Tommie's place, aren't you."

"How'd you know?"

"Take me along and I'll tell you."

Mad Dog had no intention of dragging a little old lady with him as he went into danger. "Tell me first," he said.

"We don't have time." She pointed out the window. A white Dodge Ram spun to a stop against the far curb.

She pushed the door open and ducked inside the Blazer right behind Hailey. A shadowy figure climbed out of the Dodge, reaching back for something on the gun rack. Mad Dog was convinced. Drive now. Argue later.

The chains gave the Blazer the kind of purchase he hadn't had all morning. He left sparks as he roared away from the Texaco. The man with the Dodge fired one round, then Mad Dog was too busy steering to pay attention.

"Simon musta been standing on ice," Dorothy said. "Recoil knocked him over."

Mad Dog checked his rearview mirror. Nothing back there but packed snow and the Blazer's fresh tracks. That, and the frozen miasma that already hid landmarks like the Buffalo Burger Drive Inn from view. He eased off the accelerator.

"I'd move right along if I was you," Dorothy recommended. "Simon's got the big V-10 in that Dodge and a lead foot to go with it. He'll be along in a minute."

"Then we're in trouble."

"You been in trouble since you took Tommie this morning. This is just a new phase."

"What, the phase where he catches us and shoots us dead?"

"Oh, he won't kill me. You could be another matter. That's why I'm gonna suggest we turn off up here and take a back way."

Mad Dog shook his head. "I don't know if we can make it. Some of those drifts are pretty deep."

"You got chains," she argued. "He's got you out-powered and out-gunned, but he doesn't have chains. Don't seem to me like you've got much choice. Whatever, this'd be a good time to decide. Here he comes."

She was right. The Dodge was back in view, racing the snow and beating it.

Mad Dog allowed himself one heartfelt curse. He moved his foot to the brake, swung the wheel, and skidded into the first side road headed west. The biggest snow drift he'd seen since his childhood waited, not fifty feet from the intersection. Mad Dog would have cursed again, only the Blazer was demanding all his attention. It plunged in, bucking and plowing. He didn't think they were going to make it until they broke free on the other side.

An even bigger drift loomed just beyond.

It was cold in the loft. The barn's roof needed repairs. There were shingles missing, and little piles of snow spotted the wooden floor. Worse, there was hardly any hay. Just one stack of moldy old bales over in the far corner, maybe ten feet high and a little longer. Still, it was insulation.

Heather English scrambled up the stack, surveying its construction and deciding how to modify it. The bales were ancient and rotten. The first one she tried to shift broke apart, the twine that bound it snapping the moment she began to tug.

She felt like sitting down and crying. She was sixteen. Her whole life was supposed to be ahead of her—fouled up and messy, maybe, but there. Why was some ditzy old lady keeping a prisoner inside her farmhouse? Why had she rescued them, only to turn them back out into the storm? None of it made sense, and it wasn't fair. She was supposed to go to college, have a career, find the man of her dreams.

Ice princess. That was what some of the guys at school called her. They might turn out to be right. Literally.

Heather Lane joined her on the stack. "What do we do?"

One of Two wasn't sure anymore. "Burrow in, I guess." She kicked at the broken bale. Two tried to move another. She had more success. It shifted, gained momentum, and toppled to the floor, carrying the girls along in an avalanche of moldering hay.

"That what you had in mind?" Two asked.

Heather didn't answer. She was staring at the square metal box that had tumbled out of the pile with them. It wasn't the sort of thing you normally found in a stack of hay in the loft of a barn in the middle of Kansas, though it fit right in with all the other weird stuff stored here and there on this farm.

Its black enameled surface dully reflected the dim light. A chrome handle and hinges shone brighter. It was a curious find. But even odder was the shape of its keyhole. Heather had seen lots of war movies. She recognized a swastika when she saw one.

"I don't suppose this thing's got a winch on it?" The sheriff's skull felt like it was about to split. He'd banged it against the headrest when the air bag went off.

"This is a Cadillac, not a Humvee," the chairman replied.

"You got a shovel? Maybe we can dig our way out." The pain was receding. It was merely intolerable now. If he sat quietly for a few hours before he got out and started pushing or shoveling, he might get back to just feeling awful.

"No shovel. Maybe we can collect some brush to stuff under the wheels."

"I'm all right. Thanks for asking," Judy said, loud and close to his ear. It caused a brief relapse.

"Good," the sheriff said when he could form words again. "We may need you to help push." He cracked his door. The sooner they started, the sooner he'd know how bad off they were. And maybe the cold would ease the pain in his head, or offer a different pain bad enough to make him forget.

"Hang on." Judy caught his arm.

"What for?" The closest farm was a mile away. He didn't think they could make it half that far in these conditions. But somehow, they had to get to Tommie's place, find out if his death was related to what had happened at Mad Dog's and the empty Benteen County patrol car, see if the kids were there. Since walking wasn't an option, they had to get the Caddy out of this ditch and back on the road.

"Well, hell," Judy said, "just try it first."

"Try what?"

"Try driving out. There isn't much of a ditch here. We aren't in much snow. Maybe we can just back out."

Chairman Wynn shrugged his shoulders. "Why not?" He reached down and put it in reverse. He touched his foot to the accelerator.

Judy was right.

◇ ◇ ◇

"Pull over here."

Mad Dog gave Dorothy one of those looks she was accustomed to, an eloquent way of asking the delicate question, "Are you insane?"

"Simon's probably still fighting through that first drift. He's stubborn and determined enough, he'll get through, but it'll take awhile. There've been at least a dozen more that'll cause him trouble. We got the time."

After a careful survey of his rearview mirror, Mad Dog obeyed. Dorothy surprised him by hopping out into the teeth of the storm. She looked frail enough that he expected it to blow her to Central Texas. He started to go after her but she waved him back as she skated across the road and onto a drive he hadn't noticed. There was a gate there. She opened it and gestured for him to pull through. There was nothing around for the snow to hide behind so it wasn't deep here. The spot she wanted him to go was at least as accessible as the road. He considered getting out and going over and carrying her back to the Blazer, but he didn't. He aimed it where she wanted and she closed the gate behind them before rejoining him in the cab.

"Like my shortcut?" she asked.

"You expect me to drive across this field? I guess we must be north of Tommie's place, but driving cross country won't make it a short cut, not when we get stuck in some gully or run up on a stand of trees."

"You're not on pasture. Don't you remember that pipeline they put in last fall? There was a frost just after they finished. Nothing's had time to grow on it. It cuts right back over to the highway, maybe half a mile south of where we left it."

Mad Dog did remember. It was just that he normally tried not to. The pipeline was a fresh scar on the landscape. A few feet under the frozen ground beside them, natural gas flowed to underground storage caverns a few sections southeast of here. He'd hated the idea of it when they put it in, worried over the possibility of a blowout for a few months after. Now, he hardly noticed it anymore. Once in awhile he'd seen gas company trucks near it, making inspections. Sometimes he'd glance at the scar while he was jogging, this surgical incision across the belly of his beloved Plains. It was a symbol of the awful things man did to his environment for the sake of comfort. But it had never been a way to get some place, not in his head.

"This route's probably in better shape than most roads. It runs straight as an arrow without a tree line or a fold in the earth where snow could build up to slow us. Nothing between here and the highway but one more gate we'll have to open. And, best of all, Simon won't think of it if he gets this far."

Mad Dog shook his head, put the Blazer in gear, and took advantage of some of the best driving conditions he'd encountered all day. "How'd you know about this?"

"There's no place like home." She favored him with a smile. "I come back to visit sometimes, only then I have to deal with the wicked witch."

"Witch?" Mad Dog liked Dorothy. Considering how odd most people found his own world view, he tended to be tolerant of others. He'd never argued with her claim to be that Dorothy. She couldn't be, of course. That Dorothy was the product of L. Frank Baum's imagination, a fairy tale that had been embarrassing Kansans for over a century.

Patience wasn't normally a problem for Mad Dog, but this was an unusual day. Someone had tried to shoot him. He'd found a cache of old bones on the Irons/Hornbaker property, the burial place of an unborn Cheyenne baby, and other folk. Another baby had died because someone had been molesting a little girl. All that, and the Heathers were missing.

"Don't be silly, Dorothy. You're not in Oz. There are no witches."

She sniffed and stiffened her spine. "I expected better from you, Mr. Wizard. Surely our county's resident Cheyenne shaman, of all people, isn't going to tell me he doesn't believe in witches?"

She had him there.

"I want you should show me."

Judah had caught them by surprise. He could tell from their expressions. More than that, they didn't understand what he wanted. He could tell that too.

There was a strange iron box lying in the collapsed haystack along with the Heathers. If his mind hadn't been so thoroughly on something else, he would have gone over and joined their investigation of the thing.

They were sure pretty. He'd noticed that at school. But they never had anything to do with him. Hardly anyone did, even his teammates on the Buffalo Springs Bisons. He was the strongest football player in the league, stronger even than Levi. Girls were supposed to like football players, only he didn't think they cared much for linemen. If Coach would let him play quarterback maybe girls would like him better. Pretty girls, like the Heathers.

They looked a lot alike. He couldn't tell them apart, but he didn't care.

"Come on," he urged. "Show me."

All that accomplished was to get them back on their feet. One of them raised a sharp hoe and pointed it at him. The other one looked around desperately for a minute, maybe for the scythe that was mostly hidden under a broken bale of hay. Neither offered to show him anything, or seemed to know what he meant.

He had a secret stash up here, stuffed behind a cross brace that supported the arching beams above. He kept the girls covered with his rifle as he went to it. They watched him, wide eyed. They really were scared. That excited him even more.

He was having a little trouble controlling his breathing when he reached in and got his bundle. He couldn't really cover them with the gun while he did it because he had to pull himself up with one hand and then reach behind the board with the other. It was awkward, but he managed to get back down without dropping anything and they hadn't taken advantage of him and made a break for it.

He took the rubber band off and thumbed through the stack until he found the example he wanted. It was an ad for a perfume that couldn't be bought in Benteen County. He knew, because he'd looked on the shelves over at the Dillon's one time.

A young woman stood between the pillars of an arch. Stone steps ascended in an intricate pattern of light and shadows behind her. Her hands were balled into fists that rested on her hips and there was an aggressive look in her eyes that reminded him of Gran. He didn't let himself think about that part. Instead, he concentrated on the fact that she wasn't wearing anything but the perfume.

He straightened it out and held it so the girls could see. He pointed toward the appropriate places. "Show me," he repeated. He had to stop and catch his breath. "Show me your naughty parts."

O n the bright side, Wynn Some wasn't cold anymore. Of course there was a lead lining to his silver cloud. Black Death was still on his trail.

In retrospect, he knew he shouldn't have stopped after he vaulted that fence to taunt the Brahma from hell. He should have been satisfied at being alive, not so pumped by his success that he had to strut around like some whacked-out football player doing a post-touchdown end-zone dance. It should have occurred to him that if he could clear the fence that easily, the bull could do the same.

Since then, he'd learned a lot about what bulls were capable of. They weren't sure footed on ice. Of course, he wasn't either. One of his worst moments had been lying face-to-face with a ton of thrashing muscle that wanted to kill him. He got lucky when the bull twisted, bumping him to a spot where he found traction.

He'd also learned that massive weight and sharp hooves were a disadvantage when climbing snowdrifts. As a result, that was where Wynn had been spending most of his time. There was a row of evergreens on the south side of the road across from the Irons place. Their downwind side had accumulated quite a range of drifts, all the way from waist to head high. They were tough enough for him to climb, and impossible for Black Death. Unfortunately, Brahma bulls were accustomed to dealing with problems of that nature by ignoring them.

Through, instead of over, seemed to be this fellow's motto. Luckily for Wynn, through took longer.

His problem was that the row of evergreens petered out well short of infinity. Short, in fact, of the east end of the Irons' yard. About three more drifts, and a change of tactics would be called for. None occurred to him. The Irons' farm offered lots of outbuildings where he might hide, but there were people with guns over there. Ahead, or to the south, lay a wind-swept field without any drifts to slow the bull. Behind was the bull himself, following on Wynn's heels with the kind of loyalty he'd always hoped to inspire from one of his bird dogs. So, when he tumbled off the final drift, it was to a near absence of options. His only chance seemed some promising drifts that might slow the monster over in the Irons' yard. There wasn't a Hornbaker to be seen.

Wynn waded the ditch. Facing into the storm, the wind was sharp enough to open a wound, and cold enough to freeze it shut. He fancied he heard another wind behind him, the bellows-hot breath of the beast pursuing him. He was too scared to look, and too blinded from facing into the snow to see much anyway.

That's why he was so surprised when he glimpsed the monster charging from his side. He couldn't understand how the thing had turned itself such an improbable shade of yellow, either. It butted him with a single steel horn and he stopped worrying about anything.

"**B**e damned!" the chairman exclaimed. "Road's been plowed."

He pulled into the side of the intersection. Indeed, the road leading west toward the Irons farm bore fresh tracks, and evidence they had been left by a bright yellow vehicle preceded by a blade designed to move snow, and the occasional Cadillac, from its way.

"Figures," the sheriff said. "Everything keeps pointing to Tommie's place."

"I bet Zeke Hornbaker was driving that plow," Judy said. The sheriff nodded. "I thought I recognized him."

"You really think the kids are there?" Judy's voice was an odd blend of doubt, fear, and hope.

"Let's find out," the sheriff said.

The chairman put the Caddy back in gear just in time to get out of the way of the green Blazer that grazed the same corner the snowplow had clipped. The Chevy went sideways as its rear wheels lost traction. It swiveled to face them. A familiar bald head peered from the driver's seat and nodded, then all four wheels grabbed hold and the SUV threw a spray of snow and gravel, aimed itself west again, and departed in haste.

"That was your brother in Tommie Irons' truck," the chairman said.

"Party's getting crowded," the sheriff observed. "We better join it."

The Cadillac did a nice imitation of the Blazer.

"You aren't gonna believe this," Mrs. Kraus' voice squeaked from the sheriff's pocket, "but I just found an envelope with fifty thousand in cash, and a passport and some other IDs with his picture, but somebody else's name, in Zeke Hornbaker's office."

The sheriff fumbled the walkie-talkie out of his pocket. "Whose name?"

"It don't make no sense," she rasped. "Shows him as Tommie Irons. And listen, there's some stuff about swastikas I remembered that you need to hear."

"**N**o."

Judah hadn't expected that. He couldn't remember ever refusing a direct order. It was unthinkable. He couldn't imagine what would happen if he tried it with Gran.

The one who said it was just a little shorter than the other one. He could see some small differences in the two. This one's cheekbones were more pronounced and she had paler eyes. He wondered if there would be differences elsewhere.

"You got to," he said. "I got the gun." He showed it to them in case they'd forgotten.

"You know who I am?" she said. He didn't like this one much. "You know who my dad is? He's the sheriff, that's who. You can't believe what he'll do to you if you lay a finger on either of us."

Sheriff English scared Judah, but Sheriff English wasn't here. Neither was most of his own family. Simon had taken the truck to town to help Gran. That meant just he and Levi were on the farm. If things went the way he wanted, nobody would ever know about this. Maybe he didn't need for both of them to show him their naughty parts. He worked the bolt to be sure there was a bullet in the chamber, then remembered he couldn't shoot the talkative one. She was supposed to freeze to death, unmarked. Simon had decreed it.

Working the bolt had an effect. They got even bigger eyed and more frightened than before. The little one didn't back off though. Not even when he poked the barrel at her to show he meant business, even if he supposed he really didn't. Instead, she swung the hoe at him. He took it away from her, snapped the handle, and tossed it in the far corner.

"OK. I'll show you mine," the other one said. She reached up and undid a couple of buttons on her jacket. Then she shivered provocatively. "But not here. It's too cold. If you want me to take my clothes off, you've got to take us some place warm."

The uppity one looked surprised, but she didn't object. In fact, her face relaxed a little. "Yeah," she said. "Me too, maybe, if we were somewhere warm enough."

That didn't fit the freezing-to-death plan, but the plan was no longer at the top of Judah's priorities. Blood that might have fed his brain was coursing elsewhere.

"We can go to the forge," he said. "I know how to light it."
"Show us the way, big guy," the tall one said. "Light my fire."
Judah practically ran across the hayloft. His was already lit.

The road had been plowed, but the plow had been at least a foot above its surface. There were tire tracks to follow too, but the tracks were rapidly filling and drifts re-establishing themselves. Mad Dog found it hard to believe, but the storm was getting worse. He could barely make out the trail he was following. It disappeared into a swirling froth of frozen foam just yards in front of the Chevy's bumper.

"They'll be expecting us," Dorothy said. "Or someone, anyway. And they'll be armed. I think we best go in the back way."

"There's something evil there," Mad Dog told her. He wasn't sure he knew how to explain or if she could understand, but he had to try. "That was my brother and his wife back there at the corner. They'll be along any minute. I plan to see they don't get hurt."

"Can't do that if you're dead. They'll have guns and they'll be watching the road. That's where they'll be expecting us, so it's where we shouldn't come from. Do you have a gun?"

"No. I don't believe in them."

"Oh, they're real enough. Trust me on that one, Mr. Wizard. They have racks of them on the farm, everything from .22s to Kalashnikovs."

He'd been about to explain that he meant he didn't believe in using guns to solve disputes. He had a petition in the Saab to require gun owners be licensed like drivers. No signatures on it yet, except his own. He'd been ready to launch into one of his pet political arguments until the reality of what she said registered.

"Kalashnikovs?"

"Yeah, AK 47s."

He would have looked away from the road to check the expression on her face and be sure she wasn't joking, only seeing the road at all was becoming a problem.

"Why would they have AK 47s, and how would you know?"

"They were for some little war." Her voice turned smaller, less confident. "And I live here sometimes."

"Dorothy. You live at the Sunshine Towers."

"Before that," she whispered. "Sometimes, when I wasn't in Oz, I was an Irons."

The air bags were impotent this time. They made better draperies than balloons when the bumper of the Cadillac encountered the rear quarter panel of the Blazer. The impact was harder than the one with the snowplow, but, like condoms, air bags were only intended for a single use.

It could have been worse. Visibility was so bad that they hadn't been going very fast. And both vehicles were on snow, a non-stick surface on which each could bounce away with a minimum of resistance. Still, it put Judy back on the floor behind the front seats and bounced the sheriff's head off the seat rest again. He saw double for a moment, but since he could hardly see anything outside, it didn't really matter.

"What was that?" the sheriff asked. His voice sounded far away even to himself.

"Tommie Irons' Blazer." The chairman wasn't the least shaken by the accident. He'd seen it coming, though not soon enough to get his foot on the brakes. Still, he had the steering wheel in a death's grip already and the impact hadn't thrown him around the way it had his passengers.

"Mad Dog still in it?" The sheriff could barely recognize the outlines of a pair of Blazers out there. He couldn't tell if anyone was behind the windows.

"Don't think so," the chairman said. "Let's go see." He reached down and twisted the key to start the stalled Cadillac. Nothing happened.

"I'll go check," Judy volunteered. She went out on the south side where the wind couldn't stop her from opening a door. The sheriff knew he should have done it, but he was still floating somewhere else. He knew he needed to get a grip.

"I'll check under the hood." The chairman let himself out. The sheriff was alone with his aching head and a moaning that might be the wind, unless it was him. He didn't like listening to it. He opened his own door and joined his little posse in the road. If he was moaning, no one seemed to notice. The wind screamed like a banshee. It bounced him off the fender and knocked him down. Crawling proved an efficient method of reaching the front bumper. By the time he regained his feet, the chairman had the hood open—open and tearing loose on broken hinges. He and the chairman fell back and watched it peel off and go tumbling into a nightmare sky.

"Nobody in the Blazer," Judy shouted. The chairman nodded his head to indicate he understood, then pointed at the Cadillac and shrugged his shoulders. The meaning was clear. He didn't know how to make it move again.

"Are there keys in the Blazer?" The sheriff combined the words with gestures that got him a distinct negative. "Then I guess we walk."

At least the cold air cleared his head a little. If he was having trouble staying steady, he couldn't tell whether it was because of the blows he'd taken or the storm. The wind made Judy and the chairman equally awkward. He led them behind the Blazer's mashed fender where they could duck down and he could make himself heard.

They all had their guns. No telling why Mad Dog had left the Blazer here. The sheriff believed it was for a good reason, but Mad Dog's good reasons didn't always make sense to anyone else.

"How far to the farm?" No one knew, but the chairman pointed out some tracks the sheriff hadn't noticed before.

"Looks like your brother cut across country, and he wasn't alone. They couldn't go far in this so we must be close. You want to follow him?"

The sheriff shook his head and, when his head seemed to want to go on shaking even after he'd stopped the effort, wished he'd chosen another method of expression.

"We lose those tracks out there, without any landmarks, we might never find the place. No, we stick together and we stick to the road."

They started and the wind pummeled them. The snow tried to etch icy designs in exposed flesh. The sheriff lost his footing before they were out of sight of the Blazer, one time less than each of his companions.

Heather English thought this was the stupidest thing she'd ever done. Toying with this manchild's confused libido could get them killed. Of course, so could all sorts of the other things around this farm, to say nothing of the weather. Going with Judah was like playing with fire, but however dangerous the flame, they needed its warmth.

He led the way down the stairs at the front of the loft, so eager that they could have turned and fled back and maybe found another exit. Only then what? So they followed. He wasn't bothering to point the rifle at them anymore, though he was still carrying it. Heather thought they could maybe get him to put it down, if they were willing to go far enough. Then, with two of them and only one of him, they might get the gun. Problem was, he would likely catch the remaining Heather at the same time.

He was big and incredibly strong. She'd never seen anyone do a one-handed chin up like the one he'd done to get his pictures. A couple of guys in her class bragged they could do them, but they grabbed the bar with one hand and their wrist with the other. And they weren't burdened with heavy winter clothes and boots and a rifle at the same time.

The forge was in a machine shop. It was crowded with shelves and benches, their surfaces covered with unidentifiable mechanical devices in various stages of assembly.

It was an old-fashioned forge powered by pressurized gas, the bottles for which stood in a far corner. Judah twisted knobs, adjusted flow, then brought one of those flint-and-steel welding lighters down near the nozzle. The result was closer to an explosion than Heather was expecting, but Judah just glanced from one to the other and seemed inordinately proud of himself.

"OK," he said. "Now show me."

Two smiled but shook her head. "Not yet, you silly. It's still freezing in here. Wait until it warms up some."

He looked disappointed. "How long?"

"You'll know," she teased. "When you start to sweat under all those clothes, then these can come off."

He understood. He reached down and readjusted the flow of gas. Flame spilled over the bricks and began to liquefy the piles of snow on the floor. The roar of the gas was loud, even over the roar of the blizzard.

"Sweat soon," Judah told them. Heather English was sweating already, but not from the heat.

"This used to be a hog barn." Mad Dog had expected to have to drag Dorothy into the wind, but she'd dipped a shoulder and led the way through a maze of snow dunes that lay behind every inconsequential shrub and bush. She'd known where she was going. Mad Dog and Hailey followed.

He'd left the Blazer square in the middle of the road. It was the only way Mad Dog could think of to slow down his brother. If Dorothy knew what she was talking about and there really was an arsenal fit for a small army in there, he wanted to delay them until he had a chance to…Well, his planning hadn't gotten that far yet.

"Used to keep a herd of prime Yorkshires in here, long time ago." She dropped to her knees just inside the long narrow shed, open on its south side. Under the roof, the floor was only lightly dusted with snow, ideal for her purposes. She began drawing. "Here's where we are. Here's the barn. It's right across from the house."

He knew some of it, but welcomed the refresher. "How do I stop them?"

"Like a rattlesnake. Cut off the head. The body can writhe around all it wants to and it won't hurt nothing. They're all dangerous, but you're after Becky or Zeke, whichever you can find. Once you take care of them, and let the kids know, they won't be no more trouble."

"Where do I find them?"

She looked at him, faintly puzzled. "I thought you could sense the evil." And it was true. He could. It was somewhere close.

"Be nice if you had a gun," she mused, "though I suppose that's hardly the sort of thing a sorcerer needs. Call down some thunderbolts instead." She reached in a pocket and pulled out an ugly lump of metal. "You might need this, though. Found it on the seat of the Blazer where you must of dropped it."

It was Tommie Irons' ring, the one all the Hornbakers seemed to be looking for. How had it gotten there? Then he remembered. Mary said she'd left Hailey and him some luck. Here it was.

"Don't know how you come by it. Guess that's why you're the Wizard. Magic ring, though, Wizard can always use a magic ring."

She climbed to her feet and began dusting the snow from her pants. "Where are you going?" Mad Dog asked, still wondering how to call down thunderbolts.

"Me?" She seemed surprised he didn't know already. "I'll be dealing with the witch."

◇◇◇

They almost missed Tommie's farm. They might have if it weren't for the mass of the abandoned snowplow in the front yard.

Looking to the north, facing into that gale of glass-like ice shards, was nearly impossible. The sheriff never saw the driveway, only that the path that had been plowed veered into the wind and ended at the back of a great yellow truck sitting between a pair of stick-like elms. Their branches faded until they were absorbed by a wild surge of churning white.

The sheriff grabbed the chairman and Judy and pulled them behind the tailgate.

"I think the house is almost due north. I thought I saw it a minute ago. That's where we're headed. Stay together and be ready. We don't know what we're getting into."

They nodded. The chairman massaged some feeling back into his right hand and got a gloved finger into the trigger guard. Judy drew her pistol just long enough to show the sheriff that she had chambered a round and it was cocked and ready to fire in her coat pocket.

"OK then." He didn't have anything more to say. He led them around the driver's side of the truck and checked the cab. The door hung open and the interior was deserted. He peered out the windshield over the steel blade. He couldn't see anyone out there. Not that that meant a thing. The house should be no more than a few yards away and it was invisible. He remembered a front yard filled with elms. He could barely make out the pair on either side of the plow.

"Let's go," he shouted as he led them around the side of the blade. He needn't have bothered. He couldn't even hear himself.

Crossing the Irons' front lawn felt as alien as crossing the face of the moon, only visibility would have been better on the moon, and even lunar shade was probably warmer. They found occasional trees, but didn't run into the huge drift that must be building up south of the house. The sheriff knew they'd gone far enough that its absence was a bad sign. He paused to reassess their position and be sure he still had both members of his posse. They were there, but so was something else.

The figure was immense. He might have taken it for an outbuilding except that it was moving. He thought it might come close enough to spot them.

"Down!" the sheriff yelled. He didn't know whether anyone heard.

Sweat rolled. Two of Two had peeled out of her jacket and sweater and was working on the buttons to her blouse. She had Judah's undivided attention.

Heather English was the one who was sweating. She had been deliberately slower in her own striptease. Her jacket was off, but, as bits of another Heather's flesh began to play peeka-boo in the dancing light of the roaring forge, she sidled away from the action.

She had a plan. She would put enough distance between the two of them so that Judah couldn't watch them at the same time. If he noticed and turned to deal with her, she would bolt, try to give Two a chance to grab one of the hammers that lay near the forge and make good use of it. She had a spot she planned to bolt to as well. There was a double bladed ax hanging from the wall over near the door. If she could get to it, she could do some damage. If…like if he didn't rip her head off before she got there.

Shuffling toward the ax was slow work. Two was starting to look a little nervous. She was out of her blouse and at one of those scary decision points. If she opted for modesty and removed her jeans next, she might find them down around her knees when she needed to move. If she didn't take off something else, and soon, he was likely to take it off for her.

Two reached up to the clasp that secured her bra and paused. She tried to look seductive. Seductive worked better when you weren't terrified. "I'll show you mine if you show me yours," she stuttered.

The idea seemed to appeal to Judah. He set his rifle down on the adjacent work bench and began to fumble with the zipper on his coat. "You keep going," he said. "I'll catch up."

One of Two was at the wall. She lifted the tool off the nails that suspended it. The ax was heavier than she'd expected. She choked up on the handle. This wouldn't be sudden and dramatic like in the movies. The damn thing weighed too much. But once she got it going she wouldn't be able to stop it short of hitting something—preferably Judah. She started edging back. She had to get close. She remembered what he'd done with the hoe.

She was watching Judah and her sister so closely that she didn't notice the coffee can full of hardware on the edge of the shelf. The ax hardly brushed it, but the can tumbled, slammed against concrete, and exploded nuts and bolts in every direction. Judah started to turn, only Two popped the clasp and her breasts sprung free.

Judah made a low, throaty noise, audible even over the wind and the forge. Heather swung the ax. She was going catch him in the shoulder and hurt him bad.

It didn't work. Even the wonders Judah beheld couldn't keep his attention. He spun, put out a hand, caught the ax handle just short of its blade, and ripped it from her grasp.

"You oughtna done that," he said. He swung it back at her, almost casually. It came handle first so she put up an arm to block it only a bolt slipped under her boots and she lost her balance. The other Heather was grabbing for the rifle, but the ax handle was coming fast. She had to duck, get down quick and...

A nova exploded behind her eyes. Heather, the collective, ceased to be plural.

Mad Dog lost sight of Dorothy before she'd gone a dozen paces. He knew he shouldn't let her go alone, and yet he felt she was safe here. He wasn't. Englishman and Judy wouldn't be either.

He was back at the farm he'd been so eager to leave this morning. Someone had tried to kill him less than a mile from this spot. Since then, things had gotten more complicated. He'd borrowed a Blazer and discovered the girl and her awful secret. Was that what this was all about? He should know. He was, after all, a natural born shaman. A wizard, according to Dorothy. He knew his brother was going to be in danger here, but he didn't know why. Was this because of Tommie's body? The bones Hailey found? Mary? Her baby? The ring?

On the few occasions when Mad Dog had been able to successfully practice his shamanistic talents, and he had to admit there had been relatively few of them, he'd done it by ceremonially preparing himself for the task. He fasted first. Well, he hadn't had anything but a cup of coffee at the Texaco before dawn, so he qualified there. He normally put on a breechcloth, covered himself in body paint, and spread his paraphernalia around him—a buffalo skull, his medicine bag, a pouch of Official Magic Faerie Dust he'd bought in a toy store to use in place of the corn pollen to which he was allergic. Then he would sit cross-legged on a blanket and concentrate on letting himself become one with the universe. He didn't have any of his stuff with him, not that conditions were appropriate to sitting around next to naked anyway. And it shouldn't make a difference. Those were just props, aids to help him achieve the right mind set, focus on what he was doing. None of it should matter.

He squatted on the floor of the abandoned hog shed and folded his arms and legs in an approximation of his normal vision quest position. His heavy snowsuit imposed limitations. He couldn't close his ears, though tightening the parka about his face helped cut the noise of the wind. He could close his eyes.

At first he didn't think it was going to work. Too many wild thoughts chased each other around in his head. But he'd taught himself the essentials of meditation, practiced forms of self hypnosis. He came up blank when he tried to determine where Englishman and Judy were, but when he thought about the evil…

At some level, he'd recognized the evil most of the day. Felt it in the back of his mind like an insect bite somewhere he couldn't reach. It meant to harm him and his family. He found it now, or he found something.

It glowed. He would have been hard pressed to explain what he saw to someone else. He would have been hard pressed to find anyone willing to listen. It was like looking at the sun. Too bright. Looking seared his inner eyes. He couldn't examine it directly. It was near, though. Very near.

And then he realized there was something else. Even closer. Danger!

Thunderbolts! Dorothy had recommended thunderbolts, and, somehow, he found one. Something pure and perfect and electric. He tried to grasp it, launch it, only it launched itself.

An automatic rifle exploded, one short burst. Mad Dog felt the impact. Chunks of frozen earth, shrapnel from where slugs bit the earth near his feet, slammed his chest and face. The vision imploded. His eyes flew open. An AK 47 lay just inside the building. A little wisp of smoke rose from its barrel. No one was attached to the gun. No one stood in the opening just beyond, though there were footprints. Human footprints, and a wolf's. And color. The snow was spotted with a fresh corsage of scarlet blossoms.

Hailey didn't think of herself by that name. She responded to it when *he* spoke to her, but it was only a word, not her name. Her name was somewhere in the song she occasionally sang about herself to the moon.

She knew lots of human words, more than *he* thought. But she was a wolf. Wolves respond when they want. She wasn't just an exotic dog, delighted to sit, or stay, or speak on command.

Unlike dogs, Hailey didn't like most people. She loved *him* of course. She liked or tolerated the humans *he* cared about. She didn't trust the rest. She had reason.

Hailey understood the world, perceived it, on something closer to the level where *he* went, sitting in semi-trance on the floor of the abandoned hog barn. *He* had to work at it. *He* was mostly visual. Her senses were more balanced. She could see passions, taste emotions, hear desires, smell anger, touch fear.

They were in a place surrounded by enemies. If Hailey wasn't so devoted to *him* she would have turned and run. Not from fear, but from a sense of self-preservation. Instead, she stayed and guarded *him*. And she understood, before *he* did, that one of the dangerous ones was coming.

Strange, she thought, even as *he* discovered her, and failed to recognize her for herself, how oblivious *he* was, even when *he* began to sense the world as she did. She would never understand *him*, but she would protect *him*.

The predator was almost on them, only it was as blind as *he* usually was. A dog might have barked. A dog might have growled. A wolf was more efficient.

E ven in such an alien environment, the sheriff recognized the sound. In spite of the wind, the absence of jungle, the scentless cold instead of pungent heat, he knew it. Across almost thirty years, he knew it—Kalashnikov.

He'd signaled his platoon to hit the dirt, only it wasn't dirt, of course, and his platoon hadn't noticed what he'd done. And it wasn't just dirt he hit, but the trunk of a tree he hadn't even known was there. No time for the fresh agony in his head. He reached behind him, seeking the M16 that must be strapped over his shoulder since it wasn't in his hands. His eyes swept the ground for trip wires, swept the tree line for Victor Charles or the pros from up north. There were no wires. Wasn't any ground even, let alone a tree line. There was only endless, swirling whiteness.

He looked around for his platoon. They were gone, swallowed by the roiling cloud of crystals that seemed bent on covering the world. They couldn't have gone far, but he suddenly realized he didn't want them. He'd already lost too many friends in that last village. He thought he'd been hit himself. Would have sworn he'd taken a round in his thigh, but here he was. And his head hurt, not his leg. He could do it. He could go after the little men with the AK 47s again, and this time, would go alone. He wouldn't need the radio at his belt anymore. He unclipped it and tossed it away.

The sheriff checked the load in his Smith & Wesson. He couldn't recall how he'd come by the weapon but it was better than nothing. He made sure the barrel was clear. He was ready, as ready as he'd been in the central highlands or the rice paddies. More ready than he'd been in the village.

He scrambled to his feet, threw one last glance over his shoulder to be sure his platoon hadn't come looking for him. Nobody there, for the few yards he could see. Check. He was clear.

He sprinted into the icy fog. Sprinted toward the source of that burst of 7.62 mm. Went looking for little men in black pajamas. His .38 Smith & Wesson preceded him, swinging, side to side, seeking targets.

The shots got Wynn Some moving again. He wasn't sure what had happened to him. He remembered Black Death on his heels. Then, suddenly, black had turned yellow and gored him. After that, he'd been prom king. His prom queen was an amazingly lush young woman whose face he could never quite focus on. But the rest of her. Wow! The stuff of fantasies. Literally, as it turned out. She offered to pillow him between her magnificent breasts, only they'd been icy-cold snow balls and he'd known he'd found the phantom snowballer at last, only he was lying in a snow bank at the base of some unidentifiable bush and the wind must have dislodged a clump of snow and dumped it in his face.

Wynn lay still for a minute, trying to find his way back into the dream. Prom queen or snowballer, either was preferable to the tempest around him.

The string of firecrackers seemed to go off practically in his ear. They didn't allow firecrackers at the prom and he struggled to his feet to tell them so, only to find his own prom more than a decade behind him.

Wind and snow tried to dry shave his face. He stumbled out of the drift, his sense of direction gone as a fresh explosion of snow crystals blinded him. The shots had come from behind him, he thought, so forward, even though it was into the teeth of the storm, seemed the way to go. He put his head down and charged.

Something dark loomed out of the storm. He thought it was Black Death for a moment and tried to decide where to hide. It was just an ugly little shed. Its walls looked too fragile to offer shelter, but he welcomed them, a place to lean against for a moment while he regained his breath. He hugged the rough wood, trying to shield his face from the merciless wind. There was something odd about it. It was wet. Snow grazed the shed and, instead of bouncing off, clung, turned soft, melted, and flowed down its surface.

Sweet Jesus, Wynn thought. There's heat in there. He hadn't realized how cold he really was until the prospect of warmth presented itself. He slid along its surface, fought the wind to open its door, and practically fell inside.

For a moment, he thought he was back in the dream. Only his prom queen hadn't had breasts as perfect as these. Her face glowed in the light of an open flame and was instantly recognizable. So was the fact that she was holding a rifle. And pointing it in his direction.

◇ ◇ ◇

"What is this place?" Mary asked.

What it was, was dusty and dark and cold.

"It's a library, Mary, or it used to be." Doc wasn't sure what he was doing. He just knew he couldn't sit in the empty silence of Klausen's anymore, trying himself before the hanging judge that was his conscience.

Doc's best, most trusted friend, along with his weird but honorable brother, were out there trying to solve a series of mysteries in the middle of the worst winter storm he could remember. He needed to help. He wasn't sure how, but paying a visit to the home of the "guardian of the words" seemed like a place to start. Didn't hurt that it was just down the block, within range of an aging doctor who didn't get enough exercise, and the young girl who had become his temporary charge.

"Wow. I always wanted to see a library." Mary advanced across the foyer and gaped at the stacks of books that crowded the room just beyond. Doc wondered if she thought it was normal to enter by breaking out a window so you could reach in and unlock the door. She didn't seem to have much experience with the outside world. How they'd entered surprised her less than the fact that the world held so many books.

He dusted off a seat for her on a well-lighted sofa by the windows and found her a selection of Dr. Seuss books in a pile on a cart labeled RESERVE.

Doc nibbled his lip and considered the Buffalo Springs Library. It had probably been a bank once. It had a big central room with a high ceiling that reached all the way to the building's second story roof. That room was filled with bookshelves, some of which would be impossible to reach without the wheeled ladders connected to a rail that ran just below the ceiling.

Doc's day had started with a phone call. An illegitimate baby was about to enter the world. Because of what that baby was and how it got here—and what he'd had to do with the process—Doc hadn't been able to think about much else.

Because of the mysterious swastika on its forehead, he was sure the baby was involved in Englishman's problems. But he thought it was bigger than that too. It hadn't started with the baby. It had started with Tommie Irons and Mad Dog's effort to dispose of his remains in such an unorthodox fashion. At least the combination kept it in the family.

Becky Hornbaker was Tommie's sister. Mary was what, a granddaughter of Becky's? Doc thought he had it right, now. Simon must be the baby's father. That made more sense. Tommie was already seriously ill when the child was conceived. He'd never thought Tommie was the type. Simon must have blamed Tommie to protect himself.

It was a family affair, and a family disaster, Doc decided. But he still didn't understand what Tommie might have possessed that had someone trying to kill Mad Dog, nor how a swastika fit in.

Newspapers seemed like the best place to start. A weekly summation of the history of Buffalo Springs and Benteen County was what he needed. Fortunately, Louis Henry Silverstein had been proud of his *Times*. They were gathered and bound, in leather, no less, on one of the most prominent shelves not far from the front door.

Silverstein hadn't arrived in Benteen County until the mid-sixties. January of 1966 was when *The Times* began. He wrote with an urbane wit that made Doc wish their days had overlapped, but had him wondering who Silverstein thought his audience was. The man must have written to please himself, then trusted, since there was no other local news source, he would command readership by default.

The first issue contained a prescient editorial about America's commitment to winning a war in Vietnam. It was like stepping into a time machine. Doc wondered what sort of reaction Silverstein had gotten in this hotbed of compassionate fascism. The next issue contained angry letters to the editor, and markedly less advertising. That answered Doc's question. Silverstein devoted more space to local matters after that, though occasionally the editor sounded off on the thorny issues that divided America in the days of flower power and Communist threat.

Doc got lucky because the 1973 volume was shelved out of order. He found what he was looking for because the paper thinned for several issues thereafter as businesses pulled their ads again.

The piece that had offended local merchants was an interview with a young woman. She claimed to be Southern Cheyenne. She called herself Brenda Stars-at-Night. Or maybe Silverstein invented the punning alias to protect her. She was on the way from Oklahoma to South Dakota, transporting guns and ammunition. She was part of a war party, or a relief column, bound for the standoff at Wounded Knee. The situation threatened to boil over into a second massacre if the army of federal and local law enforcement surrounding the place had their way.

Silverstein described her as a most unlikely warrior. She was young and delicate, and very pregnant. Those factors combined to make her journey more poignant. The Great Plains once belonged to the Lakota, the Cheyenne, and other tribes, she said. Then the white men came.

Her people's traditional allies were threatened by modern Custers. She and her companions would go stand with them. They would arm their brothers and resist the white man's latest efforts to wipe them from the face of the earth.

Doc remembered the rise of the American Indian Movement and the series of battles fought on the Pine Ridge Reservation in the seventies. Some lives were lost. Some ethnic pride revived. And some members of AIM were still in prison for the events that followed.

By itself, that article was troubling enough. It placed a pregnant Cheyenne girl in Benteen County, and Mad Dog was convinced that the fetal skull he'd found on the Irons farm was Cheyenne. But what made it chilling was the story in the next issue.

TRUCK EXPLOSION ROCKS COUNTY! It was a bolder headline than usual.

A few minutes after midnight, on an otherwise peaceful evening, a pickup truck and camper had exploded in a field near a stream on the west side of the Irons farm. The chief of the Benteen County Volunteer Fire Company said the truck was carrying a large quantity of gasoline. The occupants had paused for a visit at the Irons' property because the driver was Ezekiel Hornbaker, estranged husband of Becky Hornbaker, who lived there with her brother and her son. Cause of the fire was uncertain, but an unusual winter storm had produced both snow and lightning. It was thought an unfortunate bolt had hit the truck and ignited its contents. That seemed unlikely to Doc, and from the tone of the piece, it had seemed unlikely to Silverstein. His article concluded with ill-defined concerns for the Cheyenne girl and her companions. All of them were safely gone though, or so said Tommie Irons. Their truck had broken down and they'd borrowed his car. They'd left days ago.

Doc had his doubts. A pregnant Cheyenne girl staying on the Irons farm, then she's gone and the truck she was traveling in has exploded. Doc had an uncomfortable feeling he knew where Mad Dog's skull originated.

An earlier picture of the truck accompanied the article. Silverstein probably hadn't wanted to run it before because it showed the girl and two of her companions. They were headed for enough trouble without identifying the radicals among them to the locals.

The girl was dark and pretty, but she wasn't what caught Doc's eye. She was standing with a man and a woman. The woman faced away from the camera. The man was looking into the lens with the eyes of a startled bunny just realizing that shadow wasn't a cloud, it was an eagle's wings. The caption named him. Ezekiel Hornbaker.

It wasn't the Zeke Hornbaker Doc knew. This man had a deviated septum, a nose broken badly enough to be noticeable in the photograph. Doc had seen it before, on the battered ID card Mad Dog had found in a collection of bones.

J udy reached over and tugged on the chairman's arm.

"The house, it's right here," she shouted, though he probably couldn't hear her. She pointed and he nodded and they both waded through the snow in that direction.

She had no idea where Englishman had gone. It scared her. Everything about this insane day scared her, but Englishman's disappearance most of all. She was frantic about the Heathers. And then there was the senseless violence at Mad Dog's farm. Through it all, Englishman had been her rock. It would all work out because Englishman would see that it did, especially if she made his life sufficiently miserable until he set everything right again.

She couldn't imagine Englishman abandoning them on purpose, not even as woozy as he was from the blows to his head. Of course, all he would have had to do was fix his attention on something else for a moment while she and the chairman continued on their way. She remembered the stories her father had told, handed down in their family from generation to generation. Her great-great-grandfather had strung ropes from the house to the barn and other out-buildings to keep from getting lost in a Kansas blizzard. You could go thirty feet from the house and never find it again. She should have tied herself to Englishman somehow. Or noticed he was gone sooner, soon enough to backtrack and pick up his trail before the wind erased it.

It really was the house. She hadn't been sure. There was some drift snow at the edge of the porch, caught in the shrubbery that lined it. She had no patience to search for a break in the drift or the steps that must be somewhere. She just waded through snow and dormant lilacs, nearly hip deep, until she could reach out and grab the railing and hoist herself up and over. The chairman followed.

There wasn't much to block the storm up here, but the sheer bulk of the house seemed to hold the wind back a little. At least she could make out the words when the chairman cupped his hands around his mouth and bellowed in her direction.

"Don't see a door. There's one around front."

"Too far," she replied, pointing at the row of windows beside them.

The chairman bent and tried one. "Locked," he told her.

She stuck a boot through it, then used the padded elbow of her parka to clear the frame of shattered glass. "Who cares," she told him, and stepped into a room filled with scattered piles of books and magazines. Even with a window open on the storm, it was shockingly quiet in here, and incredibly warm.

The chairman was a lot bigger than Judy. It took him longer to crawl in. By the time he arrived, Judy had completed a sweep of the room. There were four cups on a coffee table in front of a working fireplace. Two of them had contained hot chocolate, two coffee. There was just the faintest trace of lipstick on one of the cups. A shade of exotic silvery red that she'd forbidden her Heathers to buy at least three separate times before they finally wore her down. They had been in this room. She recognized the scents of their perfumes, even over the smell of wood smoke that still issued from a blazing fire. They weren't lost out in that blizzard. They were here. Or had been.

"Heathers!" It came out half shout, half shriek, and brought no response.

"I sort of wish you hadn't done that," the chairman told her. "Not that you hadn't pretty well announced our arrival anyway."

"They've been here," Judy told him, gesturing at the circle of cups. "I recognize the lipstick."

He bent and picked up something off the carpet that Judy hadn't noticed. "And this is Junior's coat."

"You're sure?"

"Ought to be. I gave it to him for Christmas. Imported from Europe off the Internet. Not likely to be another of these in Benteen County."

"They must be here. We've got to search the house." Judy pointed toward the kitchen. "I'll go this way, you go the other."

He looked like he wanted to argue with her, but Judy was following her pistol through the swinging door before he could voice an objection. He didn't trail after her. Apparently he was taking her suggestion, and an alternate route, through the house.

The kitchen showed signs of recent use. A coffee percolator still issued a delicious aroma, though it no longer had electricity to keep it hot. A sauce pan filled with the dregs of milk and chocolate sat nearby. Judy looked out all the doors and windows. Someone could stand a couple of yards away and she wouldn't have seen them.

A hall led north. An empty bathroom failed to yield missing children, or clues. The door beyond opened on a wood-paneled den she liked even less than the all too masculine kitchen. There were two other doors from it, one west, one south. She decided to start with the first one. It opened on a dark staircase. Something spectral floated down it, straight at her. She got the pistol up, but not in time, and the thing was on her, knocking her to the floor and screeching in her ear as taloned claws sought her eyes.

"Could I come near your beauty with my nails I'd set my ten commandments in your face."

Judy waited for her life to replay itself. Instead, another figure emerged behind the first, took it firmly by the shoulder, and pulled it away.

"Not to worry, Mrs. English. She likes to quote things. One of Shakespeare's bloodiest threats this time, but there's no harm left in her."

◇◇◇

Being anywhere near the black tunnel that was a rifle's muzzle provided a wonderful focus for the mind. Wynn Some felt a wave of relief when he realized the gun wasn't aimed at him. It was pointed at the mountain of a man who stood almost straight between him and the bare-breasted Valkyrie who was actually a Heather.

The big guy stepped toward her, between Wynn and his view of her breasts, and there was an explosion. A little hole opened in the door beside Wynn's head, small and neat and round. Wynn tried to make himself small too.

The big guy swung around. He had the gun now, and the half-naked Heather wasn't there anymore. Wynn thought he saw something flesh-colored on the floor over where she'd been, only then he noticed there was something else down there as well. Another Heather. This one was clothed, her hair fanned out from her head like a halo on the cold concrete. Something else fanned around her head as well—something dark and wet.

The guy with the gun almost stepped on her as he came at Wynn. Wynn considered getting out of his way and finding some place to hide. No time. He also considered teleportation, sort of a beam-me-out-of-here-Scottie alternative. Mad Dog claimed you could will your body or soul to travel anywhere instantaneously. All you had to do was want it badly enough. Wynn qualified, but his soul and body stayed right were they were.

The big man stopped and looked down at him. It was Judah Hornbaker. Wynn recognized him at last. Just a kid—just a giant kid with a mean streak that terrified most of the other boys at BS High.

"I only wanted to look," Judah told him.

Wynn nodded enthusiastic agreement. Whatever Judah wanted was fine by him. Judah seemed to want to go out the door so Wynn scrambled aside. Judah pushed on the door, then stopped and turned to Wynn again. He pointed at a stain on his coat. The stain was spreading.

"She hurt me," Judah said. He seemed surprised. He seemed to think Wynn should maybe do something about it, only Wynn was still trying the teleportation thing.

Judah said something else and shoved the door open. The wind spun a cyclone of snowflakes into the room, where the forge converted them to mist. Or maybe they teleported somewhere and Wynn's aim was just a little off.

Judah let the door slam behind him. Wynn had to sit down on the floor for a moment and appreciate the fact that he was still alive before he made sense of Judah's parting words. They'd been a threat.

"I'm gonna tell!" he'd said.

"**G**et his feet."

Becky Hornbaker had already swung the blanket that held Tommie Irons' remains away from the wall and had a firm grip on it somewhere in the vicinity of his shoulders. Levi didn't want to touch it anywhere, but you didn't deny the old woman what she'd set her mind on. The feet were frozen solid and Simon had a tough time keeping hold of them. His right hand was all chewed up from that wolf. He'd shot it, and he'd managed to get away, but without his AK 47. Becky was more upset about that than what had happened to his hand.

He lost his grip on Tommie before they even got to the door to the shed. Tommie's feet landed at an angle and one of Tommie's toes chipped off. Levi just stood there and gaped, wondering whether to pick it up and try to fit it back on or just ignore the missing digit.

"Levi, you damn fool, grab the blanket instead of his feet and you won't be dropping him."

Levi obeyed and they began shuffling toward the door again.

"Where we taking him?"

"The garden shed," she said, using her butt to lever open the door. She said more after that, only he couldn't hear her over the wind.

The garden shed was between the garage and the house, a small addition that wasn't big enough to hold much other than yard tools.

On a normal day, Levi could have stepped out of this building, picked up a rock, and flung it over the top of the garden shed without any special effort. Today, he couldn't see the garden shed, let alone the ground at his feet where there might be suitable rocks. Of course, there was that toe he'd stuck in his pocket, for want of something else to do with it. The thought made him cringe, like somebody had run a fingernail across a blackboard. If anybody else had been on the other end of the macabre package, Levi would have tossed it aside, rid himself of the digit in his pocket, and run off to hide.

In a few steps Levi lost all sense of direction, but Becky didn't seem to have any doubts. She stopped suddenly and Levi almost lost his hold on Tommie's feet again. While he puzzled over why she'd stopped, she opened the door to the garden shed and led the way inside. Levi hadn't seen it.

"Let's put him over here on the bench."

The bench was nearly clear and Becky swept out an arm and knocked the handful of tools that rested there onto the concrete floor. She set Tommie's head on the side nearest the garage and Levi tried to swing his feet up on the other end. It didn't work. Tommie was taller than the shed was wide.

"Won't fit," he complained.

"Don't matter," she said. "We'll fix it so he does."

Levi couldn't imagine how until he heard her take the first pull on the starter cord. After that, it didn't matter who she was anymore. He hit the door hell bent for anywhere else. He never heard the chain saw's engine catch or what its metal teeth did to Tommie, except in his imagination.

◇◇◇

Smith led the way. Wesson came next. The sheriff followed. He had half a dozen wad cutters in the cylinder. He was confused about why. He thought they'd been on sale and he remembered hoping he'd never need them. If he did, he wanted close-up stopping power, not range, so wad cutters were perfect. Only where would he have gotten them on sale in Vietnam? And what had become of his Colt M16?

He kept low, ready to dive off the jungle trail—only there didn't seem to be any jungle, or trail for that matter. Watch out for ambush, he told himself, and booby traps.

And then one of the little Viet Cong was right there in front of him. Squeeze, don't jerk. He'd forgotten to cock the pistol and the double action was ponderously slow. The little man in the black pajamas dropped his rifle and raised his hands in surrender. He wasn't wearing pajamas either. He had on a parka, and he was big. Lots bigger than the sheriff, who felt himself go dizzy for a moment.

"Judah?" he said. "Judah Hornbaker?"

Judah didn't answer. Judah probably couldn't hear him for the wind. He had the pistol cocked, now, in case this was a trap. He moved closer. Where was he? What was Judah doing in Vietnam? And there was something about a dead baby.

"Where are they?" He shouted it in Judah's face.

"They're here. I was supposed to keep an eye on them."

The sheriff had meant the VC, only this really was Judah and it wasn't Vietnam. Why did Judah have a bullet wound in his shoulder? The world spun again, or maybe it was just snow spinning in the wind.

"Tell me," the sheriff yelled, "every damn thing you know. Anything happens to my babies 'cause you left something out, worse'll happen to you."

Judah turned just short of chatty, informing the sheriff about how he and Becky had found the kids hiking to Mad Dog's, then brought them home. How Becky had made sure they couldn't get in touch with anyone before she left to search for Mary and Mad Dog and Tommie's ring. How the girls had discovered a secret in the hall upstairs and then Simon decided to shoo them back into the storm in order to let them freeze.

The sheriff had trouble understanding. His brain felt as iced up as this altered Kansas landscape.

For some reason he latched onto the thing about Mary and Mad Dog and the ring. "What's with the ring? Why's everybody want it so bad?"

Judah plainly didn't know. "Maybe it's got something to do with bringing Jesus back. That's what Mary was supposed to do, only her baby died. Wasn't the first time it didn't work, only this time Becky seemed so sure."

"Who killed…" The sheriff had been going to ask about the bones Mad Dog found near the pond. Judah's guilt was elsewhere.

"Wasn't me done Mad Dog's animals. That was Becky. When she gets like that, ain't nothing you can do."

"How many of you here?" the sheriff asked.

"Simon's in town looking for your brother. I don't know about Becky. That leaves just me and Levi."

The slush in his mind was melting a little. And the ache in his head was coming back with a vengeance. He needed to know all this stuff, but first he needed to find his girls. And his deputy.

"Where are my daughters?"

Judah looked panicky. "I don't know." The sheriff instantly knew he was lying. Judah pointed off to the side. "Over there," he said.

The sheriff looked and couldn't see a thing. Judah turned and ran. The sheriff was about to follow when, improbably, like Peter Pan or maybe Superman, Judah began to fly.

"**D**octor Jones. I don't understand. What's this?"

Doc looked up from *The Times of Buffalo Springs*. Mary was holding an envelope, something she'd discovered inside a book entitled *The French Chef* which must have been among the children's books he'd found to keep her occupied.

"Does this have something to do with Mr. Tommie?"

Doc crossed the room to the dusty old sofa on which he'd left her. She handed him the envelope. It was sealed, but there was a symbol on the outside, one of those mirror-image swastikas like the one on the dead baby. He eased down on the cushion beside her.

"Why would you think it has something to do with Mr. Tommie?" He tried to go easy but he badly wanted an answer.

"This." She pointed at the swastika. "It's like Mr. Tommie's magic ring."

Doc waited, hardly breathing, letting her tell it without prompting.

"Mr. Tommie was nice to me. He showed me his ring. There was a secret place you pressed and it popped open with a thing shaped like this."

"Is that why you drew it on the baby?" Doc asked.

"Well," she hesitated and Doc thought he might have pushed too far. "He said it was supposed to be lucky. And it was secret. I couldn't tell anybody. I thought maybe it would make the baby well again. And, if only Mr. Tommie and I knew about it, that mark would help me find him when he got better. Was I bad? Shouldn't I have done that?"

"No. What you did was fine, Mary. I'm afraid the ring didn't have magic powerful enough to bring your baby back, but there was nothing wrong with trying. Do you have the ring?"

"No. I left it for Mr. Mad Dog and Hailey."

"Why did Tommie have the magic ring, did he tell you?" He opened the clasp and ran a finger under the envelope's flap.

"For safe keeping. What does that mean?"

There were newspaper clippings in the envelope. Maybe a dozen of them. The first was from a small-town Oklahoma paper. It was yellow and brittle with age. Someone had written the newspaper's name and the date, May 1957, across the top in a neat hand. The headline just below was a grabber. ABEL HORNBAKER MURDERED, it declared. NAZI TREASURE STOLEN!

Hornbaker. Horn. Baker. It made sense. Among brass instruments, the French Horn was commonly just called the horn. And what was a baker but a chef? *The French Chef.* The Horn Baker. Louis Henry Silverstein had been a clever man, and a cautious one.

"I'm not sure," Doc muttered, "but I think the guardian of the words is about to help us find out."

J udah was airborne, coming straight at the sheriff and he knew he should shoot the kid. He tried to get the gun back up in time and yank the trigger, no time to squeeze. Only Judah did a somersault in mid-air and landed on his butt, feet splayed, a terrified look on his face directed toward where he'd been going.

Something immense and black had materialized back there. It was plastered with blood and snow. The sheriff had a bad moment in which the thing seemed the stuff of delirium, then it was just a Brahma bull. Just? The thing was enormous. Its horns hadn't been cut and dulled the way any sane rancher should have done. It was coming closer. Coming for him, or maybe for Judah.

Judah screamed. His cry was audible over the wind, then the bull's head slammed into Judah's body and began grinding it into the earth.

"Hey! Heyah!" the sheriff shouted, waving his arms. The beast paid him no attention. It tossed Judah a few feet and charged again.

Smith spoke. So did Wesson. The bull didn't seem to care. It was busy savaging the broken figure through which one of its horns now penetrated.

The sheriff stepped sideways, avoiding the flailing body and the horns that ravaged it. He moved in close, just behind the beast's front shoulder. He pulled the trigger again and again and still the thing refused to go down.

Finally it paused, turned a burning eye the sheriff's way. He aimed at the eye. He pulled the trigger one last time. The hammer fell on an empty chamber.

The bull turned then, and trotted off into the storm. Judah flopped on its horns. He seemed to be waving farewell, a dead Captain Ahab on a great anti-white whale. And then they were gone. Only the bloody snow remained as evidence that this had been anything more than vivid imagination or too many blows to the head.

Judy struggled from under the wraith's scraggly hair and tattered clothing. Her assailant was a mere wisp of a thing. No weight to her. Old and frail, she decided. And, as the other woman, the one she'd met earlier at the Towers, claimed, no threat to a healthy person such as herself.

"My daughters?" Judy got her feet back under her. The old woman with the red tennis shoes helped pull the strange one away, but not before she uttered another baffling pronouncement.

"And children learn to walk on frozen toes."

"I don't understand," Judy said. "What does she mean."

"Outside, would be my guess," red shoes replied. "She's not as crazy as she seems. She only speaks with other people's words now, but she knows what she's saying. Her quotes usually mean something."

Judy turned to the window. It was shrouded with hurtling crystals. "Outside?"

"As frozen as charity."

Who was the hag, Judy wondered? Could she be right? Could her daughters have been here, safe and warm, then left? They weren't foolish enough to do something like that. Surely this woman must be as mad as she looked.

"No," Judy said. "They'd stay here, where it's safe."

"There's your mistake," red shoes corrected. "Hasn't been safe here since Tommie took ill. Maybe not even then."

"Where should I look?" Judy didn't trust the fantastic creature who had assaulted her, and wasn't sure about her companion. But she was desperate. She needed a place to start.

The wild woman crumpled at Judy's feet. It was as if she hadn't enough strength to go on. Only then she popped back up holding the gun Judy had left on the floor, and it was pointed straight at Judy's heart.

"I have a gub!" she said. Judy recognized the line this time. It was from a Woody Allen movie about a bank robber whose handwritten note to the teller was illegible. She'd found it hilarious when she saw it. Right now, it wasn't funny at all.

"Whoops!" her companion said. "Maybe I was wrong. Maybe there's still harm in her after all."

Doc moved the Buick all of three feet before imbedding it in the drift that had formed on its south side. Between that, and the ones sneaking into the parking lot from the evergreens that were part of Klausen's landscaping, he suspected it was trapped for the duration.

"Mary, we're going to have to walk."

She smiled. "I don't mind." It was all a grand adventure for her. She hadn't seen much of the county in her lifetime. Even the storm-swept streets of destitute Buffalo Springs must seem the height of urban tourism. She didn't understand how painful walking into that wind would be, nor how far those six blocks would seem. But he didn't have a choice. The sheriff had to know about this stuff in the envelope.

Abel Hornbaker had been murdered in Oklahoma more than forty years ago. His sons and a nephew and niece were accused of the crime. Some of their names rang bells, loud ones—Zeke Hornbaker, and Tommie and Becky Irons.

Abel Hornbaker was a successful businessman of German ancestry. A widower, he lived with his three sons (Ezekiel, Obadiah, and Malachi), a sister's children (Thomas and Rebekah), and a succession of housekeepers. He was involved in the German-American Bund in St. Louis before the Second World War. When he moved to Oklahoma to escape the hard feelings his pro-Nazi sympathies had raised in Missouri, he'd brought, some said, the organization's secret treasure.

Actually, he'd been a dealer in treasures. He bought and marketed odd collectibles. Religious artifacts were his specialty.

Nobody knew what kind of treasure he might have had. They were just certain there was one. He lived well. Visitors to the opulent Hornbaker residence recalled seeing a locked iron chest. It was memorable, they said, for its swastika-shaped keyhole. Hornbaker's friends had thought it a joke, but they'd never seen what was inside. It had seemed mysterious but not especially important, until he was murdered and it disappeared.

Then the rumors started. Diamonds, some said, stolen from the Jews, though how Jewish diamonds would have come into the possession of prewar German-Americans wasn't addressed. When his body was found, bludgeoned to death, no one was surprised that the chest was missing too.

The collection of newspaper articles told a complex tale. There'd been hints of an incestuous relationship between Hornbaker and his niece, Becky, and suggestions of hanky-panky with the Cheyenne woman who'd been his live-in caretaker. At first, people thought the rumors of Nazi treasure had lured a professional burglar and things must have gone wrong when Hornbaker caught him in the act. Only a witness turned up. Someone who claimed to have seen two of the boys, soaked in blood and in possession of the iron chest. A cache of bloody clothes was found, along with the fire iron that had been the murder weapon. Three of the kids were arrested. Tommie Irons and Obadiah Hornbaker got away.

Becky wasn't held long. She'd been at a dance with hundreds of witnesses. Her husband Zeke was there as well, though he'd left long enough to have been involved. Eventually, the state took Zeke and Malachi to trial on first-degree murder charges. In a Perry Mason moment, the Cheyenne housekeeper exonerated Zeke. She was having his baby and they'd been in the process of conceiving it when Abel was killed. Then Malachi broke on the stand and admitted killing his father. There were doubts about his confession, though, since he claimed Becky was his accomplice and she clearly couldn't have been. The state never learned for certain who was. Malachi got the death penalty. Ezekiel got life as an accessory. Obadiah was never found. Becky came back to Kansas. Tommie followed, and cleared himself with the local sheriff. Someone else's fingerprints were on the murder weapon.

Doc wasn't sure what it all meant. Louis Henry Silverstein, Guardian of the Words, must not have been sure either, but he'd been looking into it. Apparently, he'd been worried someone might discover his research. Why else hide the envelope in a cook book among children's literature on the reserve cart?

The appearance of Ezekiel Hornbaker at the Irons farm, accompanied by a Cheyenne girl enroute to Wounded Knee, had obviously intrigued the newspaperman. And one of those old articles had talked about a ring being stolen from Abel Hornbaker's finger. With it, actually, since the ring hadn't slipped off easily. It was evidently Mary's magic ring.

Englishman needed to know all this. Maybe Mad Dog, too. And Doc felt the need to ponder it, sort through all the possible Hornbakers and Ironses and work out who the guy with the broken nose was in the ID Mad Dog had found, and in the picture in the old *Times*.

There were three other interesting documents in the envelope, and no explanation how they'd gotten there. One was a list of the items Abel Hornbaker had been offering for sale. His suggested prices were phenomenal, but no more so than the items themselves. Doc had only thumbed through a few pages, but Abel Hornbaker claimed to be able to deliver pieces of the true cross, the authentic bones of saints, an original letter written by Saul of Tarsus, and an autographed presentation copy of *Mein Kampf.* Authenticity was guaranteed. Verification of provenance would be supplied to the successful bidder.

It was hard to believe, harder still considering the contents of a letter on Abel Hornbaker's stationery. Above his signature was a statement declaring his satisfaction with one order, and a request for additional stock. The merchandise referred to was scalps. Hornbaker acknowledged receiving two wavy brunettes, one Negro, and four with long, straight, black hair. He requested half a dozen blonds, and a dozen in a miscellaneous assortment of other racial types. The letter was addressed to a taxidermist in Kansas City. The scalp of Estevan the Moor (the first "European" to visit the mythic cities of Cibola) included on Hornbaker's list was more likely a scrap of buffalo hide or the like.

Finally, there was an inquiry from a collector in Argentina. As someone who claimed to trace his descent from Mary Magdalen, its author was willing to pay Hornbaker's price. But before parting with a million dollars, he wished to send his own expert to verify authenticity. The letter was dated 1956, when one million dollars was a far more staggering sum than it was today. It made Doc especially curious about what had been for sale.

Outside the Buick, the wind was worse than he'd imagined. Mary had the resilience of the young, but neither of them was up to six blocks into the face of intolerable fury. Doc explored the offerings in the used car lot down the street. He had the keys to the office, and, therefore, to all the vehicles on the lot. He had permission to borrow any of them whenever he wanted as well, thanks to a long past-due loan to "Honest But Ugly Fred," the proprietor. Fred had lots of light pickups and several sedans, and not a four-wheel drive among them. Doc and Mary pushed on.

By the time the truck pulled up beside them and threw its door open, Doc reached for its handle as desperately as a drowning man grasps at a flotation device. He pulled Mary in and fought with the door to close it.

"Thanks," he said. "You're a life saver." The chubby guy behind the wheel stared at him with an unpleasant scowl.

"This is Doctor Jones," Mary said. "He's my friend. Please don't be mad at him Uncle Simon."

◇◇◇

It was a couple of minutes before Deputy Wynn could get his feet under him. They had assumed a Jello-like consistency, too wobbly to hold him.

"Heathers?" he called.

No one answered. But for the glow from the forge, it was dark in the shed. Dim light filtered through windows that hadn't been cleaned in decades. The illumination behind them was paler than it had been. It must be getting toward sunset.

The flame in the forge was blinding. Looking toward it made seeing what was on the floor, below the level of the firebox, harder. Wynn took a couple of tentative steps.

At least it was warm. He could feel the heat on his face, noticed a little feeling coming back into his hands.

"Heathers?" Still nothing. He bent, shielding his eyes with one arm. The first girl was right at his feet. He dropped to his knees and shook her a little.

"Heather!" He shouted it this time. It was loud in there. Maybe Englishman's daughter hadn't heard him over the roar of the furnace and the cry of the wind.

Jesus! He was kneeling in her blood. He looked for a wound and couldn't see any. Nothing obvious. All of a sudden he didn't want to risk moving her again. She might have a spinal injury.

"Uhh," somebody said. That somebody sat up slowly on the other side of the forge. She was holding her face in her hands. Even in the ruddy light of the flame she looked pale.

Naked to her waist, but pale. Uncharacteristically, Wynn hardly noticed her breasts as he hurried to offer her a hand, even found himself helping her cover herself with her jacket. Later, the deputy who patrolled back roads in search of parked couples so he could sneak up and use his flashlight to peek at a naked prom queen might kick himself for not taking advantage of the chance to extend this viewing time. Just now he was too busy being scared, and not just for himself.

"He socked me," Heather Lane explained. She had the beginnings of a magnificent shiner. "He grabbed the rifle and popped me with a fist."

"Heather's out cold," he told her. "I couldn't find a pulse."

"What?" She started pulling herself down the aisle, crawling toward the place where her sister lay.

"There's blood all around her," Wynn said. Two sat on the floor and gently lifted One's head into her lap, hands exploring her skull with a feather-light touch.

"She's breathing. What happened to her?"

Wynn wasn't sure. "Judah Hornbaker musta done it," he said. "She was already down on the floor when I came in, just before you shot him. He took the gun away from you somehow, then he went out. Said you hurt him and he was gonna tell."

"Did I hurt him? I thought I missed."

"Oh no. You got him. High up near the shoulder. He was bleeding bad. The bullet went right through him. Pretty near hit me too." Wynn turned to point at the hole in the door just in time to watch it open. Judah stood there. There was no wound in his shoulder and the only blood on his coat was on one of his sleeves. His eyes stared at them, absorbing the glow of the forge without reflecting it. It was like there was no soul in there, Wynn thought. Like soul and body had somehow parted, and what was left wasn't truly human. A ghost?

Wynn wanted to open his mouth to demand that this spirit be gone. He didn't manage it. All he was able to produce was a tiny sound even he could hardly hear. "Mama!" he whispered.

◇◇◇

"I t's not loaded," Judy said. It was, of course, but she thought she was close enough to get to the gun if the hag looked down to check.

The hag didn't seem to care.

"I don't think she believes you," the lady in the red tennies said. "Lock someone in a cage for forty-odd years and it's not surprising if they have trust issues."

Judy nodded. Cage? Forty years? It didn't matter, nor did whatever issues the woman might have. Judy didn't even care who the old bags were. Only her daughters mattered.

"Look. I just want to find my girls and get out of here. I don't care about any of this. You can keep the gun if you want."

"No," the lady in the tennies said. "I don't think she should do that." She put out her hand. "Why don't you give it to me, dear?"

The crone backed up a couple of steps, swinging the Beretta to keep both of them covered.

"I'll just leave you two to work this out," Judy said. She took a tentative step toward the exit to the kitchen. The door across the room creaked as it began to open.

Now, Judy thought. She lunged, snapped her leg up the way Englishman had taught her, and kicked the spot the Beretta occupied. The wild woman swung toward the far door. Judy's foot encountered air. She felt herself losing her balance.

Chairman Wynn was pushing through the door and saying, "Judy, you've got to come look at this. I think we've found Harriet. There's a regular laboratory in here. Dead babies in jars. I mean some weird shit." She tried to comprehend as she twisted in mid-air so she'd have another chance at the gun. The woman in the red tennies was grabbing for it too.

Judy brushed the pistol with one hand as the lady in the tennies tackled the crone around the shoulders. The gun exploded. Once! Twice!

Someone shrieked and Judy fell in a heap. So did the old women. The gun skittered across the floor, just out of reach.

The far door finished opening. The chairman stumbled into the room. His eyes were wide and his mouth was open. He was the one screaming. His hands clasped the front of his jacket where a crimson stain was spreading. His legs went out from under him and he sat heavily on the floor. He opened his mouth to cry again, only this time hardly any sound emerged. Blood did though. Too much, Judy thought, for a man to lose and live.

Most Benteen County deaths were from natural causes. Given the increasing age of the population, and the decreasing economic incentives to keep young people living here, most were simply a matter of organisms wearing out.

You couldn't hang around a brother who was sheriff, though, without running into the exceptions. Mad Dog had come face to face with death in many forms—automobile accidents, farm accidents, suicides, even a brutally murdered preacher a few years back. He'd never faced it quite like this, though.

Death had assumed a persona and it stood just before him. Little puffs of steam exploded from the bull's nostrils. Blood tinged Black Death's horns. Bloody sputum dripped from the corner of his mouth and more blood flowed down his flanks and spoiled the pristine snow.

Mad Dog had left the AK 47 back in the hog shed. That's what you did when you didn't believe in guns. He wished he didn't believe in bulls either.

A lightning bolt. He needed another lightning bolt, only he couldn't begin to concentrate. Not with death so close at hand.

The bull pawed scarlet snow, dipped his head slightly. He was ready to charge.

No point in running, Mad Dog decided. The bull stepped closer. It was as if the monster wanted to look in his eyes as it killed him.

"I'm not going to let you do this," Mad Dog said. The bull didn't seem interested. "I'm a natural-born shaman," Mad Dog told it. "I can kill you without touching you."

The bull twisted his head, as if choosing which horn to use first. Mad Dog was beginning to feel a little desperate. He reached out and pointed a finger at the Brahma. "Begone!" he shouted. "I, Mad Dog, command it."

The bull nodded. Something changed behind its eyes. The angry spark flickered, dimmed, extinguished. The black giant tilted, toppled, fell, and lay still.

Benteen County's greatest shaman had triumphed again.

The sheriff was looking for the house, but when something finally loomed out of the frozen tempest, it was the barn. He didn't mind. The Heathers could be anywhere.

He slipped through the doors, from savage maelstrom into dusky twilight. His daughters didn't leap from the nearest stall to greet him as their savior, not even when he called them. No fresh Hornbakers renewed their efforts to do him harm, either.

Thinking of Hornbakers made him decide to reload. It should have occurred to him earlier. He was going to have to be careful, make himself consider the consequences of every action. His mind wasn't back to normal speed, even if he understood he was an inhabitant of present-day Kansas again. Reloading proved that. He had bullets. He just didn't have anything to put them in. The sheriff was still trying to work out what might have happened to his gun when the voice interrupted him.

"I wondered who stumbled in here. I was hoping you might be Mad Dog, but you'll make good bait for him."

Becky Hornbaker stood just inside the barn doors. The front of her clothing was spattered with something that looked like a cherry slushie. It was on her face and in her hair too. And all over the AK 47 she pointed his way.

"Or maybe you've succeeded where I haven't," she continued. "Have you found your demented brother, Sheriff, and relieved him of the key?"

"Key?" The sheriff had a theory about questioning suspects. Unfortunately, he couldn't recall it just then. Puzzled parroting would have to do. He could dazzle a confession out of her later, when he decided whether she'd committed a crime.

"No? Too much to hope for, I suppose. You just want to know about your Heathers and your deputy. You don't care about my key, even if it's what all the rest of this is about."

He seized on that one. "Where are the Heathers? Why bring them here?"

"We couldn't leave them wandering around Harriet's grave, now could we. What might people think?"

"You know?"

"Nearly every woman in this county knows Harriet, Sheriff."

"Are you…"

She interrupted him. "Am I Harriet? No. Not with Zeke championing the battle to end abortion in Benteen County. I'm just trying to claim my rightful inheritance, and an exit strategy for a situation that continues to spiral out of control. Too many people here sticking their noses in our family's secrets. And then there's what your brother stole, and what he may have stumbled on."

"I don't know what you're talking about. I haven't seen Mad Dog all day. I know he made off with your brother's body this morning, and I know your family has been looking for something of Tommie's. But that's it. You're going to have to fill me in on the rest."

"Shall I show you what this is all about? Perhaps I shall. It's heavy, as I recall. I could use your help toting it."

A moment of dizziness whirled through the sheriff's head, and this time, not just because of the blows it had taken. He had no idea what Becky was talking about, or why she was running around with an automatic rifle. "Look," he said. "Why don't you let me get my family and my deputy and leave? Then you can continue whatever game you're playing without us spoiling it for you."

She smiled without humor.

"Oh, Sheriff, I assure you. It's no game. When your brother finds the message I left him, he'll understand just how serious it is." Her grin widened. "Deadly serious, you might say."

"Wasn't me that hurt you, Judah," Wynn Some whined. "It was her." He pointed down where one Heather cradled the bloody head of another.

"You hurt Judah?" The hulk in the doorway seemed to have trouble believing that. Since the kid didn't have a hole in his shoulder, the deputy had trouble believing it too. To be on the safe side, he treated the statement as an accusation.

"Not me, Judah. Her." If he could just direct Judah's attention somewhere else.

"I'm Levi, you dumbo." The big guy punctuated his explanation by shoving Wynn against the nearest workbench. Levi sure looked like Judah.

"How could any of you runts hurt Judah?"

"I shot him," Heather said. "In the shoulder, though that's not where I was aiming."

Levi shook his head. "What you doing in here? You're supposed to be out there freezing."

"I could go now, if you like," Wynn offered.

"Go, stay. Whada I care. Only you hurt Judah. That's not right. Judah shoulda hurt you."

"He did. He hurt both of them," Wynn said. "Just look."

Levi obliged by stepping further into the room and bending down to see in the dim light below the mouth of the forge. It was what Deputy Wynn had both feared and hoped. There was a karate chop he'd seen on TV. You just stepped up behind the villain and hit him with the blade of your open hand where his neck met his skull. It worked every time, except this one. Levi should have dropped like the price of wheat at harvest. Only he didn't.

"You oughtna done that," Levi said. He picked Wynn up and threw him across the shed. "Now you made me mad."

Wynn Some would have apologized but he was having trouble with simpler things, like breathing.

Levi didn't come after him, though. He reached into a cabinet by the door and pulled out a plastic jug. He popped the lid off and tossed it in Wynn's lap. Kerosene.

Levi picked up a second jug, opened its lid as well. "You wanna get warm. Fine by me." He tossed the second jug in the forge. A ball of flame mushroomed out, engulfing everything.

Wynn was on fire. He batted his arms against his chest, trying to extinguish the blaze. He looked for a place that wasn't burning and launched himself for it. Levi got out of his way as he went through the door. He dove in the snow and let its chill engulf him. It took several minutes of rolling around and beating on himself to put it out. By then, the shed was totally engulfed in flame. That was when he remembered the Heathers.

Judy's fingers probed the chairman's throat for a pulse. He was covered with blood, slick with it.

"He needs help," Judy said. The hag was gone but the woman in the tennies was only just climbing back to her feet by the door to the hall and the kitchen.

"Honey, he needs a miracle."

Judy was inclined to agree.

"We're in luck, though. There may be one nearby."

Judy looked up. She didn't understand.

"The Wizard, Hon. He came with me. He's out there somewhere. I'll go see if I can find him for you. If anyone can raise this fellow from the dead, it'd be him."

"Wizard?"

"Oz!" the woman said, proving herself as mad as a hatter. "Though maybe you know him by his other name. Folks around here, they mostly call him Mad Dog."

Sure, Judy would take any help she could get, including Englishman's crazy brother. Maybe he knew some Cheyenne miracle cure for gunshot wounds and could free her up to search for the Heathers. "Just get help," Judy pleaded.

The woman clicked her sneakers together. "On my way," she said. "Only, if the wicked witch comes back, don't give her any more guns."

The stairs to the hayloft were steep and narrow. The sheriff knew he could launch himself back down them and Becky couldn't get out of his way. He also knew she'd fill him with 7.62 mm slugs. He might knock her down, maybe bleed all over her, but he wouldn't be in a position to benefit from it.

"You killed Mad Dog's animals? You tore up his house and left that swastika on his kitchen floor?"

"He stole the key. I had to let him know how much I wanted it back."

She made it sound reasonable, like she'd left a polite note instead of a farm full of slaughtered pets.

"Key to what? What could Mad Dog steal that would be worth that?"

"A treasure beyond price. I wonder if our Tommie told him? Mad Dog might want it for himself. He fancies himself to be some kind of Cheyenne magician doesn't he? He might think he can use it."

"Use what?"

The loft was almost empty of hay, a place turning gloomy in the twilight. The dusky floor was littered with ancient bits of straw, piles of snow, and freshly broken shingles. The wind stirred little dervishes and pried at the roof.

She didn't answer. "Someone's just been up here." She flew around him to the far corner where a few bales stood in a jumbled stack. The sheriff followed, gradually becoming aware of the black enamel box with its chrome fittings lying in a fresh avalanche of hay.

She grabbed the handle to the box and yanked. It didn't budge and that calmed her.

"It's still safe," Becky sighed. "I didn't think anyone would ever find this. I drove it straight up here and hid it the night we killed him."

Killed him?

"I stuck it over here in the farthest corner," she continued. "Lots of hay up here then. I knew it'd be a long time before anyone dug back this far. Then I made sure fresh hay always got stacked in front of this.

"Funny thing was, we killed Uncle Abel for his treasure and, you know, he ended up leaving it all to us. Everything. And there was a lot. Enough to keep this farm going through lots of lean years.

"We thought he kept money in this box. Maybe jewels. Considering what was in his bank accounts, it had to be more valuable than that.

"I let our Tommie keep the key. I didn't need the treasure then. We had enough. Enough even to carry on the family's purpose. But I kept this hidden. Something to use if things ever came apart, like they've done today."

The chest was a remarkable piece of craftsmanship. "French artisans," Becky said. "Our uncle was a member of the Bund before the war. People thought this box was related to that. They didn't understand about the things he bought and sold. Or our bloodlines."

"Bloodlines?" The sheriff was back to baffled parroting.

"You don't know, do you, Sheriff. You don't understand to whom you're speaking." She stepped back and spread her hands, carefully keeping the Kalashnikov pointed in his direction.

"You trace your ancestry to the Cheyenne, don't you Sheriff, you and Mad Dog. Well, I can do better than that. My bloodline goes farther back. And it's more noble than you can imagine."

He was cold and tired and frightened. She was probably going to kill him, but he was fed up with her senseless babbling.

"This is twenty-first century Kansas," he said. "No one cares who your great-great-great-grandfather was."

"Want to bet, Sheriff?" she said. "Mine was Jesus!"

This time it was a three-vehicle collision. The Dodge Ram slammed the Cadillac SUV, which, in turn, added fresh creases to the Blazer's bodywork.

"What the hell?" Simon complained. "This ain't a parking lot."

Doc and Mary didn't comment. Doc was just glad he'd belted Mary in and had managed to brace himself before impact since the air bags hadn't deployed.

Simon didn't let the crash slow him much. He just shifted into low and eased his bumper against the back of the Caddy. Doc felt the wheels of the truck spin and grab. The Dodge lurched forward, gradually nosing the Cadillac aside. Then it did the same for the Blazer.

The Cadillac meant Chairman Wynn was here, along with Judy and Englishman, Doc guessed. The Blazer was Tommie Irons' old SUV that Mad Dog had appropriated. So, Mad Dog was probably here as well. Simon hadn't been talkative, but as far as Doc knew the rest of the Hornbaker clan was at the farm. That meant he was headed to the right place. What with shots fired at Mad Dog and an assault on Englishman, it seemed likely he'd find need for his services here. He just wished he'd had the chance to bring his house-call bag.

"Look," Mary said. She was pointing where Doc thought the farm should be. You couldn't see more than a few yards, though, so you couldn't tell. Only Doc was surprised to see what she was pointing at. Back behind all that blowing snow, something glowed. It impressed Simon too.

"Oh shit!" he said. "Place is on fire."

◇ ◇ ◇

"**W**ho is the baddest shaman in all of Kansas?" Mad Dog shouted. He pumped his fist and twirled and jumped up to try to high five the blizzard. It actually felt like it slapped back.

"Wind, cease blowing. Mad Dog commands you." The wind didn't cease, but Mad Dog convinced himself it was a little gentler. It was hard to tell, since you couldn't actually face into it for fear the ice crystals would gouge your eyes out.

"Enemies, come to me," he commanded, still filled with himself, and with relief that the bull hadn't killed him. He didn't see the patch of ice in the low spot in the driveway. His feet went out from under him and he sat down hard. Not as hard as Levi Hornbaker, though. Levi materialized out of the miasma, trotting with his head thrown back over his shoulder. Maybe he was trying to protect his face from the wind. Maybe he thought Black Death was after him. Mad Dog just had to stick out a leg to send Levi into a head-over-heels tumble that ended with him sitting on the far side of the frozen puddle.

"You got a gun, Levi?" Mad Dog wasn't worried about it. After the bull, overcoming Levi would be child's play.

Levi just stared at him. "You won't find one," Mad Dog said.

"Uhh. I lost it somewhere," Levi admitted.

"Take off your belt," Mad Dog told him, getting to his feet and going to loom over Levi. Mad Dog was a big man, but not as big as Levi. It didn't matter. Mad Dog's looming was impressive because he'd drawn his power about him like a cloak. He was invincible.

"Your belt."

Levi did as he was told and Mad Dog bent and looped it around the boy's neck, like a leash. One Hornbaker down. What, maybe four to go? Mad Dog remembered what Dorothy had said about Zeke and Becky. Like a snake, she'd

said. Cut its head off and the rest would be harmless He was
working on the wrong end.

"Where are Zeke and Becky?" Mad Dog demanded.

The question seemed to frighten Levi. "Last I saw her,
she was in the garden shed."

"Show me." Mad Dog gave the leash an experimental tug
that helped encourage Levi to stand up.

"We can't go back there. She's making like *The Texas
Chainsaw Massacre.* She might kill us all."

"Don't be afraid, Levi. I'm armed with power from the
Maiyun, the spirits of the seven regions of the universe. The
Maheyeyuno, the four sacred guardians at the corners of
creation are also with me. The *Hematasoomao,* the immortal
spirit forms of every living thing are at my service. I can call
down thunderbolts. I can kill without touching. Nothing
can stand in my way because my heart is pure."

"You're as crazy as her. She's collecting corpses and taking
chainsaws to them. We can't go back there, I tell you."

Mad Dog gave a tug and Levi stumbled along behind, the
wind styling his hair and frosting it with snow.

"Of course we can," Mad Dog said. "I'll protect you. I'm
in complete control, Levi. Look, I'll show you." He paused
and spread his arms. "A sign. Bring me a sign," he ordered.
He wasn't a bit surprised when another figure materialized
out of the snow.

Talk about name-dropping. The sheriff thought he must
have misunderstood.

"Excuse me?"

"Our family, we're direct descendants of Jesus."

The sheriff hadn't thought Becky could shock him. "You
telling me there are some immaculate conceptions the Bible
doesn't mention?"

Becky cackled. "Hardly. Jesus was the son of God, but he
was a man. He lived in a human body. That's why he died. A

god wouldn't have to do that. But to die for us, he also had to live for us. Modern scriptures edit that part out, but he had children, you know. He and Mary Magdalen. And after he was crucified, she took them and escaped by boat to Gaul. France. And she took the Holy Grail with her and preserved it. Or so our family tradition claims. I don't think our uncle really believed it to start with, but following the legend is how he got in the business. Then following the plan got us Simon and our heavenly twins."

The sheriff was beginning to wonder whether he was hallucinating from all those head blows. Jesus' children?

"The Holy Grail? Is that what you think is in this chest?"

"It's as good a guess as any. There were references to the chalice in the old man's records. He'd been in touch with a Nazi official who was hunting it before the war. There were hints the man was successful. One letter suggested an offer had been made and accepted."

"The Holy Grail? The cup Jesus drank from at the last supper? The one Joseph of Arimathea used to catch his blood when he was on the cross?"

"It was Mary Magdalen, not Joseph," Becky corrected him, as matter of fact about it as if he'd confused Judah with Levi. "She bore his children. It was only natural for her to be there to catch his blood when Longinus speared him on the cross. It's only right we should have it, you know. Heirlooms belong in the family, and ours is still growing."

The sheriff wondered if one of King Arthur's knights might happen by to put in a claim of his own. Or Monty Python.

"Growing?" the sheriff asked, stepping dangerously near Alice's looking glass. "Are you saying you're trying to…"

"Recreate the Son of God? Yes. We're inbreeding. Uncle Abel did it. He fathered Simon. And since then, we've carried on. We may produce divinity again, or something close."

"How?" Becky, long past childbearing, was the only Hornbaker woman. The sheriff couldn't remember Simon's wife.

"Father with child, then grandchild, then great grandchild."

"You mean that dead baby…" the sheriff was shocked again.

"Our latest failure. Every generation we get closer. I thought this one…"

"Was Zeke the father?" the sheriff guessed. He didn't think it could be Tommie.

Becky snorted. "Ezekiel couldn't father a messiah. Nor could any Hornbaker."

"Then who?"

"Me, of course," Becky replied.

I t was Dorothy.

"Why's Levi on a leash?" she asked.

"Seemed like a good idea," Mad Dog responded. "At least I've rounded up one already."

"Nice start. You using magic?"

He nodded, glad someone understood.

"Good that you've been warming up. Come along then, Mr. Wizard. We got an even bigger task for you inside." The steps to the back porch proved to be only a few feet away. Mad Dog wasn't surprised that things were working out so nicely.

"What task?" Mad Dog wondered as he led Levi through the door she held.

"You recall a man named Lazarus."

"Like in the Bible?

"Yeah. We need you to resurrect someone from the dead. Just the one when I left. Could be more now. It's turning into a busy evening."

There was no way back into the shed. The walls sweated flame the way an icy beverage oozes dampness on a muggy afternoon. The door Wynn had escaped through looked like the gateway to hell. No one inside could be alive.

That's when he noticed the trail. It was a pretty obvious trail, a pair of scrapes, in some places right down through the snow to the gravel of the drive. Scrapes, like a pair of heels might make if someone were dragging them from the other end. He followed, and, sure enough, found the Heathers.

"Sheesh!" he greeted them with an overflow of relief. "I thought you guys were dead."

Only Heather Two was capable of responding. "She may be if she doesn't get help soon."

Wynn hadn't given much thought to what heels being drug had to mean.

"She's still unconscious?" From the way Englishman's daughter's head lolled, and occasional drops of blood discolored the snow, the answer was clear.

"Grab her legs," Heather Lane commanded.

Wynn was at his best when someone else took charge. He got his hands under Heather's knees and lifted her feet off the snow. He was just as glad to leave the delicate problem of supporting the injured end to Two.

"Where we taking her?"

"The house."

That gave Wynn pause. That's where they'd gotten in trouble in the first place.

"Don't you think we ought to go somewhere else?"

"You got any suggestions?"

He thought about it and decided he didn't.

"Look," she said. "From what Levi told us, the plan is for us to stay out here and freeze. I'm guessing they didn't want our bodies marked up. Well, too late. Heather's hurt bad. I'm covered with cuts and bruises. We freeze to death now, it's not going to look like it happened by accident."

"So you're thinking they might let us in?"

"Maybe. I'm also thinking they could be out here looking for us. And the burning shed. That may draw their attention. The house could be abandoned. Whatever, we've got to get out of this and we've got to get Heather some help. The house seems like the place to start."

Or finish, Wynn Some mused, but he didn't say it.

◇◇◇

J udy followed the cocked Beretta down the hall to the
kitchen. After what the gun had done to the chairman,
she hated even touching it, but she wasn't going to take a
chance on being surprised by dangerous intruders.

"It's just us, Hon," the little lady in the red tennies reassured her. You might want to keep that pointed at Levi here
while I take our Wizard back where he's needed."

It was the smaller of the Hornbaker twins, those dull
holdbacks who made life difficult for their classmates and
worse for their teachers. Only the football coach liked them
because most of the rest of the boys in the conference were
afraid to play against them. She did what Dorothy asked,
but she had something else on her mind.

"Mad Dog, have you seen the Heathers?"

He smiled and tried to look reassuring. He looked patroni-
zing instead. "Don't worry, Judy. I'm sure they're all right. I'd
know if they weren't."

Good old Mad Dog, living in a world no one else inhab-
ited. "Great," she told him, "then go with her. Work your
miracles. I'll research the subject on my own."

She could tell Mad Dog was hurt by her sarcasm. Just
now, she didn't care, and she didn't have to deal with it because
Dorothy was dragging him down the hall to where the
chairman waited.

Levi looked scared, but not of her and the pistol.

"Where are my girls?"

"They shoulda left Judah alone," he said.

She stepped a little closer and shoved the pistol under his
nose. "You know where they are, don't you?" She wasn't sure
of that, but she intended to find out.

"Yeah," he said. "But I don't think I'll tell you. Ms. English,
I want you should give me that gun."

She was standing there with the thing practically stuffed
up his nose and he expected her to give it up, and not have
to tell her about her girls?

"Are you nuts?"

"Not me," he said. He was slowly raising his hand to reach for the pistol. "That's why I need the gun. For when the one who is nuts gets here."

She tightened her hold on the weapon. "No way," she said. "I'm keeping the gun and you're going to tell me what happened to my daughters."

He shrugged. "They hurt my brother," he said. "So now they're burning in hell for it 'cause I sent them there."

Judy felt like he'd punched her in the solar plexus. She couldn't breath. He gently began prying the gun from her fingers and she was paralyzed with the agony of what he'd said, unable to resist. He began to grin. The bastard who claimed to have killed her daughters was slipping the pistol out of her hand. Fuck you, she thought. She pulled the trigger.

Nothing happened. Nothing except that he finished taking it away from her. "I didn't think you'd do that," he said. He was turning the gun this way and that, trying to figure out why it hadn't fired. The hammer was cocked. That wasn't it. He peered down the barrel from the muzzle end. "Looks like it should work to me."

Levi was right eye dominant. She could tell, because that was the one the 9 mm hollow point tore out on its way through his brain pan when he tried the trigger himself and this time it worked.

S imon stopped the Dodge near the inferno that had been a tool shed. He fumbled behind the seat and came out with a fire extinguisher. It was the kind they sold at the Texaco, not much bigger than a can of spray paint, and, Doc thought, for a fire so out of control, similarly effective.

Simon didn't ask Doc's opinion. He grabbed the can and hustled around the truck toward the blaze. Doc couldn't help noticing that the truck was still running and Simon had left his rifle behind. He'd been hoping opportunity might knock. He hadn't expected it to use a sledge hammer.

Doc clambered across Mary, slid behind the steering wheel, and put the gear selector into drive.

"What're we doing?" Mary asked. "Shouldn't we wait for Uncle Simon?"

"He might need help," Doc explained. "Let's go see if we can find some."

Simon made a misty silhouette against the flame's ruddy glow. It was too hot for him to get close. He extended one hand, pointing the extinguisher at the blaze. It didn't seem to make a difference.

Doc kept his foot off the accelerator. Wind and fire were making plenty of noise, but he didn't want a change in the truck's exhaust note to compete for Simon's attention. He might have left his rifle behind the seat. That didn't mean he wasn't carrying a pistol. Doc just wanted to creep away, not get into a shootout, not with Mary there.

The truck began to roll. Simon didn't notice. Like the rest of the world, his outline was soon absorbed by the blast of snow crystals smoothing Benteen County's already flat surface.

Doc was peering over his shoulder, taking one last look to reassure himself that Simon wasn't hot on their trail before he started speeding up. The metal hood of the truck rang as something slammed against it, nearly sending him through the roof. It was the fist of a snow-suited figure standing only inches from where he sat. Another was beside it, a box cradled in its arms. The one who hit the truck had a gun and was pointing it straight at Doc's window. It seemed to want Doc to stop. He thought that was a good idea. Only the other figure lunged at the one with the gun and the two of them fell out of sight. Doc rammed his foot down on the accelerator. The truck lurched forward.

It probably would have worked if the barn hadn't been in the way.

◇ ◇ ◇

"**B**astard!" Judy said.

She heard Mad Dog come running back down the hall. Bone and blood and hair and other pieces of Levi Hornbaker were leaving smears on the cabinets as they dripped on the counter. Levi's body was similarly spoiling the kitchen floor. She felt like she'd had a dozen cups of coffee, totally buzzed. She hadn't killed him but she'd tried. And she wasn't sorry he was dead. In fact, Judy decided, unless Englishman appeared to take over and put the world back the way it belonged and Mad Dog started producing miracles, she was prepared to round up every single Hornbaker and blow each of them away. If her daughters were hurt, someone was going to pay.

"Judy, see, I told you," Mad Dog said. An icy breath caressed her cheek and she realized the back door was opening again. She let her gaze shift, saw the door admit a swirl of snow, and Deputy Wynn's butt, backing in, awkwardly carrying something.

"Oh God!" Judy said, recognizing his burden. It was Heather.

The baddest shaman in all of Kansas was suffering a crisis of confidence. One look at the chairman had been enough to start his doubts. Judy had covered the holes in Supervisor Wynn's torso with compression bandages, but they were soaked. So was the floor of the den. Mad Dog couldn't imagine how to heal something like that.

"Aren't you going to do something?" Dorothy had urged.

He tried, but the magic had failed. How could he hurl thunderbolts and kill with his mind one moment, then fail utterly the next? Now Levi was dead in the kitchen. And Heather, his beloved niece, lay there unconscious. He didn't seem to be able to do a thing about that either.

"What's going on in there?" It was Becky. The doorway opened yet again. The kitchen was turning as popular as Bertha's on all-you-can-eat catfish days. She and Simon came in herding Doc and Mary and Englishman. Both Hornbakers had AK 47 assault rifles, and Simon was carrying a curious iron chest.

"Hard to see," Simon said. It was getting dark fast. The sun must have set and the gloom under the clouds was finally holding sway. "Looks like all hell's broke loose. Somebody killed Levi."

"Englishman! Heather's hurt. And Chairman Wynn's been shot." Judy was on the floor hovering over one daughter while the other tried to help. Mad Dog couldn't get near. Filled with self-doubts, he hadn't tried very hard.

"How bad is it?" Englishman joined them.

"Let me see," Doc said, plunging into the crowd.

"Where's Dad? Is he OK?" Wynn Some demanded.

Simon interrupted them with half a clip. That put everybody but the Hornbakers down onto the linoleum.

"You just shut up now," Simon said. "We'll do the talking."

Simon had aimed high. His bullets stitched a seam across the ceiling and caused a brief hail of plaster.

"How sweet," Becky remarked. "A family reunited." She turned her attention to the far side of the room. "Dorothy dear, what happened?"

"I'm afraid we've had some accidents, and the Wizard hasn't healed any of them yet."

"No, dear. That's not what I mean. I put you in the home with Tommie. You failed me. Now I'm very cross with you."

"Always liked him better than you," Dorothy replied.

Becky curled her lip in a snarl, but her attention was already shifting to Mad Dog.

"You do have Tommie's ring, don't you Mad Dog?"

He nodded, reluctantly.

"Pull it out of your pocket," Becky said, "slow, so I'm sure you aren't drawing a gun."

"I don't use guns," Mad Dog said.

"So I've heard. Slow all the same. This isn't the moment I want to find out different."

Mad Dog climbed back to his feet and slowly dug it out. "Why all the fuss? This can't be worth much."

"You don't know? What were you doing with his body then, hiding it up in a tree like that?"

"Tommie wanted a Choctaw burial."

Becky smiled. "Mad Dog, you are a caution. He wasn't a Choctaw. Wasn't any kind of Indian. Hell, he wasn't even Tommie."

"The Indian thing, that was how he planned to keep the ring from her, Mad Dog," Dorothy said. "He was gonna swallow it and you'd hide it along with him, only then, at the end, he couldn't choke it down anymore."

"I thought he might have swallowed it," Becky said. Then, "What else did you find at the pond, Mad Dog?"

"Bones. And an ID card that looks like Zeke, only it isn't."

"There are your Indians, Mad Dog," Becky said. "Ezekiel's Cheyenne slut and their mongrel. A sinful pollution of the holy lineage. I was afraid they weren't buried deep enough. But that doesn't matter anymore.

"Feel the edges of the ring," Becky told him. "There's a protrusion, just a tiny one. Can you find it?"

Mad Dog did. It gave when he pushed against it. As he watched, the metal lump blossomed. Wings unfolded, sprang from where they had hidden in the meaningless contours of the ring's surface. A reverse swastika!

"Give it to Simon so he can open the case," Becky said. Let's see if I have what I think I do."

"What is this? Some Nazi trash?" But Mad Dog handed the key to Simon, who fumbled it into the lock. In spite of decades in a stack of hay, it turned easily. When Simon pulled on the handle, the hinges folded open without protest.

"What's in there?" Becky demanded. It was too dark to see more than outlines across the kitchen.

Simon reached inside. A pottery cup lay on a thick bed of velvet. He took it out and peered at it curiously.

"Dorothy, get it from Simon and bring it to me," Becky said.

"She thinks it's the Holy Grail," Englishman said.

Mad Dog thought that was idiotic. But then, maybe, so was trying to heal the chairman.

"Imagine," Becky whispered. "What if Uncle Abel actually found it? What if it really is the holiest relic of all? They say the chalice is capable of miracles. That it can heal the sick and injured, feed the hungry, erase the weight of years."

She reached out a hand and touched the cup. "Look! It made me younger, didn't it?"

It was very dark, but Mad Dog thought she might be right.

"**D**on't nobody move!" The voice blew through the open door at Becky's back. "Can't see who's who in there," it rasped, "so if anybody starts something, I'm gonna open up with this here Glock and let God sort you out."

"How'd you get here, Mrs. Kraus?" the sheriff called.

"Commandeered me a snowmobile," she replied. Then, "Ah, ah, ah! Don't you move none, Becky Hornbaker. It's dark in there, but I see you turning that gun my way. Hold still now, or they'll be cleaning your brains off that ceiling."

"Everybody accounted for in there?" Mrs. Kraus continued.

The sheriff responded. "All of our side. I think Zeke Hornbaker passed us in the snow plow on our way here. He must be around someplace."

"There's a crazy old woman out there too," Judy added. "Don't know who she is, but she's dangerous. Watch your back."

"Sheriff, can you help me out here?" Mrs. Kraus wondered.

"I've got Judy's Beretta, Mrs. Kraus. Simon's covered. You concentrate on Becky."

"I'll empty this weapon in your daughters at the first shot," Becky said. "Might do that anyway, if you don't give me the Grail and let me go."

"I'm willing to discuss it," the sheriff said. "Only we need some light in here. Anybody got a flashlight?"

"There's a coal oil lamp in a cupboard next to the sink," Becky said, "and matches to light it."

"Simon, you get it," the sheriff said.

"Who's gonna make me?" Simon retorted.

"Do it," Becky ordered. "Set the lamp on the counter, then tell us before you strike a match. We don't want any surprises setting off a war."

The wind tore at curtains and pelted them with flakes previously confined to the back porch. The sheriff could hear noises over where Simon should be, but he couldn't tell if Simon was pulling out the hurricane lantern or wadding up a spitball.

"I'm ready to light the match," Simon announced.

"Go on then," Becky said.

"Wait!" There was a no-nonsense quality in the sheriff's voice that required obedience. It worked, even on Simon.

"Can't you smell it?" the sheriff asked. "That's propane."

"Careful," Becky shouted. "A shot might set it off." The odor was becoming pervasive. "Simon," she commanded. "Check the stove. Turn it off."

"Stove's off." Simon sounded a little desperate. "Gas line's been cut near the wall. Someone must have turned off the propane, cut the feeder pipe, then just now turned it back on. What should we do?"

That, the sheriff thought, was an excellent question.

Judy wasn't worrying about a shot setting things off. She could see a ghostly figure emerging from the billowing clouds of snow behind Mrs. Kraus. Scraggly hair whipped about its head. Stick-like arms protruded from the quilt of rags that wrapped it, insufficiently, from the storm.

Judy recognized the apparition. It was the hag, the one who'd shot Chairman Wynn. She shouldn't be visible out there in the dark, but the woman was surrounded by a glowing aura. Its source was an old-fashioned blowtorch. It was lit and she was pointing it at the house as she advanced across the yard. If she got close enough...

But she didn't have to get close enough, Judy realized. There was a fire in the hearth in the living room.

"We need to get outside," Englishman told the assembly. Judy wondered if he'd seen the hag, wondered if she should tell Becky and Mrs. Kraus what was behind them.

"Lord, it's the witch!" Simon howled, absolving her of the responsibility.

There was a brief moment of confusion as everyone looked to see what Simon was talking about. Judy was already grabbing one Heather and whispering to the other. They had to escape before the gas found the fire, or the old woman found the gas. And then everybody was moving. Bodies threw themselves about like Keystone cops in choreographed confusion. Someone sprinted down the hall to where the chairman waited for a miracle. Someone tall went through the swinging door to the living room. Becky, Judy decided, since her silhouette was no longer blocking what little light came through the back door.

"Now," Judy told Two as she began hauling One toward the exit. Mrs. Kraus had stepped away from the doorway. Judy and the Heathers cleared it as the old woman held something up to her torch. It looked like she was lighting a candle.

"Dynamite," the second Heather cried. "I think that's dynamite."

Mrs. Kraus opened fire. She was a few steps from the back porch, windward of the house and the propane. The Glock bucked. Judy kept moving, dragging one daughter with the help of the other, as far as she could get from the disaster she expected. Dorothy was right behind her with Mary in one hand and Wynn Some in the other, urging them on for all she was worth. Englishman followed, pushing Doc.

Judy hoped they could get far enough. It wasn't going to matter whether Mrs. Kraus was accurate. Not when the gas found those flames.

Mrs. Kraus emptied the Glock and the specter staggered and went down. Then it got back up again. It still held the torch.

The hag lighted and hurled the first of her bombs. More were stuck in a belt holding her rags about her waist.

The explosive hurtled toward the back door. And then its course was altered by the snowball that intercepted it. Dorothy had stopped, once she got the deputy and Mary clear. Now she was bent over, scooping up a second snowball even as her former companion lit another stick of TNT.

The first one tumbled and landed, still sputtering, almost at Judy's feet. While she tried to decide what to do about it, Wynn Some hurled her violently aside. "Run for your lives," he shouted, throwing himself on top of the explosive. "I'll absorb the blast." Then Englishman was there, pulling him off and Judy could see that the fuse was out and Deputy Wynn, of all people, had saved their lives.

The hag let fly again. This time Dorothy's makeshift missile defense failed to intercept. The stick of dynamite tumbled through the air. Mad Dog came pounding out the back door, the chairman over his shoulder, just ahead of it. Simon was hard on his heels. The TNT glanced off the side of the doorframe as Simon came through. He dropped his AK 47 and frantically grabbed it out of the air. He looked around, deciding what to do with it.

"Hey, you Englishman's Bastard," Simon shouted. "Catch this!" He cocked his arm to hurl it. Then he disappeared. Along with the house.

Judy felt like she was at ground zero of a nuclear blast. Her shadow etched the snow. She tried to throw herself between the explosion and her injured daughter. Something slammed her in the back. She never knew where she landed.

The first thing Mad Dog noticed afterwards was that he couldn't hear anything. His ears were ringing, not the constant singing of summer cicadas that was his tinnitus. This roar rivaled a Kansas tornado.

He struggled to sit up and saw Englishman ask him something. Probably, "Are you all right?" He nodded an uncertain yes. Doc was scrambling toward Judy and the Heathers. Englishman followed and that left Mad Dog alone with the chairman, who had already proved beyond his help.

It was no longer dark in the yard. He couldn't make himself turn to look at the house, but flickering shadows indicated that pipes back there still vented gas. And there were little piles of burning debris scattered about, adding their own fitful efforts to light the scene. It was surreal, like something Dante Alighieri might have imagined.

Dorothy had the cup. She wandered around touching people with it. Becky had claimed it could heal. Dorothy touched Mad Dog and Chairman Wynn, then mouthed something in Mad Dog's ear. He heard enough to understand her. She still thought he could heal too. Only he wasn't any more Oz than that pottery bowl was the grail. Still, maybe he should try.

Mad Dog willed himself to that other world, the one no one here but Dorothy seemed to believe in. It wasn't easy. His body ached. Wind and snow stung him. Cold seeped out of the earth. He closed his eyes and tried to ignore it all, tried to find that other place where his soul sometimes escaped.

And suddenly he saw two who were one and yet not one. He didn't understand, except that they were a danger on either plane of existence. Again, Mad Dog needed weapons to fight them. He remembered that moment in the hog shed. He'd searched for a thunderbolt and found one. He looked for it again, begged its help. He thought it agreed. And something, or someone, else agreed as well.

Mad Dog opened his eyes and tried to comprehend. Judy was coming around. Dorothy went over and touched her with the cup. She touched the injured Heather as well. He was surprised when Heather's eyes flickered open. But he didn't have time to celebrate because they were fixed on something behind him.

It was the hag. She was back. She was soaked in her own blood and she'd lost her torch, but she still had plenty of candles. And lots of places to light them.

Englishman fumbled with his pistol. The witch bent over a pile of flaming debris, tried to light another bomb.

Englishman dropped to one knee, used a two handed grip, squeezed. Nothing happened. Mad Dog watched him frantically rack the slide to eject the failed round. It jammed. Englishman looked about for something else to use against her, only there was already something there.

Hailey seemed to materialize out of nothingness. The witch gave up on the stick that wouldn't light and tried another as Hailey limped toward her. The wolf's flank was caked with frozen blood. She could barely move, wasn't capable of attack in the usual sense. The hag didn't notice, not until Hailey snapped a jaw full of fangs within inches of her face. The witch recoiled, fell into the flaming wreckage and emerged, aflame herself.

Hailey glared at her. For a moment, the woman stared back. She didn't seem to realize she was on fire. Her hair vanished in a puff of acrid smoke. The rags she wore glowed and flickered in the wind. Hailey began to move. Ears down, fangs bared, she advanced. The hag turned and ran. Mad Dog saw the woman's eyes go wide, her mouth fly open in terror. The flames engulfed her, and the fuses on the sticks in her belt burned as well. She vanished into the storm as Hailey sank to the ground. Then the north turned bright and the earth shook, and Mad Dog ran to see to his lightning bolt.

Blazing headlights were the sheriff's first clue that another danger was on them. They were mounted on an old green and yellow John Deere tractor with a cab around the driver's seat.

Old John Deeres don't move fast, but they move more surely than most things in Kansas blizzards. This one moved straight for where the sheriff's family lay. Judy, his Heather, they weren't mobile yet. He couldn't get them out of the way in time.

A snowball exploded against his chest. It drew his attention. Dorothy, who else could have thrown it. She threw him something else and he understood.

The sheriff ran to meet the tractor. He dodged its front wheels by inches, but as he did so, he showed the driver what Dorothy had given him. He knew who guided the tractor, and how badly she wanted the pottery cup. The tractor veered away from the others and twisted to follow him. He ran.

In his mind, he saw the figure in the tractor as a thing that burned, much the like the hag had, though this one's fire was internal. The sheriff burned too. He felt pure and perfect and electric, capable of saving the world, or a small part.

The tractor closed fast. The sheriff wasn't sure where he was. Then it didn't matter. In spite of dark and snow, he saw every building. He tasted the trees, heard the fences, smelled the anger behind him, and touched its fear. He dodged and the tractor followed, no longer gaining.

He stretched himself, flattened his ears, and ran. He felt long and lean. His feet clawed through the snow and found earth. His tongue lolled across sharp canines.

The tractor followed. He knew the frustration of the thing guiding it. And its resolve that he would not get away. He had no intention of getting away.

He leaped a fence, then trotted slowly to give the tractor time to follow. He hadn't been here before, yet he knew the place. This land had never felt the plow. Generations of beef and sheep had altered its vegetation, but the earth was the same. The prairie recognized him. They were old friends.

The pasture was flat and empty. The tractor could go much faster here. Faster than a man, but not so fast as what the sheriff had become. He circled toward his goal, came at it from the north. The terrain gave little hint of where he led. He crashed through clumps of thicker vegetation, jumped a low mound of earth and felt the surface change beneath him.

Ten strides more, and then he spun and stopped. The tractor followed. It nearly reached him. Then the earth opened and swallowed it whole.

Only it wasn't earth, of course. It was ice, the pond's surface. Frozen thick enough to let the tractor come all the way to the deep end. But not thick enough for more.

The sheriff felt human again. Human and winded, utterly exhausted. He found his way to the edge of the pond, a place where the dam had begun to erode. He sank down beside an icy cut from which old bones protruded.

Behind him, something scrambled from the frigid depths. Somehow, a shape pulled itself from the water and onto a place where the ice was still thick enough to hold. It wobbled toward him, the chill of wind and water stealing its life as it came. It had Becky Hornbaker's face, but it wasn't Becky. Somehow, it had lost most of its clothing escaping from the submerged cab of the John Deere. Its hair was short and dark and frozen. So was the longer gray wig it grasped in one hand and held in front of its genitals.

The sheriff reached out and knocked the wig aside. Though shrunken by cold and trauma, it was clearly male. The face was Becky's, but it was Zeke's too.

"Tommie Irons, I presume," the sheriff said.

The figure reached for the sheriff. Its eyes locked on his, pleading. The sheriff understood. He looked down at the cup for the first time. It was decorated with a ring of alternating swastikas and swavastikas around the rim. The cup looked ancient enough, but it didn't look worth dying for. The sheriff shrugged and handed it over. Eyes blazing, the figure grabbed it. But its fingers were frozen, too stiff to hold on. The cup dropped to the ice…and shattered.

The thing that had been Becky, and sometimes Zeke, collapsed onto the shards and slid down among the bones. The sheriff felt its flame extinguish, felt the spirits of those who lay in the earth reach out and claim it. Something, never

wholly human, died. That's when he noticed. The wind had
died also. And snow had ceased falling.

Stars hung, twice as bright as normal, over Buffalo Springs.
It was good to have horizons back and appropriately
distant beneath that endless vault of sky. The MEDEVAC
helicopter lifted off. It carried Chairman Wynn, still clinging
to life by a tenuous thread and accompanied by his son,
toward the nearest trauma center.

It was too cold to stay out and watch them disappear into
the distance. The sheriff had checked a thermometer. It was
just over ten degrees in Buffalo Springs. With cloudless skies,
the mercury would fall farther before morning.

He picked his way around snowdrifts and pushed through
the doors and into one of the town's few lighted buildings.

"Any word yet?" he asked.

They occupied the lobby of the Sunshine Towers Retirement Home, its residents and staff having been shooed elsewhere. Doc had chosen it as a worthy emergency medical
facility. It had a well-stocked nurses' station, a generator to
supply its own power, and was closer at hand.

"Doc's still back with Heather," Judy said. "What's taking
so long?"

No one ventured an opinion. The other Heather sat with
her arms folded tight to her chest. Mary dozed in one of the
big chairs near the birdcage. As if they understood, the birds
kept their songs soft and comforting.

Judy paced near the door that led to where Doc had taken
her daughter. "Why won't he let me in there?" she demanded.

"She'll be fine," the sheriff and Mad Dog told her simultaneously. She looked at them and shook her head.

"What's that," she countered, "the expert opinion of our
local witch doctor and his brain-damaged brother?" But she
stopped pacing and leaned against the wall.

The sheriff's head throbbed, but he felt surprisingly good. The people he loved had all survived. So far. Chairman Wynn was yet to be determined, but keeping him alive until the MEDEVAC team arrived already constituted a miracle, or so Doc had told him. Equally miraculous was the fact that he'd managed to get a cellular call through and start the chopper on its way. Since that one call, his phone had gone stubbornly out of service again. And there was Mad Dog, who had lost the beloved pets that were killed at his farm. Only animals, some people would think, but he knew his brother's pain was intolerable.

"I'm the sheriff," he announced. Saying it reassured him. "I've still got a job to do. People died. I need to know why, clear up loose ends." He looked across the room to where Dorothy hovered protectively over Mary. "Let's start with you."

She didn't seem surprised. "OK," she said. "I confess. I'm the phantom snowballer."

"After seeing you pick off that dynamite, I already worked that out. But the snowball case is the least of my worries. Why did this happen?"

She stood there, nervously clicking ruby-tennied heels.

"Silver," Mad Dog said.

Everyone looked at him curiously. Mad Dog shifted in his chair. Hailey lifted her head to check for threats, didn't find any, and put it back on her paws. The wound along her shoulder had stopped bleeding. Mad Dog had made Doc promise to see to her as soon as he could, even though Doc had already assured him it wasn't serious. Mad Dog ruffled the fur on her neck with his hand and the sheriff wondered which of them drew the most comfort from it.

"You're trying to go home, right?" Mad Dog asked. "Well, they changed those shoes for the movie. Ruby slippers were more photogenic. They were silver in the book."

Dorothy smiled and turned to the sheriff. "What do you want to know?"

"I've got most of it," the sheriff said. "I know that Becky and Zeke were actually the same person. I know the real Becky was the one locked up in that cage all those years. I know you're her sister. I even think I know who Tommie really was."

"Yeah, that was Tommie who followed you down to the pond," she admitted. "And it was Tommie who passed himself off as Becky and Zeke all these years." She looked down at Mary and sighed. "He believed all that lineage stuff, us being Christ's children and all. It was our legacy."

The sheriff nodded. "Doc said he read about the legend of the Magdalen's offspring somewhere."

"That's where it began. Tommie and Becky thought it meant they could live by different rules. Like when they were kids. They baptized that boy until he stopped breathing. After that, she and Tommie got shipped down to Uncle Abel in Oklahoma real quick."

"Doc found a file at the library," the sheriff said. "There were newspaper clippings about your uncle's murder. What really happened?"

"Becky, the real one, the witch. She and Tommie persuaded Abel's three boys, Ezekiel and Obadiah and Malachi, to help her kill Abel. Abel was Simon's father. Becky hated Abel for making her a brood mare for the new Messiah. She was married to Zeke, but it was a sham Abel came up with to explain Simon and the others he intended. Abel was rich. Made a fortune selling collectibles. Had that chest you open with the ring and she told them he kept a treasure in there.

"Becky and Tommie were about the same size. Looked alike as well, and resembled their cousins. All that inbreeding, I suppose. Becky needed an alibi. There was a dance that night. She sent Tommie, dressed up as her. Zeke was his escort. Obadiah and Malachi stayed to help with the killing.

"When it was done, they split up. Zeke got the ring. Tommie tossed the chest in a truck and drove up here to hide it. They never looked inside. Things were too frantic at first, then Abel left Becky his fortune and it didn't seem important.

"Zeke and Malachi and Becky got arrested," Dorothy continued. "Tommie and Obadiah got away."

The sheriff let his eyes slide around the room. They were like a little band of primitives, gathered around the wise woman as she told them there really were things to be afraid of out there in the dark.

"Abel had a housekeeper, a young Cheyenne girl. She helped Tommie and Obadiah hide out till Becky got cleared. Then Becky and Tommie came home to Benteen County. Tommie was laying low since the law wanted him. His fingerprints were on the murder weapon 'cause he hid it for Becky. He'd been at the dance, only as Becky. None of the witnesses were going to admit they might have danced with him.

"They threw the book at Zeke and Malachi. Malachi got the death penalty. Zeke would have, only that Cheyenne housekeeper came forward. Claimed Zeke was with her when the murder occurred. She was convincing, especially since that was when she conceived his baby. Zeke got a life sentence, just the same."

Mrs. Kraus interrupted. "How could Tommie live here with a murder warrant out for him in Oklahoma? I mean the Tommie we knew. Who was he?"

"Obadiah, of course. He came along with Tommie and Becky, keeping his head low like Tommie at first. Only Becky had a taste for murder by then. She decided if she killed Ma and Pa, she'd inherit our farm."

"You mean that car crash wasn't an accident?" Mrs. Kraus asked.

"She beat them to death with a tire iron. Came after me and Tommie too, only Obadiah stopped her."

"That's why she was caged," the second Heather said.

"Right," Dorothy continued. "Tommie and Obadiah piled the folks in their car and went off and wrecked it to hide what she'd done. Bunch of my stuff was in there too, so everyone decided I'd died with them. After that, they couldn't let Becky run loose. But folks knew she and little Simon were here. The law was still looking for both Tommie and Obadiah and Abel's inheritance belonged to Becky.

"Tommie got the idea. He'd impersonated Becky once. He could do it again. And Obadiah had got scared and run out before they killed Abel. His fingerprints weren't on anything incriminating. He looked a little like Tommie, enough to get by in Benteen County where nobody had seen Tommie since he was a kid. So Tommie became Becky and Obadiah became Tommie. As Becky, Tommie contacted the local sheriff. Told him her brother was innocent and wanted to turn himself in. The new Tommie got his fingerprints checked. They didn't match. From then on, Tommie was in the clear, and, from then on, that was who Obadiah was."

"Sounds like something out of daytime TV," Mrs. Kraus observed.

The sheriff agreed. But nothing seemed surreal when you might have spent part of your evening as a werewolf.

"You've had a miscarriage, Heather. You're not pregnant."

"Oh God, Doc!" Heather English turned her face to the wall and cried like a little girl. He sat on the edge of the bed and gathered her in his arms and comforted her. Hell, she was a little girl. She was just sixteen.

It took awhile before her sobs subsided. He'd known there would be tears. That was part of the reason he'd gotten her back into the privacy of the examination room and barred Judy, or anyone else, from joining them, even while he was still patching Chairman Wynn and pumping plasma in him.

"It's OK, Heather. You're going to be fine. You're too young now. It's just as well. You can have more babies, but when you're ready."

"Oh Doc, you don't understand," she sniffled. "I wasn't going to have this one. I was going to kill it. That's why we were out there. I was going to…"

"You were going to see Harriet. I know, Heather. I'm Harriet."

That shocked the last of the tears from her eyes. "You! You can't be. I mean, you're a doctor. You can do abortions if you want. They're legal."

"Legal, yes. But not acceptable. Not in this county. That's why I became Harriet. With Harriet, nobody knows who the women are and nobody knows who the abortionist is. It's a lot safer for them—and me—here in Benteen County."

He watched a look of horror descend across her face. He'd been expecting it.

"Does that mean you…"

"No, Heather. It doesn't. Your miscarriage was natural."

It wasn't true. He might have been able to prevent it. But he hadn't. He'd made a decision, but there wasn't any reason for her to share the guilt.

"The miscarriage was a result of what happened to you today, not something you chose. And there hasn't been any permanent damage."

"Oh Doc," she whispered. "I'm so ashamed."

"Of what? Getting pregnant? It can happen to anyone, Heather. Ask Harriet. She knows."

"I feel stupid. Forgetting to take my pills sometimes. Thinking he really loved me. But what shames me is that I wanted to get rid of it. It makes me feel like a murderer. Even if I didn't get to carry out my intention, I tried. But I'm glad it's gone. I didn't want a baby now. Only that makes me feel evil."

"That's how I feel too, Heather, every time. Like a murderer. And yet, there are so many unwanted, uncared for children." He sighed.

"You would have cared for this baby. Your parents would have helped, and given their love and support. But you might not have gone to college. Your mom might not have been able to keep her job. Your dad might not get reelected, not in puritanical Benteen County. That's why I would have performed your abortion if I could have met you at Harriet's stone."

She sniffled some more. She would need time. The blows she suffered from the Hornbakers were nothing. Adjusting to the presence, and then the absence, of the life that had begun inside her—that was what might leave scars.

"I still can't believe you're Harriet," she said. "I mean how could you be? Everybody always knows where your station wagon is."

"That's why I arranged for access to other vehicles," Doc said. "Listen. This has to be our secret. You've got to promise me, just the way your Grandma Sadie made me promise when I took over being Harriet from her."

"Grandma!" Another shock for her, but the fact that her grandmother had supported decisions like the one she was on the verge of making obviously helped.

"I made her quit when I found out who she was. If secret abortions were being done in this county, I thought they ought to be done by someone with a medical degree. Your grandmother agreed, though not because I was more qualified. I think she had a premonition she wouldn't live much longer. She was afraid there wouldn't be anyone to carry on."

This time it was Heather who embraced him. "Thanks, Doc," she told him. "Thanks for everything." This time, the tears were his.

◇◇◇

"The dam?" the sheriff said. "That's where the real Ezekiel Hornbaker and his Cheyenne family ended up?"

"That's right," Dorothy said. "See, the real Zeke had the ring. The authorities kept it with his effects while he was in prison. That's part of why no one ever looked in the box.

"I wasn't around much then. Simon was growing up, none too bright and unloved. He was a mean kid. And his momma was caged up in that room at the end of the hall. Worse, Tommie took over from Abel trying to breed a new Messiah.

With crazy Becky at first, then with one of their daughters he kept and raised. Then a granddaughter, then Mary. You should have explored more. There were cages in the basement, and more graves. Eventually, Tommie kept Judah and Levi and pretended they were Simon's, but plenty of others just got disposed of or stuck in jars in Tommie's lab.

"So, I traveled, clicked my heels and took off. But Obadiah and Tommie stayed, adjusted to their roles. Obadiah even grew to like it. He spent most of his time in the fields or with the animals. Didn't have to put up with the animals in the house. He got to like the way the land renewed itself and provided, year after year. When I did come back, he and I got to be close, closer than I ever was to Becky or Tommie."

"Then Zeke got out of jail," the sheriff prompted.

"That Cheyenne girl never stopped working to get his case reviewed. Not even after they ran a zillion volts through Malachi and planted him in a potter's field. She finally got Zeke pardoned.

"Zeke had a half-breed daughter, a lot like you, Mad Dog. She might be just half Cheyenne, but that was the part that mattered. Zeke thought taking her up to Wounded Knee might help win her over."

"I thought about going up there myself," Mad Dog said.

"Zeke started out," Dorothy said.

"Then ended up in that dam with his family," Mad Dog continued. "The girl was pregnant, wasn't she?"

Dorothy nodded. "The baby's father was supposed to be among the defenders. Her momma and Zeke and her, they loaded themselves in an old pickup with a camper. They got hold of a case of AK 47s through connections Zeke made while he was in prison. Had some boxes of TNT as well. And Zeke knew one of Abel's curiosities the family had inherited was Custer's scalp. He didn't believe it was real, but Abel made convincing imitations. Zeke told his woman and daughter and they decided to pick it up along the way."

"Custer's scalp." Mad Dog shook his head. "Why not, with all the other stuff out there?"

"Zeke figured they owed him. Obadiah agreed, and promised to get him some cash as well."

"Did Tommie kill them?" the sheriff asked.

"In a way," Dorothy said. "Tommie seldom did things himself. He liked to persuade somebody to do them for him. Usually, Becky.

"Obadiah welcomed Zeke and his family. Tommie and Simon didn't. That's why Zeke camped in the pasture by the slough while Obadiah raised the cash. Then Tommie let Becky out of her cage."

"So Becky murdered them," Mad Dog said.

"Obadiah cleaned up after her. His life would have unraveled if people investigated. He liked being Tommie Irons. To go on with that, he had to cover for her. He buried the bodies, hid the weapons, cleaned out their belongings and packed them in his own car and drove it to Wichita. Left it in the parking lot of some go-go joint with the keys in it. Obadiah used a couple of sticks of that dynamite and some gasoline to blow the truck and camper to smithereens. And he and I locked Becky back in her room.

"Obadiah and me, we considered doing the same to Tommie, only Zeke's arrival and disappearance opened a door for him. Zeke's death turned into Tommie's escape.

"All those years hiding behind a dress and pretending to be his sister had taken a toll. He'd begun obsessing about the treasure, wondering if what was in that chest could buy him a different life. When he turned Becky loose, she was supposed to get him the key. She left it on Zeke's finger. Obadiah found it and kept it then, so Tommie couldn't have it.

"That upset Tommie at first. Only somewhere in there it occurred to him that Zeke and he resembled each other. After a few weeks, Tommie worked up his nerve and tried it. Cut his hair down to a burr like the one Zeke wore, dressed in some of Obadiah's clothes, and tested himself on downtown Buffalo Springs. He was Zeke Hornbaker, come back to reconcile with Becky and take charge of the family, even though Simon was already growed up. If anyone noticed Zeke had lost the broken nose he'd had last he was here, they never said. Becky—Tommie under a fresh wig he picked up in Wichita—vouched for him. So did Obadiah. It got Tommie out from underfoot."

"I never suspected," Mrs. Kraus said. "Don't seem possible things like that could go on in a place like Benteen County and nobody know."

"He'd done the hard part. He'd passed as Becky for years. The new Zeke was popular. He was so glad to be released from life as his sister, he turned generous, big spender of the family fortune. There was enough. Obadiah didn't object.

"Fellow picks up your tab at Bertha's a few times, you put up with what annoys you about him. It worked for Tommie. Got him elected, as Zeke, to the County Board, didn't it?"

Indeed, the sheriff realized. It had.

"And Tommie didn't take the key from Obadiah because he couldn't," Dorothy continued. "He tried. Even in the Towers Obadiah made a fuss, said things that didn't make sense, except to Tommie. Tommie figured he better wait. He had a back-up plan. Me. Stuck me in the Towers as a charity case so's I could keep an eye on Obadiah. Bag the ring when I got the chance. Only Obadiah was my friend, so he was the one I tried to help."

"And that explains it," the sheriff said.

"Yeah," Judy agreed, "but for one big thing." She looked across the room at the figure over whom Dorothy hovered. "What becomes of Mary?"

"**H**eather's doing fine," Doc said, pushing through the swinging doors and into the lobby.

Judy started toward him. "Can I see her?"

"I don't think that's a good idea," Doc said. "Not for a while, anyway. I just got her to doze off. Nothing better for her than sleep right now. And she's pretty concerned about how you're going to react to what she did today—from pre-dawn toilet papering of a classmate's yard to skipping school for unauthorized driving lessons. I've got her in a free room with one of the residents who used to be a nurse keeping an eye on her. Heather should get some strength back before she faces an angry mother, or a protective one. For now, Judy, best you can do for her is leave her alone."

Doc watched the internal struggle. The mother who planned to take over fought it out with the one who wanted what was best for her child. It was a near thing, but the latter won. Judy slumped a little.

"She's afraid of me?"

"Your daughter got seriously knocked around out there. She has a mild concussion. She got kicked in the abdomen and she had some internal bleeding. It's under control, but she was a little hysterical about having to face you and explain how she got herself into this. She'll be fine. With a little rest, she'll be just as anxious to see you as you are to see her. Only, not right now."

Judy dropped into a chair beside the door. "You know best, Doc." She didn't sound convinced.

He wished he believed it himself. "Sheriff," he asked, "what day is this?"

The sheriff looked surprised. "Geez, I don't know Doc. Still got a couple of hours of Thursday left, if that clock behind the reception desk is right."

"What was your mother's name?"

"Sadie," the sheriff said. "Why?"

Doc came over and shone a penlight in the sheriff's eyes. "You seem to be recovering nicely, Sheriff. Anybody disagree? Anybody notice signs of confusion?"

"No more than usual," Mrs. Kraus muttered.

"He's being the sheriff again," Mad Dog said. "We were just getting quite an interesting story from Dorothy before you popped out here."

"Where'd she go?" the second Heather wondered. "She was here a minute ago. And where's Mary?"

Doc and the sheriff went through the swinging doors together. A little old lady sat at the end of the hall. She wore bright red tennies, but she wasn't Dorothy. Same shoes, different senior.

"Where's the woman who gave you these shoes?" the sheriff demanded.

"Dorothy? Why she just traded with me. Wasn't that nice? Those others never fit right, and these red tennis shoes are so soft and comfortable."

"Where?" the sheriff repeated.

She pointed across the hall. "She and the child just took the elevator."

Doc looked at the indicator. It changed from two to three as he watched. "Why'd she run out?" he asked.

"The question of Mary's future came up. I expect that troubled her. And maybe she worried some about her own." The sheriff reached out and punched the elevator button. "You better come with me, Doc. Reassure her, in case she's decided I'm some kind of threat."

Doc nodded. "You think she's gone to her room?"

"Where else?" The elevator was coming down. Doc watched the indicator return to ONE. The doors opened on an old man.

"You know Dorothy?"

"Our Dorothy. Sure, Sheriff, everyone knows her. Why?"

"Where'd she go?"

"I don't know. Haven't seen her since you and those blamed Hornbakers left this morning."

"She didn't get off this elevator before you got on?"

"No. I punched for it and it came up. Nobody in it when the door opened."

The sheriff looked at Doc and Doc looked back.

Mad Dog joined them. "Ma'am," he asked the woman who had traded for Dorothy's tennies. "What color were those shoes you gave her?"

They all knew the answer before they heard it.

"Silver. Does it matter?"

Evidently, it did.

◇◇◇

Heather Lane was impressed. Boris had waited. He was too desperate with the need to relieve himself to more than wag his tail a few times, briefly drench his people with kisses, and poke a curious nose at Hailey's butt as she limped, heavily bandaged, beside Mad Dog into his brother's house. Hailey snarled, but it was more a matter of form than content. The two canids cautiously watched each other across the room as Judy went around lighting candles and starting the fire that was laid on the hearth.

Englishman and his brother fell into a pair of easy chairs and Two curled up on the couch beside Boris, where she reassured him about Hailey. Judy brought them all quilts to huddle under and took orders for coffee or hot chocolate, or some of the brandy she kept for special occasions and emergencies. This qualified.

Judy fussed and mothered them until she couldn't hold the question in anymore. "Heather, do you know about Harriet?"

If Judy hadn't been digging in the bureau for more candles, she might have noticed Heather look away. She missed it though, and the quick lie that followed.

"Harriet? No, who's she?"

"I thought she was long gone," Judy explained. "Abortions used to be illegal here. Even after that changed, none of the local doctors would do them. According to the grapevine, though, they were available. The way I heard it, if you were in trouble you went to Harriet. I never knew who she was until today."

"You found out today?" The idea worried Heather.

"On the road to Mad Dog's place. Not far from where you left the cruiser in the ditch. There's a little cemetery, remember."

"Yeah, I think so." Heather sounded doubtful.

"I never paid it any attention," Judy said. "Until today. As we were going by, I noticed a red flower by a headstone. Harriet's stone. That graveyard, that particular grave, was the place abortions were arranged in this county. I think Becky, or Tommie as Becky, was doing those abortions. The chairman said something about a laboratory in the house, and jars with dead babies, before he was shot. Oh, Heather! Forgive me, but I thought..."

Heather knew exactly what Judy thought. She avoided her foster mother's eyes and got busy petting Boris.

Judy didn't quit. Evidently she still had doubts. "You aren't, are you Heather? You aren't pregnant?"

The accusation hurt, no matter how close it came to being accurate. What hurt most was that she was the one Judy assumed had gotten in trouble. She was the outsider, the perfect Heather's imperfect twin. Her parents had experienced sexual abuse, maybe practiced it as well. That made her the bad seed. It was tough, but the anger she felt at the accusation helped. She locked eyes with Judy.

"No," she said. "I'm not pregnant. I've never been pregnant. If you want, you can get me tested to see if I'm lying."

Judy looked away. "No. I'm sorry. I was just so afraid that you, or maybe Heather...It wasn't Heather, was it?" Judy couldn't let it go. There were tears in her eyes, as well as a silent plea for another negative reply.

"No!" Englishman said to Heather's relieved surprise. He sounded certain. "Something happened to me today, I can't explain it. Concussion, I suppose. But for a little while, I went where Mad Dog tells us he goes as a Cheyenne shaman. Like I said, I can't explain it, but I'm as sure about Heather as I am that I'm sitting here. Neither of our daughters is with child. They didn't go to Becky, or Tommie, for an abortion. That rose you found, Judy, it had to do with someone else."

"It's not the abortion," Judy tried to explain. "I'd support my daughters in that. Or help raise a child if they wanted. It was that they might be afraid to tell me. That they might go to some crazy, evil, unclean place just so I wouldn't know. It made me feel incompetent, like my failure to understand, and make our girls understand, contributed to something awful."

"You've done fine," Heather said. She wasn't angry anymore. She went across the room and into her mother's arms. Not foster—just a daughter to her mother at that moment. "We'll turn out OK, Mom. Really we will."

◇◇◇

Heather Lane was in bed. Judy had turned down the sheets in the guest room. Mad Dog would stay with them until he could seal up his house again. After Doc radioed with an update on the other Heather's condition, Judy's anxiety level gradually diminished. She abandoned the brothers to their companionable silence, the fire she had lit, the glasses of brandy she'd poured them, and followed her daughter's example. Boris and Hailey curled at their respective person's feet, almost muzzle to muzzle, drifting in and out of canid dreams.

"You're troubled," Englishman said, "and not just about Buffalo Bob and your wolves."

Mad Dog wondered if his brother was simply being perceptive or if his spirit still wandered that other realm. He nodded. "There were abortions in Benteen County. I should have known."

"They're not illegal."

Mad Dog nodded again. "True, but that doesn't make them right. Abortion is unacceptable."

"Is it, Mad Dog? Is it really?"

"Every foetus is a returning soul."

"Not every," Englishman countered. "You've told me how Cheyenne souls recycle. You've also told me most people don't have souls. We're only meat."

"Not you, Englishman. If you ever had a doubt, you should have lost it tonight."

Englishman sighed. "Yeah. What are we, one-quarter, one-sixteenth? Our Cheyenne blood's pretty diluted. What about my daughter? Is she meat? Is Judy? How about Two of Two?"

"Not meat," Mad Dog said.

"How can you be sure, Mad Dog? Today was my first experience with any of this. But you, you're a man who wants to serve the spirit world. You've told me you're a natural-born shaman."

"I may have exaggerated."

"But you have visited that other world. Many times. You said you recognized that skull you found today as Cheyenne. If you could do that, you should be able to recognize the soul of any Cheyenne, right?"

"I think so."

"So you would have known if one of our Heathers was pregnant," Englishman said, "unless there wasn't any soul there to recognize."

"Actually," Mad Dog said, "I think I knew."

"And was there something there? Did you recognize a returning soul?"

"What are you really asking me, little brother?"

"I don't know, Mad Dog," Englishman said. "I've believed in you for a long time. There've been too many things you understood that I can't explain away. I think you're right, but I think you're wrong too. I think you've latched onto a nineteenth century world view. You've grabbed hold of our mother's people's religion as it was in that brief time they were horsemen on the Plains running headlong into Manifest Destiny. I don't believe in meat, Mad Dog. I understand why the Cheyenne did. That's how they were treated, as if they were animals instead of people. That prevented them, and now you, from being able to recognize the rest of us, however flawed, for what we are. This philosophy of yours is narrow-minded and ethnocentric. It's Cheyenne to the exclusion of being human.

"You, me as well...at least today...we touched some of what exists beyond the visible world. I don't know what to think about that yet. But I don't believe you've begun to comprehend it all. And I don't think you can decide whether all those girls who went to Harriet were murderers."

"I'm just trying to do what's right."

"Don't you think they were?"

Mad Dog swirled the brandy and stared into its depths. "Isn't truth eternal, Englishman? I have to follow my beliefs, even when they aren't easy."

"So does everyone," Englishman said. "But you can't hurt my daughter or any of those women. Believe what you want, Mad Dog. Don't harm anyone with it."

"I wouldn't," Mad Dog assured him. "My responsibility is to tell the truth as I understand it, not punish people."

"I know," Englishman said. Then he surprised Mad Dog one more time. "You told me about a place up on Pawnee Rock. A little spring where you said the spirits sometimes whisper. Let's you and me go there when it warms up. Offer some tobacco, sit and listen, maybe ask the spirits for guidance about the things that trouble us."

"I'd like that, Englishman. I'd like that a lot."

"Maybe we can take the girls with us. Judy too."

"And Doc."

"You thinking he, especially, needs guidance?"

"No more than me," Mad Dog replied.

Englishman poured more brandy in their glasses and changed the subject. "You worrying about Dorothy and Mary? A resident of the Sunshine Towers confessed. The elevator's emergency exit opens on one of their secret escape routes. We'll probably find them tomorrow."

"No. I don't think you will, and I'm fine with where I think they've gone. It's…"

"What, Mad Dog, come on?"

"It's that cup."

"Jesus, Mad Dog. You don't believe it was actually the Holy Grail?"

Mad Dog rubbed his hand against his chin. "Well…"

Afterword & Acknowledgements

Mad Dog & Englishman, to which this story is a sequel, was my going-home-again novel. Thomas Wolfe says you can't do that. Singer/songwriter John Stewart (who has been scoring my novels, without his knowledge, since long before I began selling them) was more specific. In his song "Kansas" on *The Phoenix Concerts* album, he says, "...you can't go back to Kansas..."

In spite of that sage advice, I not only went, I have returned a second time. I didn't expect to. Residents of the real Kansas, to which my Benteen County bears only an exaggerated resemblance, were probably thinking once was quite enough. Not that they would have easily found my book. There aren't many bookstores in the heart of the Plains anymore. They've gone the way of the Buffalo and the family farm.

Perhaps that's why it felt like the residents of Benteen County were so eager to escape onto the pages of another manuscript. They don't get out much. When they do, they do so with a vengeance. Benteen's residents took my plot hostage and began throwing me twists from the opening page. They spent a few thousand words relating their adventures, exaggerating a little, a lot, and maybe even indulging in a few tall tales. I juggled what they threw at me and tried not to leave any balls in the air at the end.

This is a novel, so its truths aren't limited to those confined by fact. Kansas is real enough, though Benteen County is a mix of personal memories and perceptions from irregular visits to Reno County over more than thirty years. The Sunflower State is prone to extremes of weather, but recent winters have been mild and the blizzard of January 2001 struck only Benteen County. Curious? See for yourself. Kansans delight in tourists—they see so few. Old friend and fellow expatriate Kansan Mike Jacobs presented me with a t-shirt a few years ago. "Kansas Trek: to boldly go where no tourist has gone before" (Top Art Inc. © 1991). There's more to see than even the giant ball of twine and the Pretty Prairie Rodeo. Visitors really do pull off to the side of the road and wonder at that endless vault of sky. And Kansas has mountains more majestic than Mt. Sunflower, highest point in the state. They're mountainous thunderheads, and while they inspire fear as well as awe, they rival any natural wonders to be found at our national parks and monuments.

None of the characters are real. Except Hailey, but she's a German Shepherd and not a wolf hybrid. The two Haileys' resemblance is limited to the circumstances surrounding their rescues. The real Hailey is more a threat to Frisbees and tennis balls than bad guys. The character of the Hailey in this book is based on another pair of German Shepherds separated by forty years—Sherry and Kimba—and an unfortunate wolf hybrid, Casey Jones, I came to know in Albuquerque. Anyone considering wolves and wolf hybrids as pets should reconsider, or enter into the relationship only after very careful study. There's a difference between our companions and our competitors.

There also was a real Louis Henry Silverstein. He was the acquisitions editor at Poisoned Pen Press to whom I submitted *Mad Dog & Englishman*. Louis passed away while I was writing the sequel. The Press sent an announcement and asked authors who knew him to write up their memories. We never met, except by email, though he had a profound impact on my life. I thought I might offer a small memorial of a different sort, and so "The Guardian of the Words" came to Benteen County.

There are those who truly believe in the family of the Magdalen. A German SS officer named Otto Rahn did search for the principal religious artifact in this text, and claimed to find it before dying in the snow of the Tyrolean Alps. After that, why not on to Kansas?

Mad Dog's Cheyenne philosophy is as accurately depicted as possible. Dr. Karl H. Schlesier, author of *The Wolves of Heaven: Cheyenne Shamanism, Ceremonies, and Prehistoric Origins*, helped me keep it so. Where Mad Dog may err in interpreting that philosophy, it's because he was misinformed by me.

Further credit where it's due. The quotes from the witch at the end of the hall, as well as Two's response, were all borrowed from Shakespeare *(King Lear, Julius Caesar, Macbeth, King Henry V, King Henry VI)*, except and in order: Yip Harburg ("Over the Rainbow"), Franklin Delano Roosevelt *(First Inaugural Address)*, Ned Washington ("High Noon"), Tennessee Williams *(Camino Real)*, Emily Dickinson *(Part I, Life)*, Virgil *(Aeneid)*, Henry Van Dyke *(The Prison and the Angel)*, Oscar Levant, an epitaph quoted by William Camden *(Remaines Concerning Britaine)*, William Ernest Hedley *(Echoes)*, Mark Twain ("Note to London correspondent of the New York Journal"), Edwin Arlington Robinson *(New England)*, Robert Southley *(The Soldier's Wife)*, and Woody Allen *(Take the Money and Run)*. Oh, and Judy's line, though not an accurate quote, is from the film *The Treasure of the Sierra Madre*. As for Oz, L. Frank Baum's imagination forever linked it to Kansas in 1900. Unless it wasn't imagination. Might Baum have actually visited these magical realms and reported fact instead of fiction? Mad Dog's expert opinion can be solicited over a slice of chocolate pie at Bertha's. Or we'll ask Dorothy, if we find her.

The usual suspects should be rounded up and thanked. You know who you are.

My critique group worked miracles and helped keep me on target while the citizens of Benteen County ran wild. They include Sheila Cottrell, Elizabeth Gunn, Mary Logue, and E.J. McGill; all, in one way or another, there from beginning to end. Margaret Falk and Bill Capron passed through and were significant contributors. Friend and author J.R. Dailey also read the manuscript, listened to me whine, and offered encouragement or suggestions, as appropriate.

Thanks to J.C. Martin of *The Arizona Daily Star*, and perhaps Bruce Dinges of The Arizona Historical Society, for the title. It's perfect.

Special thanks, again, to the wonderful people at Poisoned Pen Press. Without editors and publishers like Barbara Peters and Robert Rosenwald, who care enough to pick up the slack left by the big-box, one-size-fits-all publishing houses, there would have been no sequel, nor anything on which to base it.

Without my wife, Barbara, none of this would be possible. She helped shape whatever might be of value in these pages. For the flaws, I alone am responsible.

JMH
Tucson, by way of Hutchinson,
Darlow, Partridge, Manhattan,
Wichita, Sedna Creek, et Tabun,
Albuquerque, and a yellow brick road